Faux Ho Ho

"The setup is simple: fake boyfriends for the holidays, started as a lie to get someone out of a dreaded family event, but snowballs into a more elaborate ruse. A tried-and-true formula really. But, *Faux Ho Ho*, 'Nathan Burgoine's new holiday release, is anything but formulaic or contrived. The execution is original, and the story is an utter delight. It's charming, fun, and sweet, everything a Christmas romance should be. And, it's also a little bit nerdy! Which, in my book, is a bonus."
The Novel Approach

Exit Plans for Teenage Freaks

"Burgoine (*Of Echoes Born*, 2018, etc.) has created a gay teen protagonist who is a bit goofy at times but who is comfortable in his own skin... Overall, a feel-good, contemporary read with strong LGBTQIAP rep and an unusual fantasy subplot."
Kirkus Reviews

"READ THE BOOK. NOW. IT IS AMAZING."
Book Princess Reviews

Of Echoes Born

"Burgoine assembles 12 queer supernatural tales, several of which interlock... The best tales could easily stand alone; these include 'The Finish,' about an aging vintner whose erotic dalliance with a deaf young man named Dennis gets complicated, and 'Struck,' in which beleaguered bookstore clerk Chris meets Lightning Todd, who predicts his future wealth and romance. A pair of stories set in 'the Village,' a gay neighborhood, feature appealing characters and romances and could be components of a fine *Tales of the City*–like novel."
Publishers Weekly

Stuck With You

"…hilarious and an all-around enjoyable read... Highly recommended for hi-lo readers who loved *Heartstopper*."
School Library Journal, ★ *starred review*

"...two charming leads readers can't help but root for... An adorable romance with strong coming-of-age elements."
Kirkus Reviews

UPON THE MIDNIGHT QUEER

TALES RETOLD

BY

'NATHAN BURGOINE

UPON THE MIDNIGHT QUEER

All stories in this collection previously appeared on apostrophen.wordpress.com, with the exception of "Folly," which is original to this collection.

Cover art and book design by Inkspiral Design

ISBN 13: 978-1-7773523-8-7 (audiobook)
ISBN 13: 978-1-7773523-7-0 (ebook)
ISBN 13: 978-1-7773523-6-3 (paperback)

DOMINANT TRIDENT BOOKS

PREFACE

OR. DONNING SOME GAY APPAREL

THIS BOOK YOU'RE holding—be it physically or as ones and zeros via your device of choice—came about out of an accidental Christmas holiday tradition. If you've read any of my other holiday stories, especially "Handmade Holidays," it won't surprise you to learn I've long approached Christmas with a mix of trepidation, frustration, exhaustion, and the grim resolve to make it into something good.

That resolve was tested the first year I had a Christmas tree. I'd bought the floor model from the Christmas store in the mall where I'd worked Christmas Eve at the bookstore. I'd taken the tree home, set it up, and then realized I'd made a particularly foolish mistake.

I had no ornaments.

By coincidence, a friend gave me a cross-stitched ornament that year inside the Christmas card she sent, and I hung it on the tree alongside a bunch of candy canes, and while the following year I did buy some plain ornaments, I also received another ornament as a gift from a different friend. I added ornaments to my tree as memories of the year, and ornament by ornament—some years more than one— my tree turned into a reminder of how far I'd come.

Instead of that first year, where it was a rather stark reminder I was flying pretty much solo and had very little to work with, decorating the tree these days has become my favourite part of the holiday season, because as my husband and I pull out ornament after ornament, we relive our vacations, laugh about funny moments, sniffle over people (or pets) no longer with us, and thereafter spend a great deal of our holiday season looking at our tree and seeing the wonderful life we've made for ourselves.

And then, inevitably, someone turns on Christmas music or a holiday classic movie, and I die a little inside.

Okay, that's overstating. A bit.

In my defence, having worked retail for decades and being forced to listen to "Rudolph the Red-Nosed Reindeer" and all the other holiday songs from mid-November onward, I think it's quite fair that I loathe the return of the rotation of holiday noise. Someone give that chipmunk his goddamned hula-hoop and put me out of my misery, would you?

More than that, though, it's all so damned *heteronormative*. The holiday ads, the holiday songs, the holiday movies. If we queer people do exist, we're the sassy elf-like friend who cheers on the clueless heroine about to bump into a lumberjack in some small town and fall madly in love with him and give up an amazing career she worked her ass off to achieve, all so she can help him save his family Christmas tree farm.

(Okay, I admit it. I watch these movies like I mainline candy canes, but I wish we had the same volume of sugar-coated holiday movies for queer people. I'm so glad they're *starting* to exist, but more please. They're not immortal Scotsmen. There can be more than one.)

The music, though? The classic stories? Oof. Take the way Rudolph is so freaking ill-treated by everyone else right up until he becomes *useful*. It just makes me cranky, and I was having a conversation with some queer friends about exactly that ten years ago when inspiration struck. Over the space of a few evenings, I wrote "Dolph." A queer take on a holiday tale.

Mostly as an amusement, I put it up on my blog. To my surprise, quite a few people *really* liked it.

A year later, as my social media reminded me I'd written "Dolph" the year before, I got it into my head to do it again, and that year "Frost" happened. Then "Reflection" the year after that. And so on. I got asked quite a bit if I'd considered releasing "Dolph"—some people printed the story out and told me they re-read it every year, even—and then "Frost" got picked up for a year's best anthology, which was pretty awesome. Continue this accidental tradition year after year, each year a new story on my blog, including one bonus story from about five years ago, when I was asked to take part in a publisher event, and, well, here we are. Ten years later, eleven stories, with "Folly" brand new for this collection.

It's been a tradition of mine for a decade now to don this particularly kind of gay apparel on holiday cheer which hasn't often included queerness, and I'm happy to be able to finally share it this way. I hope you enjoy it. Also, I must take a moment to acknowledge two pieces of public domain holiday cheer: "The Christmas Hirelings" by Mary Elizabeth Braddon and "The Romance of a Christmas Card" by Kate Douglas Smith Wiggin. Excerpts of the former are used in "The Doors of Penlyon" and excerpts of the latter—and the poems inside the titular cards in question—are used in "Not the Marrying Kind." Those are both lovely stories and I suggest you check them out, but given their time and place, they weren't exactly donning any gay apparel of their own.

Oh, and one final thing. One of the stories in this collection, "Most of '81," takes place in 1981, in Toronto. For those outside of Canada, it's important to note that year a massive police raid on bathhouses called "Operation Soap" happened, kicking off major protests and leading to what's often called "Toronto's Stonewall" and then the end of the year levelled a particularly rough kick at the throats of queer people when the Ontario Legislature voted against including sexuality in the human rights code. And, of course, the end of 1981 was also when news of the "Gay Cancer" in New York was starting to be heard elsewhere. This is why the hero of that particular Christmas is retreating into a solo holiday as the story opens.

Merry Christmas. Or Bah Humbug.

I'm partial to either.

NATHAN BURGOINE.
NOVEMBER 2024

For
Matthew Bright,
Anthony Cardno,
Nicci Robinson,
Victoria Villasenor,
and **Jerry L. Wheeler**,
all of whom—probably without
even knowing it—
said things that made me
keep going when I
faltered on this one.

CONTENTS

DOLPH

HE WAS NAMED Rudolph when he was born, but like so many born different, he eventually shed the name he was given. And if it hadn't been for a foggy night and a hard decision, the rest of us freaks would still probably be tucked out of sight, waiting to be useful in some way, and in the meanwhile, to hell with us...

But wait, I'm telling it out of order.

It doesn't actually start with Dolph. It doesn't start with Klaus, either, though it involves him.

If it's not about Dolph and it's not about Klaus, then where does the story really start, you wonder. Well, it starts with a woman. A woman both powerful and visionary, which is probably not the way you've heard it told before. Most of the time, in most of the stories, she doesn't even get a name when she appears, but I promise you, she has one. And I promise you, she's the one who matters the most in this story, even if we usually only hear about the others.

Every one knows about Klaus and his gift, though we'll get to the truth of that in a second, but not very many know about her. It's important to know where she came from, though. See, this woman, she was the one and only daughter of Father Time.

And, like most of the people in this story, she was gifted.

So when people talk about Klaus and his wife—and that's always her role, isn't it?—they never seem to mention how she's one of a kind. And she truly was, for damned sure. And it's her gift of holding time at bay that makes everything possible. She saved Klaus's life, and she helped him find a purpose when he was ready to walk out into the snows and take a nap.

The thing about the big guy that no one really gets is he's up there in the frozen nowhere because it's where a guy like him needed to be to stay sane. To my mind, that's just more proof of how special she is. I don't think I could run away from the world to be with someone that broken for a lifetime, let alone a forever.

Yeah, you heard me. The big guy? He was broken. Understand, Klaus is a man with a curse. He takes one look at people, and he knows. He knows the colour of a human soul. That takes a toll on a man, and so… snow. There's no dark stain anywhere to be had on the endless snow. He'd always been a builder—keeping his hands busy helped keep his eyes from knowing too much about the people around him—and together they built a home.

And then he started making toys.

You ask me? I think the toys were her idea. The big guy, he has great hands for that kind of thing, and with her gifts, all the time in the world. Together, they made for a happier couple than most I know. But I also know he was done with children. He'd seen too many of them start out so good and end up not. She, on the other hand, loved children. She can't have any, of course—no baby will grow in a body that lives outside of time—so I always figured she does the next best thing she can: she tries to do good by all the kids of the world.

Now, if you're noticing most of the magic is in her, and only a little to do with him, and thinking that ain't much like the story you've always been told, well, welcome to a world where some stories get retold more than others, and some truths aren't found to be worth retelling.

Holding on to moments is one thing, but using them proper is another. In her endless time in an endless home, Klaus surpassed apprentices and tradesmen both, and soon he was an expert craftsman of nearly every kind. And though he'd been an older man when they'd met, he grew no older, and in between her ongoing forevers, the light in his eyes came back.

They were happy. And when he was happy, she asked that they might take all those beautiful crafts he'd made and give them to the world. To children. And because he was happy again, and it had been so long since he'd seen a bad soul, he agreed.

Given enough time, any living creature can learn. And it was not too much for her to spread her reach a little wider and snare a dozen reindeer. Klaus never worried about animals—his gift only ever worked with people—and the longer those reindeer existed out of time, the more they learned. Eventually, they were as smart as you or me. Inside her reach, they kept their antlers, they earned names for themselves, and, in time, they even learned simple words they could send to Klaus's mind or hers or each other.

They could see the other reindeer outside her reach, and sometimes they even wanted to go back, to grow older, and to pass on from this world. And though it made her sad, she let them go. As the daughter of Father Time, she was well aware that for all things that breathe there will come a time of breathlessness, though she herself might hold it off for as long as forever for some.

Klaus made bells and harnesses and a beautiful sleigh, and she wrapped timelessness in the ringing of the bells, so powerful that the air itself would hold still around their sound, and the reindeer could walk right up into the sky, their hoofs on the edge of air as solid as stone. And so it was she and Klaus would visit the world, all between an infant's blink, and leave behind wonderful treasures inside all those homes, for all the children. When the world was asleep, and time didn't pass, Klaus didn't have to look at any man, woman, or child if he didn't desire to.

He only looked at the children, and only the good.

That's how it was for a forever for them, centuries for the rest of the world. Sure, the reindeer would sometimes ask to be released, and though she mourned, she always allowed them to go and live out the rest of their lives with others of their kind, though they might not have the speech or understanding of Klaus's former team.

And that's how Rudolph came. Always a little different, a little more courageous at some things, but shy about others. Klaus watched him grow, and he swore he caught something of a light from him. Not like seeing a soul—Klaus had never been able to read the souls of animals, only his fellow humankind—but something else. Something palpable. Something visible to all.

The light was soft at first, but it became brighter as Rudolph grew to adulthood. From the window of his home inside timelessness, Klaus watched Rudolph's light grow stronger. It seemed to happen in a blink, not long enough for Klaus to know how difficult a time Rudolph had. But when he saw the creature use his light to scare a wolf pack away from a stray youth, Klaus decided. Even though he had the dozen reindeer he'd always maintained, he brought the lightbringer into their fold.

If neither Klaus nor his wife saw how these proud and ageless reindeer also treated Rudolph, it is perhaps not their fault. For the reindeer speech was mind-to-mind, and what the others said to Rudolph they would never dare to say to Klaus, nor especially to the woman who had made them what were.

Rudolph, in the way of the different, believed their claims that he could be cast out at any time for his differences, and thus never spoke of his fears.

The other reindeer tormented him. Lied to him of how others like Rudolph had come and gone through the forevers, and how every time, Klaus took pity on the different one and tried to teach it not to be different but eventually gave up in disgust, banishing them back to the world where they would lose their speech and their thought—and, of course, their light.

In response to this harshness, Rudolph tried to learn the limits of his light in order to have better control over it, and to learn how, someday, to leave that light behind. But the light had other ideas. It started to show him things and cast shadows from elsewhere. Rudolph saw how others—especially others like him—were treated. Kittens born without tails, or puppies missing an ear or an eye; little human girls who cared nothing for dresses or frills or babies; even wolves, who Rudolph struggled to like, chasing off their own when their own were all black or all white; or little human boys who knew from the start they they were *different* and that *different* meant *wrong*.

Mostly, though, Rudolph saw people. People pushed others to the side so often. Children who were not what their parents desired were as tormented as he was, and they didn't have his Klaus or the woman who made time stand still. Some of those people ran. Some were silenced. All were alone.

Rudolph watched, and Rudolph learned.

Then came the fog.

To Klaus, the fog seemed born of the castoffs of dark souls: a mist made of all the hurt and bad people had been doing to each other. To the daughter of Father Time, it seemed the stain of too many horrible yesterdays, memories of bad times trying to force a way into their home. To the reindeer, it cast a blur over the eyes, and a wail in the mind, drowning their kindnesses to each other, and making them all the crueler to Rudolph. But it was opaque to all of them. The lady rang one of the bells, and though the fog froze, there was no seeing through it. It gathered around their home, and she looked at all the gifts that her husband had made, and for the first time in her piece of forever, she grieved.

Her sadness brought a bravery to Rudolph, who had an instinct this stain was not immune to everything. And so, despite the merciless threats of the others year after year, Rudolph brought forth his light, as bright as he could make it, and as he'd somehow known, they could see into and through the fog.

Klaus asked Rudolph, mind-to-mind, if he would lead the rest of the team with his light to pierce the fog and guide the way, walking on air held apart from time.

And oh, the things those other reindeer said to Rudolph to frighten him, but Rudolph agreed. There was steel to the lightbringer's thoughts. And the lady? She was happy, then, knowing the gifts would find homes, and she thanked him.

Rudolph did not meet her gaze.

Klaus made him a harness and bells. She brought time to heel and bound it in the ringing. Rudolph tried on the harness, shook the bells, and learned to walk into the sky, casting his light before him to lead his way to, and from, their home in the snow and ice surrounded by the fog.

But the night they were to go, when she pulled on the thread of the year to draw a whole world into one moment of a single night, Rudolph was gone. His bells, his harness, and—the biggest betrayal of all—many of the gifts had all vanished with him. In the passing of a breath or two, Rudolph had acted and returned, showing no sign of shame. In fact, Rudolph's head remained high right until he saw her, and only then did he kneel before her in apology, though he still didn't speak of what he'd done or why.

He did not reply when Klaus demanded to know where the gifts were. The others tried to incite him the only way they knew how, but Rudolph was stronger than their games. Only when the lady asked him kindly and patiently what he had done, did Rudolph find himself unable to hold his quiet.

Rudolph had visited only those his light had shown him, the cast-offs, the broken, the unwanted, and the unloved. Those who woke each morning knowing they were wrong, and prayed each night they would not wake up so the next day. Those who fit in the roles of others, or who missed fitting at all. Those who hurt. Those who cried. Those who had forgotten how to do either.

She listened to him and asked him why. She was a woman aware of infinities, and knew the power of a 'why.'

Rudolph admitted he could not break his light, and knew it was only a matter of time before, as the other reindeer had explained to him, she and Klaus would send him away for being so different. And he had wanted, just once, to make a difference for others like himself, so he left each of them a little of his light.

He would not do more. He would not help them deliver the rest of the gifts to those he knew had allowed so many to be left aside. He would not help the other reindeer. And he would not apologize for what he had done.

Rudolph waited to be punished, knowing it must come.

But it didn't. Both Klaus and his wife agreed on that much, though Klaus wanted to send the other reindeer away. The lady, though, prevailed upon him to wait until they showed no ability to change, or at least until there were others capable of taking their place.

But the night would have to stand as Rudolph had left it. The thread of time, pulled so taut, would have to be released, and even she did not know what it might mean. And with the fog and Rudolph refusing to lead the others, she had no reason to hold on any longer. She let go, and the night resumed until morning came.

Those who woke to Rudolph's presents were the ones most affected. It didn't matter the gift itself, the presence—and the light Rudolph had left—was the thing. To be singled out, and celebrated, and rewarded, and seen, and heard... And to see others, others like themselves with the same gifts, was to many the first time ever knowing they were not alone. The light Rudolph had given them drew them to each other. They gathered, and they spoke, and they found in each other something they had never had before: a family.

But the world around them saw no joy in this, only anger.

That the broken and strange and weak and different were rewarded when the strong and the normal and the common and the celebrated were not? An outrage. And a particularly dark confusion. None could deny how the gifts had been bestowed, and yet the world refused to see the reasons why these people held a light of their own. More, that same light revealed some who the world had always believed belonged among their own. Such revelations tore more than one apart.

In the fog, the lady and Klaus and the other reindeer could not see these things happening, but Rudolph could, and the pain of it—of his own making, his own actions—left him so broken, he went to Klaus and the lady and begged for their aid.

He called his light and showed the lady and Klaus and the reindeer all the shadows of the people he had helped, and those who he had angered. There were joys, yes, but the hatreds were there, too. Klaus looked away first. He knew where these things were likely to go, having seen dark souls enough during his life where time passed.

As what Rudolph's shadows revealed grew worse, the lady couldn't help herself. She reached out and snared another thread, calling it all to stop before another fist could fall.

Holding forever in her hand, she asked for help. The reindeer, knowing now they'd had no small part in making this happen, agreed. Klaus, wanting to make her smile again more than anything, agreed. And Rudolph, poor Rudolph, seeing that the other reindeer were terrified of what might come of them and knowing those he'd helped had only been singled out for violence, agreed.

She was not her father. Holding time still, standing between moments, making a second count more than years, those were her gifts. And so, when she wound the thread backwards, she knew it was done imperfectly. Some things would have to be allowed to remain, lest the whole thing unravel, but she chose them carefully.

Rudolph led Klaus's sleigh of gifts out into the fog, bolstered by the knowledge that his difference was welcomed by the lady and Klaus, and that he need not fear what the other reindeer had told him. They broke the fog away into nothingness as they rode the time-hardened air, circling a world in which the same night replayed again, differently, but also the same.

The second morning of that same night, some woke knowing the day had happened before. The ones Rudolph had visited opened their gifts knowing what would be inside, and knowing that the real present had nothing to do with what was in their hands, but in a kind of light they could see in others. They left the places they slept, whether they were homes or shelters or the streets, and they saw that light reflected inside other people they had already met on another version of this same day. They knew each other again, for the first time.

And this time, the presents given to all, each home visited, and everything delivered as it might originally have been, the world around them didn't notice.

At least, not at first.

The broken, and the strange, and the weak, and the different, and those who fit the wrong role, or missed fitting at all had found each other, and in each other a strength. They brought their own light, and found they were not alone.

The world around them would notice, of course. And now and then, they'd even have a moment that almost felt like a memory: an almost-dream they'd seen these people before, and had faced them in numbers, and had done them wrong. The memory would be uncomfortable and unreal enough to ignore, and easily forgotten. But it would return. It did return. Often enough, sometimes, to make them think a little differently.

Though sometimes not.

Now, Klaus and his wife and his animals all live outside of time. Dolph—he calls himself Dolph now—shows Klaus and his wife shadows of those who might need an extra special gift, and Klaus and his wife are more careful now about a lot of things. But she and Klaus and Dolph, they'll remember both nights forever.

The rest of the world? Well, they're still growing old. Fewer and fewer of us are still here from the night that never was, the night that happened twice, the night a light guided us through a darkness to each other, and the story—like all stories—is fading in the retelling. We try to find those born like us in the new generations, but sometimes we miss some, and with so many of us having our own memories of that night, the details change.

After all, ask three people for the truth and you'll get three stories.

Sure, it makes for a happier tale when everything rhymes and the only villain is a bit of bad weather, but I see these other folk like me getting shoved aside. I even see those of us who are different stepping down hard on those who are *more* different than us. I see fewer folk happy to welcome them in. Fewer folk happy to see any difference for what it is: a gift.

As for me? Well. I still see the light in my people. I keep telling this story. But I look around, and I see the way the world is treating the different, and I can't help but think another fog is rolling in.

I just hope Dolph is willing to shine his light again.

FROST

I T WASN'T A magic hat, and it certainly wasn't about laughing and playing—though there is dancing—but if you'll let me, I promise there's a story worth telling.

It's not just about the snowman, either. Or the magician—who, by the way, was a woman, not a man, but that should surprise none who've watched history shift as it is passed along.

Mostly? It's about a man who most considered a boy.

He was a man, though, and that's important to know. They called him Little Jay. He was scrawny instead of strong, short instead of tall, and took so much after his mother that his father would routinely tell others at the pub his wife must have made Little Jay all on her own.

Certainly, Little Jay was of no use to his father, who was a woodcutter and a carver and who had five other strong sons who learned his craft and worked with him every day. Together, the six Carver men filled the fireplaces of all through winter. They were a cornerstone of the village.

Little Jay was more like a crack in the cobblestone path.

So, Little Jay helped his mother in the house. They had no daughters, so Little Jay learned the skills his mother taught. He could mend and sew and cook, and the straw brooms and baskets he made were as good or better than her own. He had a knack for building patterns from scraps since he was always inheriting them, taking broken things and mending them. After all, when one of his brothers or his father would rip or tear their clothing beyond a simple repair, his frame was small enough that undoing the stitches meant he could fashion a new shirt or trousers from the pieces, carefully avoiding the ruined bits.

He often found enough torn leftovers to make small colorful patchwork hats, gloves and scarves, or small dolls for the children of their village. He also mended for the villagers, and his repairs were often pretty. His mother called this his magic, but Little Jay knew making a pleasing pattern out of castoffs wasn't magic.

It was practical, perhaps. Useful, even. And certainly a way to pass time in the winter.

But magic? No.

Magic was rare and wonderful and often done by those the village didn't mind inviting when times were dire or needs were great, but otherwise preferred to leave unseen. Such was the case of the traveling wizardess who came through with the first snows each winter.

The families of the village fed her, housed her, and asked her to bless the fields. She always smiled, never telling them magic was not a blessing, and she worked the spells in exchange for their hospitality. Even Little Jay's father and mother would have her spend a night. Little Jay would sleep in a nest of blankets by the fire, and after a meal of a nutty bread and thick stew, the wizardess would walk through the woods, touching the small saplings the family planted, tying small silk ribbons to ensure they grew tall and strong. Then, she would sleep in Little Jay's bed until morning.

She stayed only a night with each family. And she was ever careful not to cross paths with the parson, who made it no secret she was not welcome.

She saw the way even those who hosted her frowned at a woman who wore silk trousers and seemed to feel nothing of the cold, though she expected they cared more about the trousers than the enchantment she had woven into her silks. She knew full well that when she had done the things they asked of her, it would be wise to go, and quickly.

On the last night before she left the village, the wizardess would perform for the children, making things appear and disappear, and doing other minor magics that were as much trickery as they were spells. Little Jay waited for this night every year, and though often his brothers would mock him for attending, many of the other parents liked that Little Jay was present at these shows, watching over the other children who attended.

None wanted to offend the wizardess, after all, but if a respected adult joined the audience, it would seem too much like approval in the eyes of the parson.

As her final trick that winter, the wizardess threw her black silk shawl into the air and meowed like a cat while it floated down in front of her. The silk was shredded, midair, though none saw anything touch it, and the children applauded as the segments landed on the straw-covered floor of the barn.

When the wizardess picked up the pieces, pushing them into her closed fist and then pulling the scraps back out as one long braided scarf, the applause was all the louder.

This, she explained, was the most important rule of magic there was. Anything broken might never be what it was, but in the right hands and with enough heart, it could always become something else.

And as she wove the scarf around her neck, gathering her things about her and getting ready to leave, Little Jay noticed the small scrap of black silk still left in the straw.

He tried to stop her, holding the piece in his hand, but the wizardess merely winked, and was gone. Wizardesses are often present to begin a tale, and far less often to see the end of one.

But that scrap of silk?

Little Jay worked it into a silk cap he'd made of scraps.

Change had come to the village.

His mother praised the pattern Little Jay worked into the scraps. His father criticized the dye on Little Jay's hands and the uselessness of a silk cap in winter. His eldest brother joked that only a snowman would wear a hat so useless.

After dinner, when his father took the rest of his brothers to the pub, and after he and his mother had finished the dishes and placed the hot stones in their beds, Little Jay went to his small room filled by the large bed he'd never grow into, pulled the quilts over himself, and found himself awake.

He heard the other men come home and take themselves to their beds. He heard their laughter, and their cheerful wishes for good dreams, and he heard their snores that followed.

After, as quietly as a small man who has learned to avoid notice could be— which is very quiet indeed—Little Jay dressed, wrapped himself in a scarf he'd made from scraps, shrugged into his patched jacket, carefully slid his feet into boots after layering two thick socks on first, and found his best, warmest gloves.

Little Jay went outside into the snow.

He loved the snow and the patterns it made. Drifts were like waves, and the ice on the pond sometimes looked like large snowflakes. He would catch flakes on the end of his scarf, so he could peer at them, holding his breath, and see the star-like patterns—tiny, beautiful things—before they melted away. Tonight, the sky was full of snow, and the dim lights from the village below and the single winter lantern his mother kept lit overnight, were barely enough to chase off the darkness.

But Little Jay had no fear of the dark and much love for the dance of the snow, and so he twirled, arms wide, knowing the scorn he'd invoke for what he was doing if anyone had been there to see.

When he saw the way his footsteps remained in the snow, he knew it was the kind of snow he could build with, so he set to work. What his brother had said—only a snowman would wear a hat so useless—struck him as a dare, and he took pains to craft a man of snow as large as Little Jay himself was small, as wide as he was narrow, and as strong as he was gentle. He took care and time to craft a jacket of snow, with pond stones for buttons. For boots he wrapped pale orange leaves he found under the trees, and he used needles from the evergreen trees as though the man's white trousers were stitched with green thread. For the face, he took two slivers of coal for the eyes, which he placed under a strong brow and a square jaw nothing like his own face, and then he wove his patchwork scarf around the snowman's neck.

Now he was done, the smile slipped from his lips.

The large man of snow was nothing like him. And while that had been the point, now Little Jay couldn't help but think this was the sixth son his father would rather have had.

He pulled the silk hat from his head.

To have a man like this, a man like his father and his brothers, who would look at him and respect him and—yes—love him, even though he was small and narrow and gentle.

What that might be like.

He wiped a tear on the hat, then fit it on the top of the snowman.

Then, Little Jay went to bed, which was how he missed the snowman's first breath.

The next morning, a man came to their door. A stranger in the village was rare and not often welcome, but the tall, broad-shouldered man was eager to work, and possessed good humour and an easy smile. Even in the midwinter, such a man had opportunities. For a place by a hearth and a plate at the table, he agreed to chop wood, clear snow, or haul what needed hauling. That he was handsome, with eyes darker than anyone in Little Jay's family had ever seen, and that his clothing was so unusual brought some pause—especially to Little Jay's father—but the man put them all at ease within moments, and soon it was settled that he would breakfast with them, work the day together, and join them for dinner and warmth thereafter.

When Little Jay and his mother brought out the morning food, Little Jay nearly dropped the wooden bowls of warm oats and brown sugar.

The stranger wore a white fur coat with carved stone buttons, and white breeches sewn with green thread. His leather boots were a pale orange, and most importantly, atop his head was a silk cap made of dyed scraps, and a scarf almost to match.

Little Jay looked out the window, but the snowman and the cap and scarf, were not there.

The man met his gaze, nodded once, and smiled.

His father introduced Little Jay the way one might mention the spoon a cook stirred with, and if his father or brothers noticed how warm and kind the stranger's greeting to Little Jay was, it went unmentioned.

His mother asked the stranger his name, and with a short pause to once again meet Little Jay's gaze, the man said his surname was Frost.

They ate, and then they went to work.

Little Jay fretted the day away, and more than once his mother had to bring his attention back to the blankets they were mending and the baskets they were weaving. Making patterns out of castoffs felt dangerous now, and Little Jay's fingers trembled.

Could it be true?

He wove another round of the basket's rim. The women who would later buy the basket would swear it held more than it should.

Could it be true?

He patched a faded blue quilt with small yellow scraps, making a bright star on an otherwise cloudless sky. The child who would later sleep under the mended cloth would always dream of flying.

Could it be true?

They started the evening meal, and Little Jay found himself weaving bread in knots, something he rarely bothered to do unless the meal was a special one. His mother, seeing him work, considered whether or not her son might be apprenticed to the village baker.

But of course, he had two broad-shouldered sons of his own.

She returned to her work, swallowing the familiar fears of what futures might be there for her youngest, smallest son.

When the men returned, Little Jay's father's report of the day was something close to a celebration. The stranger had done work almost equal to the rest of them, and their wagons were full of wood for the village days before they could have expected. His father and brothers tore apart the knotted breads, telling stories of how the stranger felled trees with half the blows it would have taken them, and only Frost himself paused to compliment the bread itself.

They laughed into the dark hours, knowing that the next morning they could have the rarest of rewards: a later start. His father offered the stranger Little Jay's bed, saying Little Jay himself would sleep by the fire in blankets—he was the only one small enough to fit in the nook. And though the stranger protested, Little Jay thought nothing of it, and eased his concern with a smile and a bob of his head.

The others went to sleep, his brothers one by one, then his mother, and finally his father. Little Jay cleared the table with Frost's help, and they worked side by side in silence. When what work that could be done was done, Little Jay found himself looking at Frost again.

His brow was strong, and his eyes were as dark as flecks of coal. He still wore the silk cap, though he'd shed the white fur coat with the carved stone buttons and beneath that wore a plain cotton tunic. Broad and strong, he seemed so very real, and yet...

Frost reached out, took Little Jay's hand, and thanked him.

Little Jay listened in silence as Frost explained that anything broken might never be what it was, but in the right hands and with enough heart, it could always become something else. Magic from a piece of a scarf meant to keep a wizardess warm could not be a scarf again, but it could bring warmth of another kind, enough to make what was snow into something that was, though still snow, alive. Something crafted with love might, with that little bit of magic and a single tear, be given the freedom to return the love. He drew Little Jay into an embrace.

14

There was room enough in Little Jay's bed, though Little Jay was careful to return to his little nest of blankets and pillows by the fire come morning, and the next day, while he and his mother worked, she noticed the patterns he wove into the baskets were truly things of beauty, and a second blue quilt was mended with whole constellations of snowflakes.

On the market day, the village met Frost, who charmed them all by helping them carry their firewood to their wagons. He was the talk of the village by the time the sun hit its peak. Even the parson stopped at their family stall, ostensibly to pick up one of Little Jay's excellently woven straw brooms, though his mother knew he'd already purchased one only two weeks earlier.

Frost's laughter, dark eyes, and warm voice put the village at ease, and in some small way, Little Jay felt welcomed as he'd never felt before. Indeed, Frost had a way of mentioning Little Jay's talents to those who browsed their stall, and a few times the other villagers looked at Little Jay like they were seeing him for the first time.

But neither the man born of magic and a longing for love, nor a youngest son who made that wish, however, knew how dangerous being noticed might be.

There were few so easily slighted as the eldest Carver son, used to all the attention and praise. And after days of being placed second to a stranger, Little Jay's eldest brother had begun to study the stranger.

The cap he wore, for one, was familiar.

The eldest son went to the parson with his firewood and asked if he had ever seen clothing like the fur coat Frost wore, and the parson had to admit he had not. The eldest son asked the parson if it was perhaps odd that a man so strong would need to wander from village to village to find work. Having planted the sapling, the eldest son returned to his family, and tried hard to remember where he'd seen that silk cap.

The parson had never come to dinner before, but his request could hardly be turned down. Little Jay worked beside his mother, once again braiding bread dough while she worked to craft a meal worthy of the respected man's standing. The brothers were not happy to have to wear their finest, except for Little Jay, who liked the way the collar of his shirt made him seem a little older.

At the meal, it was soon clear that the parson wanted to know more of Frost.

Why would a man so strong and so generous of spirit need to wander from village to village?

Frost dipped his bread, took a moment to thank Little Jay for his efforts, and suggested that anyone with a gift should seek to spread the gift as widely as possible. If strong arms made for shorter work, there would be more gained from them for many if those arms were to travel.

Was it not hard to keep such beautiful white fur clean? And what sort of fur might it have been?

Frost sipped his tea, took a moment to thank Little Jay's mother for the lovely blend, and suggested that everyone had surely seen a white furred creature at one time for another. It only took patience and fingers as clever as Little Jay's to make large things from small things, and cleanliness was a goal worth seeking.

And how long would the village be granted the strength and giving of such a man?

Here, Frost paused longer still, taking the last bite of his meat. Having come with the snow, it seemed fitting he'd leave that way, too.

Little Jay clenched his hands under the table. His father, uncomfortable with the directness of the parson, suggested it time for hot gin and lemon, and his wife went to set the pot to heat.

And that hat, the parson wondered aloud. How unusual it was.

Little Jay's eldest brother remembered then. He turned to his youngest brother and asked him plain if he had made it.

From scraps, Little Jay agreed, with a measure of pride.

And this was how the parson's gaze was turned to Little Jay.

After all had eaten and drunk and said their goodnights, the parson left. Little Jay and Frost cleaned the table and kitchen, and then, as had become their habit, they made up Little Jay's nest of blankets and pillows by the fire, and then left them there alone. They went outside and danced in the snow together, which Frost could call and conjure to play, before heading back inside to Little Jay's bed.

From the hilltop, unseen, watched the parson.

The sheriff and the parson came for Little Jay after the Carver father and brothers and Frost had left for the morning's work. His mother, standing in front of her youngest son, tried to refute what they were saying.

Little Jay, however, was tired of scraps. He was tired of mending the broken things of others and watching others have lives he might never have. So he stepped forward and told them of a scrap of magic, of a wish and a tear, and of how a man made of snow was the most loving thing he had ever encountered, of a man who loved him despite his size, and who danced with him in the snow and made the snow dance with them in kind.

Little Jay had been loved, and he did not care if magic had been the seed of that love.

They took him.

Little Jay's mother ran to the woods and found her husband and her sons and Frost, and it was as though she saw Frost for the first time. Eyes as dark as coal, more handsome than should naturally be, skin unreddened by the cold, unlike her husband and sons, and a simple silk cap that could have done nothing to keep the cold away.

She wanted to hate him, and though she told him what had happened and how it was his fault, she knew the words were untrue even as she said them. Her eldest son, appalled, threw himself at Frost, and so surprised the big man that he did not stop the eldest son from tearing the silk cap from his head and flinging it far into the woods.

The eldest son turned, sure he would now see a snowman where Frost had stood, but Frost remained. Frost pushed the man aside, and began to run. Though Little Jay's father and mother and the other brothers tried to chase after him, the snow itself seemed no impediment to Frost, and soon he had left them behind.

Frost paused at their home, grabbing one of the unfinished straw brooms— just the broomstick—and then was once again on his way.

Down he went, to the village.

The villagers had seen the parson and the sheriff pass by with Little Jay between them, and many had heard the whispers spread in the wake. They lined the street and parted before Frost as he approached. Each time his broomstick touched the ground, a tremor ran through the village.

The sheriff, seeing the large and angry Frost approaching, held out his hands and called for the man to stop, but Frost raised the broomstick and thumped it against the ground, and a wave of snow and ice burst forward, knocking the sheriff aside.

Frost drove his stick into the ground by the doors of the parson's church, and the doors were driven from their hinges win a spray of cold.

Little Jay lay inside. Fingers snapped, each a refusal to recant; back bleeding, each stroke a refusal to speak of Frost with anything but love; feet broken, a refusal to apologize for magic.

The parson's words of condemnation died on his lips when he saw Frost's coal-dark eyes and the fury within them, and he stumbled aside as Frost lifted Little

Jay and carried him from the church to the street, from the street to a field, and from the field, away.

While they walked, the snow parting and rejoining behind them, Little Jay reached up a broken hand and asked for one more kiss.

In the mountains, where the snow fell thickest, Frost knelt down and gathered Little Jay into his arms again. Little Jay was shaking with cold, and his body all but finished, so broken at the hands of the parson and the sheriff. Frost, created out of love and a wish, shed his first tears, and held Little Jay tight while he kissed him.

With that kiss, Frost and Little Jay both were reminded that anything broken might never be what it was, but in the right hands, with enough heart, it could always become something else. Even hands and a heart first made of snow. A scrap of a scarf and a tear had seen to that. And now, a tear and a kiss were magic and heart enough to restore some of what was lost.

A magic twice mended, first for love and now for life, could only go so far.

Still, Little Jay took a breath. And then another. He sat up, and felt none of the cold around him. He smiled, looking at the man who had carried him from his village, and he understood.

Little Jay rose, and when his restored hands brushed a tree, patterns of ice spread up and down the bark, like scraps of winter mended and woven into something beautiful. He turned to Frost, who nodded.

Their hearts were now the same, winter born and winter sustained. And since that day, they travel together, loving and loved, wherever the winter snows might take them. They leave patterns behind for those who might need to see beauty when things are cold.

Little Jay left the name Carver behind with his village, taking Frost as his surname instead. In all the places the snow falls, there are none quite as happy as Frost and the man who used to be Little Jay.

But you likely know him as Jack.

REFLECTION

I ONLY KNOW my own part, but that's all any of us can say. But before I begin, I need you to understand one thing above all: I was rescued twice, not once, but I was never kidnapped.

But I should start at the beginning, which I guess is the garret.

If you live in a garret, you get two views. One is the view through your window, where you can see the whole city, up high like a bird. The other is the way people view you, which is the complete opposite. Poor people lived in the garrets, where even as young as I was when all this began, I had to duck down on one side of our room so I wouldn't hit my head on the slope of the roof.

And in my case, I had a third view but it had barely started. A glance in water, a moment in front of the small mirror my mother kept, or catching a glance at the side of a teapot.

I'm getting ahead of myself again.

I did have a grandmother, but I lived with my parents and brothers, too, all of us in our two rooms with one window, but if people talk about my family they only talk about my grandmother. I had friends—we garret kids had the top set of stairs to ourselves, after all—but mostly there was Gerda.

Gerda didn't live in my building. Her family was in the one next door, but if I scarpered out my window, I could climb into hers, and between the windows her papa built a box where my grandmother grew vegetables, some herbs, and sometimes even a flower or two.

They weren't roses. You don't grow roses in garret flower boxes.

I guess that's the first thing you've been told that's wrong. They were pansies. And it's more important than you'd think. Pansies are tough.

It took me quite a while to figure that part out for myself.

WHEN WINTER CAME, and the last of the things that grew in the box were gone, my grandmother would tell me stories by the light of the window or read to me from the only book we had in our rooms. My parents worked most of the day—my father chipping away deep in the stone of the earth, my mother keeping one of the great houses fed without being seen. Two of my brothers were already working with my father—I imagined that would have been me, too, if not for everything that would come—and my third brother was out selling, carrying his tray-box around his neck and stomping his feet in the cold.

My brothers always looked at me like I'd done something wrong being born last. Like somehow, staying home with my grandmother and holding the yarn while she knitted, or cleaning the floors while she cooked up a stew from bits and pieces was a great life they'd missed out on for having been born before me.

Me? I watched them climb down all the stairs every day and go out into the city and walk through the streets and thought they had freedom.

We were both wrong. They were no more free than I was, they just got a different view and had more people to talk to.

I should say my grandmother never meant to be cruel. When they say she loved me, I suppose in her way, in a fashion, she did. Same with Gerda, really. But there's love and there's love. So, when my grandmother warned me about the Snow Queen, she thought she was doing me a good deed.

I HEARD THE same stories year after year—my grandmother only had so many— but when frost started to draw patterns on the glass of our window, she'd usually tell me about the Snow Queen. The frost reminded her, I think.

"She's a queen, like bees in their boxes have queens, my boy. You have to watch the snow. Sometimes what seems white and pure and delicate isn't—that's her."

My grandmother would trace her finger on the glass, pressing it against the surface until the frost melted.

"Watch for the snow. Sometimes it's not snow. When you see the snowflakes gathering in the light, make sure they're not hers. They're more like bees, my boy. Like bees made of ice so sharp, they'd cut you like glass."

After that, she'd knit for a while in silence, and I'd watch the ball of yarn grow smaller and smaller until the candles grew dim and it was time to start the evening tea. I would go downstairs to fetch water or sweep the room, and I'd look at the frost on the window and wonder about bees made of glass.

"Beware her kisses, my boy. One kiss and you'll be as cold as she is, two and you'll be as heartless, and if you allow a third…" Here she would pause and look over her glasses at me. "A third is death."

That winter, the winter they talk about, I barely slept. I lay by the fire in my blankets, shivering with a cold that had little to do with the drafts of an attic room. My grandmother had started to ask about my friendship with Gerda.

My eldest brother would soon be married, and he would leave us in spring.

I knew what she was asking, and I knew I couldn't answer.

I gave up trying to sleep and paced the small room, wishing the movement and stoking the fire would warm me inside where the cold fear was settling. To the window. Back again. In the other room, the rest of my family slept. I tried whispering rhymes to myself. Gerda had a silly rhyme about pansies she liked to sing to me, and sometimes that would help.

But that night it didn't.

The cold inside me only grew worse the more I thought about the days ahead.

So, I went to the window.

It was just a glimpse. A woman, tall and beautiful, in a cloak as white as freshly fallen snow was walking through the street, and the angle between the two buildings from our garret window meant my glimpse was brief.

But she turned, and she met my gaze.

Her smile seemed kind.

I pulled away from the window, went back to my bed by the fire, and pulled the cloth over my eyes. I should have been terrified.

Instead, for the first time in months, I finally felt warm.

That night I realized I liked the stories of the Snow Queen better than the ones from the book, which so often made my insides twist, desperate and terrified, even as my grandmother swore we'd all be welcomed in paradise. She said she knew our hearts, and we were all worthy.

I knew better. I only had to see a mirror to be reminded.

And I knew better than to say so.

FOR ALL THE warnings my grandmother made in winter, it began in summer. I had brought a bucket to the plant box between our garret windows, and Gerda had a picture book. I don't know where she got it, but it seemed like a very beautiful thing to me. There were dancing ladies and men in great coats and so many birds.

I was using a ladle to water the plants. If that seems silly, understand I didn't want to carry a second bucket all the way up all the stairs to the garret when I could carefully water each vegetable enough with just one bucket and a ladle.

"Look at these two," Gerda said. She pointed to a group of pipers, each man playing music. Her voice was hushed, as though she was telling me a secret.

I looked at the picture. Two of the pipers were holding hands.

Heat and cold warred inside me, despite the summer day. I opened my mouth to say something, glancing down at the bucket, and I saw Gerda's reflection.

She was recoiling from me, pulling away and shaking her head. Disgusted or afraid or just pitying. It was hard to tell on the surface of the water, but I was sure of one thing: like every reflection I happened to look into, it was telling me a truth.

It was a warning.

"It's a terrible thing," I said, meaning one thing but knowing Gerda would hear another. She gave me a little nod and closed the book, and helped me water the rest of the vegetables.

I watched as every ladle lowered the water in the bucket. Gerda seemed to get farther and farther away.

"Gerda," I said, before there wasn't enough water left to show her face. "Are we friends?"

She smiled at me. It was a sunny smile, as warm as the day. "Of course we are."

Her reflection shook her head.

I poured the last of the water into the garden. The pansies were bright and pretty, even though the wind had been strong for days and many were a little beaten down. I wished I had half the courage they had.

IT WAS EASY to catch my grandmother's reflection, too. Between the basin where we washed the dishes, and the small mirror in the garret, it just took a little forethought. When I allowed myself to think of myself as I was, and whisper a word out loud, her reflection would turn from me. Or raise both hands to the heavens, pleading and afraid. Or weep.

That was the worst.

After, I kept my own counsel, and I tried to avoid anything that reflected, but it wasn't always possible. My grandmother noticed. So did Gerda. And my grandmother even noticed how little Gerda and I spoke, and that concerned her more.

"Have you argued?" she asked me, one autumn afternoon.

"No, grandmother," I said. I was always respectful. I did nothing to give her any reason to worry about me. But I knew it couldn't last forever. Her face was full of concern.

"Good," she said, but I knew she felt it was anything but. Her stories turned to tales of those who didn't allow love in their hearts, and the various cataclysms befalling them. Every story seemed to begin with someone who lost love from their heart and become cruel, and ended with someone who loved them bringing them back from some dark place.

I learned to close my eyes when I passed the garret mirror and keep my gaze above the water when I washed plates or watered the plant box.

BY WINTER, THE tales my grandmother told were once again of the Snow Queen, and I was barely sleeping. I could not find enough blankets, and I singed myself by sleeping too close to the fire. Nothing thawed the fear every mirror, window, or pool of water revealed to me. If they knew, they would turn away.

And worse, I knew *if* would eventually be *when*.

After a particularly heavy snow and a productive morning, my grandmother suggested I go outside with my sled. I knew she wanted me to go with the others my age, especially Gerda, but I took her at her word and carried my sled outside by myself. Between the fear in my chest and the snow that was still falling, I was soon chilled through, though I did ride down the slope of the lane a few times.

And at the end of our lane, I saw the carriage sleigh. It was beautiful: its wood painted white, trimmed with fur and bells and somehow stately in a way I couldn't explain. And on it, as though she had been waiting for me all this time, was the beautiful woman herself, in her white furs and smiling her kind smile for me.

Children would hitch their sleds to carriage sleighs like this to have a ride. But this was *her* carriage sleigh, and I looked around and saw no other children and the snow in the air seemed to swirl in and on itself in little circles, less like snow and more like bees.

My grandmother's warnings conjured nothing. I should have been afraid. I shivered, but it was not born of fear of this woman. I tied my sled to the carriage sleigh, and her smile stole any shred of worry I might have had.

The ride out of the city was incredible. There were no crowds of people in our way. Everyone seemed to step aside just in time, and I found myself laughing as the snow itself blew into people's faces and made them turn or twist or pause. We flew through the streets, and when we came to rest outside the gates, I was panting from laughter.

I untied my sled and went to thank her.

The woman on the carriage sleigh was no longer just a beautiful woman in white fur. She had cast aside her fur coat, and beneath she wore snow and ice gathered like a fine gown. Her eyes were the palest blue I'd ever seen, and I could see my own reflection in them.

And just for a second, I saw myself smiling and happy.

"You are the Snow Queen," I said.

She nodded once. "I am."

"Are you here to hurt me?"

Those pale blue eyes filled with a sadness so familiar I ached for her. "Do you think I am?"

I shook my head.

"Most people can't see me," she said.

"I see things," I said. "In mirrors. In glass. In water. In..."

"Ice?" she said.

"Reflections."

"You see a person's heart, then?"

"I think so." I swallowed. "Yes. Truths, I think. Words in my head make truths in reflections."

The Snow Queen waved her hand, and snow whirled in a circle beside us, a swarm of flakes that wove the air itself into ice so perfect and smooth I could see both of us on its surface.

"And what do you see of me?"

I looked at the reflection, and I allowed myself to imagine telling her more about myself. Not just the things I could see in mirrors.

In the ice, the Snow Queen opened her arms in welcome, and I stepped into her embrace.

"I do not love," I said. "Not as they want me to."

When the Snow Queen embraced me, she kissed my forehead. And finally, the cold fear that had lived inside my heart was gone. My grandmother was right. I was as cold as she was.

It was just that she wasn't cold at all.

"They'll never understand," I said. It wasn't a question.

And so the Snow Queen kissed me again.

I was not made heartless, either. The second kiss drew a distance in my thoughts and memories, though, and a knowledge that I could not be what they expected. It wasn't heartlessness. It was understanding some hearts could not be pleased.

Enough understanding to know it was time to leave.

THE SNOW QUEEN took me to her palace, tucked away in the northern woods where snow and pines reigned around us in a peaceful and beautiful rest. She had friends, people like us, who would visit a while from time to time, but mostly she lived alone, content and happy with her own company.

She took me to a lake frozen mirror perfect and began to teach me.

"I work with snow and ice and memory," she said. "You work with words, reflection, and potential. I'm not sure how much of what I know might guide you, but for me, it always comes to a thought—a word as a truth—and the magic takes the rest."

It was like that for me, too. I had only to imagine words of truth on my lips, and I could see the reactions those words would bring in the reflections of those around me, but to do so with a purpose beyond discovering how others would react?

We started with simple things.

The Snow Queen would speak of winter, and for her, the snow would shift and twist and fly around in squalls about us, covering the world in a layer of white that no longer left me cold.

And when I spoke those words, the surface of the lake beneath us showed me winters around the world, where people woke and shared greetings, or where those who were alone would gaze out upon the snow-covered beauty of the season, and perhaps see something in it worth knowing. And, a few times, I even saw others like us—a valiant antlered deer who seemed to be fighting off wolves with a blazing light, and a woman who could pull time taut and hold it steady, and a young slight man who drew patterns of frost on every surface he touched with his bare hand—and I knew there was much to learn in the simplest words and truths.

I would often spend the whole of the night outside, for it seemed to me that the reflections I saw in moonlight were different from those in sunlight, and I had no fear of the cold thanks to the Snow Queen's first kiss.

If I was not happy, it was not that I was unhappy. If I was alone, it was worth saying that I was not lonely. The Snow Queen would visit, and she would see what words I had uncovered, and often join in for a while to speak them herself and see what, if anything, they would do when she used them.

When I said "home" under the sunlight, I saw my family, who believed I had drowned in a river. When I said "home" under the moonlight, nothing would appear beyond swirls of light and colour.

When I said "escape" under the sunlight, I could watch myself hitch my sled to the Snow Queen's carriage sleigh, and ride off to the freedom I now enjoyed. Under moonlight? The same word showed me myself, sitting on the lake, speaking word after word, trying to find the right one.

One morning, the Snow Queen came to me and draped a beautiful white cape across my shoulders. I tied it closed. "Thank you," I said, though I was confused. "It's lovely."

"It's a day for giving gifts," she said, and I realized just how long I'd been working my magic on the lake.

"I'm sorry," I said. "I keep thinking there is a word I'm missing. Something I could say that would show me where in the world there is a place for those like me." I smiled at the Snow Queen. "And yet here I sit, in a place you've brought me to that is place enough."

"This is mine, and it is perfect for me," the Snow Queen said. "But for you? I'm not sure. I think you're right. There's a word you still seek."

"I'll keep trying. But for you?" I gestured to the lake beneath us. "Gift," I said.

I kept my eyes away from the ice, for it felt private, but seeing the joy that crossed her face at whatever she watched play out beneath us was a gift in and of itself. Her laughter made beautiful snow zephyrs dance around us.

"You're talented," she said, once the vision had ended. "Perhaps tonight you will join me for a dinner?"

I said that I would, and I did. But come the morning, I returned to the lake and the hunt for my words.

And just before sunset came Gerda.

"THE PANSIES WOULDN'T die," Gerda said.

She stood facing me. I had no idea how long she had been there, watching me conjure magic from the reflection in the lake, but when I finally saw her, the expression on her face was exactly as I'd seen it in the bucket. Disgusted. Afraid.

Well.

Now she knew, and I knew I'd been right not to tell her.

As victories went, it was hollow.

"How?" I said.

"The pansies... and then I went... I went to see a woman. She... She was like you, but I thought, to save you, it was worth the risk... She tried to stop me, but the pansies, again..." Gerda was shaking her head. "They broke through, and I knew it meant you were okay."

A coach stood by the edge of the lake. I hadn't even heard it approach. It must have been how she'd come here. We never spoke of the rest of her journey to find me, so I never learned if what's said about her time with a prince and princess is even a little true, but her adventure had served her well, even if my "rescue" was not at all to be at her hand.

And she did look so fine, dressed in beautiful winter clothes. She couldn't feel the cold in those layers of furs.

"Aren't you cold?" she said. It was like she was reading my mind.

"No," I said. "It's part of..." I bit back the words. "It's part of all of this."

"Will you come home?"

"Home." I repeated the word, and the magic of it escaped me. Beneath us, the lake showed us my family in their garret, gathered for a meal. Gerda gasped, stepping away from me, her eyes on the magic.

And then the sun set, and the lake changed to the swirls of light instead.

"Why are you doing this?" Gerda said. Then, angrily, "Why are you like this?"

Snowflakes began to swirl around the edge of the lake. The Snow Queen, protecting me.

"Gerda," I said, not sure what else to say.

"Come home with me," Gerda said. "Come back to us. We're your family. We love you."

"Say that again," I said.

Gerda frowned, but repeated herself. And when she did, I caught her words and let the magic free.

Beneath us, she saw the truth of her words reflected in the ice. She saw my grandmother weep and pull away, my brothers full of scorn and spit, my mother turn her back, my father's anger... And her own disgust.

"It's not true," she said, shaking her head. "We do love you. If you just free yourself from her. From what she's done to you."

Around the lake, the snow swirled faster.

"She rescued me," I said.

"No!" Gerda stomped her foot, as if wishing her fancy new boot would break the ice and drop us into the frigid water deep beneath. "No, you are not... This isn't you. You're not..."

"A pansy?" I said.

She turned away. "You don't have to be."

"But I am," I said. "And I always will be."

The ice beneath us filled with the swirling light again, so bright the snow swirling around the lake seemed like lace curtains in motion. Gerda took my hand, frightened.

"It's okay," I said. I tried repeating the word that had set the magic in motion. "Always?" The light flared. It wasn't quite the right word, but it was in the same family as the one I'd been seeking all along.

Gerda was crying now.

"It's okay," I said. She buried her face in my shoulder. I tried another word. "Forever?"

Closer, still.

"Please don't," Gerda said. "Kai. It's like her. It's the snow. It's the Snow Queen!"

"It's not," I said. It was so close. Almost the right word. I could rescue myself, I could find the way to a home, if I just got it right. "It's not her. It's me. It'll always be me. Forever. It's…"

"Kai!"

"Eternity."

Light again, a moment between breaths, and then we saw all the places where I belonged.

IN THE STORY you were told, we came back together changed, adults in the space of the fallout of a single magical word. And I suppose, if you look at what happened a certain way, that might be true for me at least. But it took me time to go to all the places I saw, and it took me a bit longer to figure out what it was I was looking at.

But Gerda went home without me.

The lake showed me a pretty house in the woods, planter boxes on the windows, but also a row of stone houses in a city much bigger than the one where I'd grown, each colourful door with a basket hanging above. An inn decorated with a candle and a robin. A farm. A beautiful manor home with a large stable. Docks lined with barrels. And so many gardens, one even by a palace.

I thought one of those places might be where I belonged, and so I went to them. It took days, then weeks, then months. I grew stronger, and taller, and in each of those places, my magic was welcomed by one or two people, and I used it to help them speak truths and see things they didn't yet know.

And I would say the word *Eternity* and I would see all the places I had been already before the rest. Sometimes the order was different. Sometimes some of them were gone, replaced by others. It was a different kind of riddle, but as I traveled, I met others like myself.

It's possible you're wiser than I, and have spotted what it took me years to notice.

The pansies.

Pansies in flower boxes or baskets outside houses and stores and even the inn with the candle and the robin on the sign. Pansies on the hillside of the farm. Pansies on the docks. Hardy things, those flowers. And they're everywhere. They make it even when the wind breaks them down. They bloom, and grow, and thrive wherever they can.

It's possible all the various mirrors who'd shown me where I needed to go to find a home where I could belong could have been a bit more clear, but, well.

They reflect. It's what they do.

People come to my home from all of those places: the city where I was born, the farms, the row of stone homes, villages, and ships. Over water or glass I help them find the words they need, and outside, I hang a mirror. Each morning I stop, face it, and say the word.

Eternity.

The mirror is there for people who need it. People who need to look and see a truth they might not know themselves.

There have always been people like us.

There always will be.

And as for where we belong?

Everywhere.

You're tougher than you think.

Just like pansies, children who live in garrets, and the Queen of the Snow.

THE FIVE CROWNS AND COLONEL'S SABRE

"**A**S A GOOD soldier, he ought to know the wounded are not expected to take their places in the ranks."

My father's words were a cold comfort, spoken years before about a toy and yet could have been said now, were my father still alive, with just as much merit.

Now, as then, I couldn't help but feel some shame.

A good soldier. I had been that, in duty and effort and action if perhaps not always in heart. And now I rode a train back to a place I scarcely remembered from when I'd been a boy until the day I'd told my father I would not be joining his practice, but would instead be taking my skills to aid in war.

Ahead, I saw the city, lit in the failing light of the early winter afternoon.

The wounded are not expected to take their places in the ranks.

I exhaled, putting my father's words out of my mind as best I could.

"I NEED A sword." Marie sounded positively terrified. I saw the bandage on her arm, and I tried to have patience with her. She'd had a few rough days, and though our godfather had meant to entertain her, I think we'd both found his story more terrible and mean than anything else.

You'll be turned away if you are different, that story said. *Even if you bring a magical nut, restore a princess, and fulfil a prophecy.*

"Fritz?" Marie asked again.

"Pardon?"

"My nutcracker. He needs a sword. I can't... I can't protect him, and..." Tears filled her eyes.

I thought of my father and mother and our godfather, all of whom had been very, very clear that Marie's flights of fancy needed to stop, and indulging them was childish. Her story of the battle between the dolls and the mice—my own soldiers doing abysmally—had been a dream, of course, it had to have been, but...

I looked at her tears again.

"Did my hussars really perform so poorly?"

She sniffed. She was always such a considerate girl. "I'm sure they were just unprepared. It was a frightful thing, the battle."

"Well," I said. "Soldiers should be brave, not unprepared." I eyed the cabinet. "I may have just the thing."

She hugged me, and I hugged her back. Surely it wasn't an unkindness to set my younger sister's mind at ease?

I tried not to think of what my father might say. He didn't need to know, I thought.

He didn't need to know.

THE WALK FROM the train station to my home—so strange to think of it as my home—was done without fanfare, for which I was grateful. My leg kept me at a certain lacklustre pace, but it pained only a little, and I carried my bag in one hand to free the other for my cane. The absence of fuss was a welcome piece of rare luck.

I had my key, and my eldest sister Luise had arranged for someone to come by the house and ensure it would be stocked well enough for me to spend a day or two acclimating before having to see to anything of a grand effort.

I lit a lamp left at the entrance and eyed the spare entryway. With the door closed behind me, the worst of the cold and snow had retreated, though surely it would also be cold inside once I had not the contrast to consider.

I eyed the great staircase, but the weariness of that particular trek was too much. So, I pinned my hopes on my father's penchant for resisting all change and made my way to a room on the ground floor.

It was, indeed, unchanged enough for my purposes. The silent, unwound clock in the corner and the tall cabinet with glass doors were still the most striking pieces in the simple room, but it was the daybed I looked on with true relief.

Had I gone upstairs, I might have cleaned myself, washing away the lengthy journey before sleep, but instead I went to the hearth, lit the waiting tinder, and barely took the time to change into a sleeping shirt before I fell into the little bed, pulling the blankets up around me and resting my head with a sigh equal parts relief and worry.

Much was going on in my head, more in my heart, and still more in my soul, but a good soldier learns young how to sleep no matter the noise, whether internal or external.

I closed my eyes, the last sight of the evening a cabinet and a clock by firelight, and the last thought uneasily of both.

I woke to the sound of an unfamiliar cry. Bolting upright in my bed, the shadows of night all around me, I peered into the darkness and waited.

A bad dream? Damn godfather's story, I thought, he has put such awful ideas in my head.

Another cry. And another. Different voices. And… a whinny?

I crept out of my bed, a skill I'd had long practice with when waking in the night in need of something sweet, and left my bedroom.

The sounds came from below, growing louder not quieter. Did the others not hear? I eyed the doors to their rooms, wondering if at any moment Luise or Marie or mother or father would come into the hall and demand to know what was making a din, but…

Nothing.

I descended the great staircase, skipping the spots that squeaked or groaned, though it seemed to me if those above slept through what was growing all the noisier below, they'd not hear a misstep.

In truth, it was frightening, but I kept thinking of what Marie had said about my hussars, and as such, bravery was at the forefront of my mind.

The noise, once traced to its source, was at once both clear and impossible.

A battle was being fought in our home. My soldiers and cannons and—yes, the hussars—were leaping from the cabinet now, despite being inanimate, simple things. And leading the fray, holding a colonel's sabre in the air was the Nutcracker.

Across the room, tiny lights glittered in the darkness, and it took me a few seconds to understand I saw eyes.

So many eyes.

I took a step forward, unsure, and caught sight of my retired colonel in the cabinet, watching from his shelf. He reached out a hand to me, a hand that should not have moved at all, let alone on its own. I took it.

My world shifted, and I had a sensation of falling, almost, but not quite that. It was sudden, and so near to immediate I scarcely had time to cry out.

But after, I wore the colonel's uniform, and he was nowhere in sight, and I looked down and saw a battle where soldiers were outnumbered by those glittering eyes, and despite that, the Nutcracker held his blade high, and cried out.

"For Marie!" he said. "For her sacrifice!"

And so, I ran into battle beside him.

SETTING THE MANOR to rights filled my days, and Luise was invaluable. Sheets were removed from the furniture, curtains opened, and what few updated amenities my father had allowed were put to rights and, with my blessing, plans were made for further changes as well. Though it was late in the season, I found wood enough to keep my fireplaces burning until the spring from a woodcutter Luise knew who she said came and went with winter, but always offered fair prices. And that man— Frost, his name was—was a giant of a fellow like so many woodcutters, and he worked with another, far slighter man who sold scrap rugs for the kitchen's cold stone floors that honestly seemed finer than some of the floor coverings formerly on display in more public rooms.

Lastly, I visited the graves of my parents to pay respects, found an institution in need of a surgeon, and tried to adjust to the thought of a life outside the military.

"Dear Fritz," Luise said, touching my arm. "You do hold yourself so tight."

I tried to relax my posture, but it only made her laugh, bringing colour to her cheeks.

"Never mind," she said. "Never mind." She invited me to eat with her husband and family, and it was a good evening. When I came back to my own home—for another habit I intended was to think of the manor as such—it felt all the emptier, and once again I retired to the smaller room.

The clock ticked now, and the announcement of the hour was a comfort of noise, if not melody. I opened the tall glass cabinet and pulled free a particular clockwork castle, winding it and watching as the figures moved about their slotted paths, endlessly performing their routines, the clicking of the clockwork piece almost a kind of heartbeat.

I smiled now, as I hadn't much smiled then. It was a clever piece of work, from a clever godfather's hands. With perspective, I saw now the effort and care and intellect required to make such a beautiful thing, where in my youth I saw only repetition and a lack of whimsy.

I sipped a brandy, stoked the fire, and my eyes traveled the rest of the cabinet. A few hussars remained, though most of the other pieces had been long passed on to Luise or Marie's children. Tucked in a far corner, a colonel stood.

"Retired, with full honour," I said to the small soldier. "And pension. I thank you for your duty."

My hand shook with the next sip.

The colonel did not wear his sabre.

MICE.

We fought mice, which would seem so simple and unthreatening, but was neither. Their teeth flashed so quickly, and they leapt to deadly effect. The hussars struggled to outmanoeuvre them, and failed so quickly my own heart leapt into my throat as they were to a man surrounded with speed.

I had the benefit of my own agility, and though distorted, a notion of the layout of the battlefield such as it was. Beneath footstools and between the legs of the cabinet and the shadow of the clock, I wove my way through the battle, trying to reach the Nutcracker, though I scarce knew what I would accomplish once I arrived.

The cries of the soldiers were terrifying. The Nutcracker could only repeat his weak call to action again and again, but a reason to fight was not enough.

"Form a rank!" I found myself crying, giving away my position in the shadow by standing upright in what little light there was. I pointed. "You are better than this! Have you learned nothing from our drills?"

My soldiers started, twisting free from sharp teeth and furry bodies, and over time did as I said, with much effort and fear plain in their painted and molded eyes.

Soon, we had a simple, basic line.

"Advance!" I cried.

All too soon it became clear to the mice this new influence on their foes must be me, and I was soon dodging attacks of my own.

Those teeth. I was not made of tin, I was not carved of wood. One good bite could end me here on the floor of this little room.

They leapt for me, and I tumbled as best I could away from their reach. It was harder and harder to keep the battle clear, to remember the layout of the land, to keep sight of the goal—or, since I'd joined this sortie so late, my assumed goal of the far end from whence the mice came—and hold the tenuously formed ranks of soldiers.

I was so very afraid.

"Hussars!" I pointed, and they sprang to action.

"Cannons!" I pointed, and instead of the "pop!" I knew, there were deep, chest-shaking booms.

Mice screamed. They were enemies, yes, and they wanted me dead, but oh… Oh how they screamed.

MARIE ASKED ME to dinner next. We hugged carefully—each convinced the other more fragile than we were—and broke apart to smiles just shy of laughter. It was good to see her. Her husband had inherited my father's practice after working with him a number of years. He was quick to offer me a position if I so wanted one, but I assured him I had plans to teach, and would be doing so come the spring.

As though the pain was conjured by our amiability, my leg set forth to ache in such a manner that no amount of my best training could hide, and so Marie asked her husband to take me home early.

"I'm fine," I demurred.

"You are not, and so I dismiss you," Marie said, imperious, and in that moment, we shared a glance of *knowing*.

I maintained my pride well enough to thank them both and accepted the offer, cane in hand. I would need to arrange my own transport eventually, but as yet it was another thing on a long list growing ever longer each day.

Dismissed.

"She orders you around like a princess holding court," my brother-in-law said, though only once we were alone together in the carriage.

"More of a queen, I would say."

He laughed, and I joined him.

I imagined he didn't know.

AND THEN I was beside him. The Nutcracker, tall and strangely built, with his short, white beard and large eyes and a colonel's sabre in his hand, now wet with mouse blood.

"You are with me?" he said, sparing a glance.

His voice seemed to reach inside me, to find something there and hold it tight.

"I am with you," I said. I wished I had a sabre of my own. Then, over my shoulder, "Grant cover! Sortie! You, to the right!"

The final stretch was a fury of screams on all sides, mice, teeth, sabre, cannon… We ran and dodged and slipped, and more than once fell and rose with the aid of the other. I had never been more afraid in my life, but I learned fear and bravery were companions, and how the fellowship of someone else tipped the scales to bravery's side every time.

Our goal should not have surprised me, and yet, when I saw the foul creature rise, I was struck dumb at the sight of him.

Seven faces loomed above us, each one bearing a crown, each one with sharp teeth and glittering eyes.

"I won't let him terrorize her again," Nutcracker said.

"Agreed," I said, the only word I could force past lips otherwise failing at the sight of the beastly king.

"You are with me?" he said again.

"I am with you."

And we charged.

When it was done, seven crowns lay at our feet, and the remaining mice were scattering back to their holes. The colonel's sabre was finally still inside the beast that lay at our feet. I stood shaking from effort and the echo of fear.

He wrapped his strong arms around me, holding me tight.

"Dear Fritz, you were with me, and you gave me that blade, and now, now I am as a free as I dare hope to be."

If he saw I was crying, he didn't mention it. Soldiers aren't supposed to cry, I thought, but I was a boy, too. And I was being held, and it had been so very long since I'd been held like this.

"Are you really his nephew?" I said, once my voice returned. My godfather's terrible story had lived up to its horror in so many other ways, it now seemed simple enough to believe. As Marie always had.

"Here, I am this," the Nutcracker said. It wasn't quite an answer.

"You are brave," I said. "And if it were up to me..."

He waited, watching.

"You are so brave," I repeated. "And I am lucky to have fought with you."

The Nutcracker held me again, and I was not the only one with tears in his eyes this time.

He held my hand while we walked back across the battlefield, and the hussars and soldiers and cannons bowed as we passed, then followed. They formed their rows and ranks back on the shelf, and I watched each pass by, commending their courage in turn.

Finally, the Nutcracker and I were the only ones left.

"You are quite fine, Nutcracker," I said. "You are quite fine as you are."

His short white beard tickled my ear as he leaned in.

"Those are good words to remember."

After that, I swooned, falling and rising both, and come morning, I had no idea how I was restored to my bed, but I had aches and bruises and was much fatigued, as though from battle itself.

EVEN IN A city this large, there is only so much time one can hope to have without certain company. In my case—and how suitable—it was on Christmas Eve my path crossed with my godfather's nephew.

Walking home from Luise's house, my attention had been on my cane and my gait, and of the pleasure of waking up tomorrow morning to my own small tree and the few things beneath it gifted me by what remained of my family. I was not unhappy, I had realized with a start, pausing to look up at the sky and watch snow falling around me.

I am not unhappy, I thought again.

I lowered my head, and there he was. He looked smart in his jacket and coat and scarf, and his eyes—those cunning green eyes—distracted my attention from my step so completely I nearly fell.

He caught me with some effort, and I remained upright as much by luck as by the strength in his arms. He had always been slighter of build than I was, and the years had not broadened him much beyond his youthful frame. The beard though, was new, and it suited him.

"Fritz," he said, turning what had been a lunge to keep me upright into a tight embrace. "Fritz," he said again.

For half a breath, I returned the embrace, then managed a half-step retreat.

His gaze wandered over me, cataloging me with his quick intellect and leaving me feeling bare and broken before him.

I was neither, I reminded myself. I was neither.

"Theodor," I said, not without warmth.

"You're back," he said.

THE MOCKERY AND disdain of the adults only paused when Marie returned to the room with the seven tiny crowns on her open palm.

"See?" She said. "My valiant Nutcracker defeated the Mouse King, and here are his seven crowns!"

My breath caught in my throat, and I had to clutch the wall not to swoon, but no one noticed. All eyes were on Marie, and the tiny crowns in her hand.

"Where did you get these?" my father asked, his voice quite cross.

"But I've told you!"

My mother picked one up and eyed it carefully. "It's so finely made…"

"Watch chain," our godfather spoke suddenly. "From my watch chain. Do you not remember me gifting it to the children?" He spins a story of a gift from years ago, and once again tells Marie not to be so childish.

I open my mouth. I want to yell. *You never gifted us these crowns*! I will say. *Marie is right*! But instead, I close my mouth again. My mother, father, and godfather all took to Marie now, telling her to be an adult, to not be so fanciful, to admit it was a dream.

She catches my eye then, and I think she sees. She knows.

I shake my head, and I think I see something break between us, but I don't know another way. I don't think we can win this battle.

I'm not sure any child ever has.

It is another afternoon, only weeks later, that we are sitting together in the room as a family, and almost out of nowhere, Marie declares that were she royalty, she would never reject someone brave and true just because of how they looked.

I'm not sure either of my parents realize quite what she was saying, but no sooner has she declared it than we hear both a crash and a knock at the door.

The crash is from inside the cabinet, where a shelf has inexplicably given way and scattered most of the soldiers and dolls. Marie and I set them to rights while my parents answer the door.

"He's gone," she says, her voice barely above a whisper.

I look, for there's only one toy she could mean. And she's right. There is no sign of our—no, *her*—Nutcracker.

I look at my colonel.

His sabre is gone, too.

"Children." My father's voice is, as always, a command. "Godfather Drosselmeier's nephew has come to the city. Come say hello."

We both recognize him, of course, though he is much changed and so handsome. He grins at Marie, and they hug as though they've known each other for years and are close as family, much to my father's surprise and consternation. My mother jokes they hug like betrothed—and the adults laugh at the notion of children so young marrying.

All I can do is be polite, to offer and shake a hand now trembling.

"Fritz Stahlbaum," I say, and to my credit, my voice doesn't shake as my hand did.

"Theodor Drosselmeier," he says.

★

IN THE ROOM, Theodor smiles first at the clock, and then at the cabinet. I hand him a glass, and we toast the season, then fall silent into an awkwardness that feels as much shame as habit.

"I'm sorry—" I say, just as Theodor says, "I wish—"

We regard each other, grown men amused by our mutual cowardice. "Please," I say. "Let me."

He looks as if to argue for a brief moment, then nods.

"I'm sorry," I say again. "For how I left. For how I… *refused.*" It's not quite the right word, but it's the best I have. "I didn't dare. I wasn't brave enough, I think. I couldn't have done what she did. I couldn't have had and *not* had." I look at him, and every part of me wishes I could gather him into my arms again and let him know with touch instead of useless, weak words.

I have always wanted him, I realize. Even as his presence reminds me of another time, when I was still in medical school, and I and another student living together at the same rooming house found each other's company, and kept it for the years we studied. I had those happy years, and until tonight, I don't think I'd realized I'd come to believe those years the sum total of what I'd ever expect to have. I'd left for the military, and he'd left for a hospital, and I'd imagined that had been the end of any possibility of…

Of *what?*

"I still have the sword," he says, and the memory of the boarding house and companionship is pushed back to its place.

"I'm glad," I say. And I am, oddly. He kept something of mine. It settles gently in my heart, that knowledge.

We sit, and after a sip, he pauses. "I can fashion a brace, if you'd let me. I'd like to."

"The watchmaker's nephew is as clever as he was, then?" I say, because I can't quite bring myself to accept plainly.

He smiles. "I'm told. Out here, I do well enough."

Out here.

"So, you still..?" I say. It's as much as I dare. My chest tightens.

He nods, and I wonder what he was going to say originally. "I wish—" What, exactly?

"And Marie?"

"Queen Marie comes and goes as she pleases." His smile is a genuine one. "And she brings her children, too. They were delighted."

I can well imagine.

Finally, I can hold my tongue no more. "You said 'I wish.' What do you wish?"

Theodor turns his handsome face to me. "That I'd shown you then. That you knew it could be more than battles and screams and blood." He pauses. "Most of all, I wish you would let me show you now. I hope—I wish—it's not too late."

★

"But we can go there whenever we want, Fritz! Theodor said he will take us." Marie's delight is clear. "When he comes back. He *promised* to come back. I'll be a queen there."

It stings. If she is queen, then what could I be to Theodor? It's unfair. It's all so unfair. Every moment we spent together in that little room is a kind of torture.

"You have to let this silly fantasy go," I say, though I'm not speaking to her. Not really. I hug myself and squeeze, though those aren't the arms I'm thinking of.

"I know you're his friend," she says. "I know it."

"It's dreams and childish and father says—"

"You know it isn't. You *know*." Her tears are no easier to ignore this time than before, but I can still hear my father and my mother and my godfather. They will throw her toys from the windows if she keeps this up. If I join in, it will only make things worse.

And if the toy is thrown, what would become of the boy? Because after Theodor left, there it was: the Nutcracker on the shelf again.

I can't allow that. I will be brave. If the only way for him to be okay is to turn my back, then isn't that my duty? A soldier protects. A soldier is brave.

"It's just a dream, silly goose," I say, meeting her gaze and speaking so carefully, hoping she will hear what I daren't say. *I can't have this. I can't. But you can, if you're careful.*

Marie's eyes spill over, but she nods.

We don't speak of it again, and when Theodor returns to the city, sometimes I see them sneak into the small room with the cabinet late at night. I count to ten before I follow, finding only an empty room.

Marie is always back in the morning, and night by night, she becomes *more*. Calmer. Assured.

Regal.

I don't dare speak to Theodor, and I don't chance being alone with him. Our parents joke that perhaps one day he and Marie will marry, given how sweet they are together, and I have to smile along with them.

After a few visits, Theodor realizes I am avoiding him, and though I sometimes catch him looking, he defers. I tell myself it is best Marie have something special for herself. I will have great things of my own as an officer someday, but for her, with her whimsy and imagination and great heart, life will never offer anything like this.

I tell myself it's not that I'm afraid.

When it's time to be sent away to medical school, it is a relief that aches like shame, but it is a relief nonetheless. The boarding house, the smile of a fellow student, the slow awareness of what we could be to each other, for a time. But *only* for a time.

After school comes war. It's a choice that ends that temporary companionship, but I do my duty, take my place, until…

Until.

The wounded are not expected to take their places in the ranks.

THEODOR AND I go as far as the castle, and up a tower so I can see out over a land of spun sugar and deep brown ginger and powdered snow. There are dancers and swans, and this world is full of bright, warm things. My heart is pounding in my chest, and I fear my cane will crack the candy floor with every step, but it doesn't.

We are welcomed by faces both familiar and unknown—some ageless faces I remember seeing as a boy on the battlefield—some I did not meet in that terrifying night, but who have heard of me.

Theodor has told them of me.

He holds my hand while I look out over this whole other world.

There have been moments like this, I think. Even after the boarding house. Snatched seconds between battles. Kindnesses, touches, but always with the understanding of their nature always being so: found, impermanent moments, however sweet and wonderful. But here—*Inside? Elsewhere? Wherever we are?*—time, I think, will allow us much more than a moment.

"It's wonderful," I say, though I'm looking right at him.

"I still have five more crowns," Theodor says.

I glance away, remembering the seven crowns he'd taken from the mouse king's lifeless body. One he wears now, himself. One, I assume, is on my sweet Marie's head whenever she is here. Theodor has pointed to her kingdom, barely visible on the horizon.

I wonder if we will visit her there.

"I'm no prince," I say, knowing what he's offering, feeling it in the way his hand squeezes. "But I am with you, if you want it."

"That settles it," he says, and kisses me. "My soldier king."

FIVE SHILLINGS
AND SIXPENCE

ONE OF THIS is right, thought Peter when the turkey was delivered.

It wasn't the bird itself, though to be sure there was no way his father could have afforded such a large turkey. It was... everything.

Peter tugged at the collar of his father's old shirt, standing back while his mother and father and even Tiny Tim exclaimed over the turkey. The address, clearly printed right on the label, left no arguing it had been intended for anyone else but them.

"But who?" asked his mother.

"I think..." Tim said, then paused as though he was reconsidering his words. But, after only a slight hesitation, he smiled. "I think it was Mr. Scrooge."

As his parents exclaimed over that particular unlikelihood, Peter eyed his brother and noticed the shadow around Tim had grown thinner.

"Well," his mother said. "I expect I should start it now, though I'll confess I'm unsure I've a pot large enough."

His whole family laughed. An unexpected joy, and on Christmas Day no less?

Peter put a well-practiced smile on his face, and as Tim passed, he rested a hand on his brother's thin shoulder for a brief moment of contact. Tim smiled up at him. Peter, after all, rarely touched anyone.

The shadow around Tim had grown lighter still.

None of this is right, Peter thought again. He bit his lip.

"FIVE SHILLINGS AND sixpence," his father said, finishing his announcement.

Peter lowered his head, feeling a swell of pride as his family cheered for his good fortune. It wasn't much, but the first time his father had told him of the position, Peter had felt the shadows move around him. Most especially? The darkness looming around a lone crutch by the fireplace shifted. Moving farther away. Not gone—Peter wasn't sure he believed anything could send a darkness so inevitable away—but farther. And farther he'd take.

The difference of five shillings and sixpence.

Their meal, later than usual thanks to the morning's turkey changing a great deal of the day's plans, also lifted some shadows from the Cratchitt home, and they were shifting so quickly Peter stumbled a few times through the meal, answering the wrong questions and only realizing after that he was having conversations others weren't. He caught Tim staring at him, and had to stop himself from returning the gaze in kind.

The shadows around Tim—the ones he'd seen since he'd first started seeing them—were nearly gone.

How?

Surely not the five shillings and sixpence. He'd already known that meagre increase to the family fortunes would not be enough for more than a stay of...

He distracted himself from that train of thought by remembering Tim's voice: "I think it was Mr. Scrooge."

As though Peter's rumination had conjured Scrooge to his father's mind, at that moment his father led a toast, and included the man in question. The cries of outrage from his family—earned, deserved—still somehow rang *hollow*. Peter couldn't quite join in. He glanced at Tim again, and found Tim looking at him, a small frown on his face.

"Peter?" he said. A quiet aside, the sort Tim spoke best. His voice had always been soft and gentle.

"It's nothing," Peter said kindly, and Tim turned back to the passing of the cup. But by the time the cup had passed around the table, Peter could barely keep up the pretence. Everything was changing.

And it hadn't been him, his new position, or his wages.

After the meal, Peter excused himself, wrapped his neck with his muffler, and went out into the snow, saying—no, admitting—he needed a walk to clear his head.

PETER CLOSED HIS eyes, recalling how the street had appeared only the day before, and when he reopened his eyes, the difference stuck as all the more obvious. It was like someone had washed some stones clean from the dark layer of coal smoke that coated them. And though it wasn't just his family's home, it *was* the cleanest.

It wasn't a real stain, and the real stains were still there, of course, but to Peter's other eyes, the sight that had opened wider and wider over the last couple of years, the dark smears of pain, and sorrow, and loss he'd gotten used to seeing everywhere had lessened.

Remembering how they'd appeared the day before reminded him of how overwhelming it had all seemed at first, but it hadn't been long before he'd noticed he himself might *shift* the darkness, ever so slightly. A kind word. A connection. Doing unto others.

He pushed his hands into his pockets, took a moment to consider, and followed the shifting in the patterns of darkness. The path was hard to follow—as a rook might cross the sky, not how a young clerk-to-be might walk—but he found his way through alleys and crossed narrow streets as he needed until he faced a graveyard.

What now?

Peter had long learned to avoid graveyards. Here, the shadows were often the thickest yet. Losses, inevitable losses, those he believed not even the power of five shillings and sixpence might delay often tangled and twisted themselves thickly in places like this.

But no.

No, not this one.

To Peter, parts of the graveyard almost held *light*. Indeed, a single space where no gravestone yet had been placed burned brightest of all.

Peter's breath hitched, a cloud of white tugged away on the cold city wind.

If this much might change, what about him?

He turned back to the whorling ropes of darkness, pausing to note where the darkness frayed ever more around the edges before following once again. In truth, he was almost unsurprised by the time he reached Ebenezer Scrooge's home. It was not a beautiful place, and he'd never have known it in passing, but it all came from here. Every weakened braid in the twisting ropes of shadow, every loose thread in the weave of potentials Peter had been fighting for the better part of two years began here.

"*I think it was Mister Scrooge.*"

Tim's voice again, in his memory. Peter breathed on his hands, unsure what to do now. He couldn't as well as use the knocker, not if he wanted his father to know nothing of the route of his evening walk.

The knocker.

It, too, existed not only clear of shadow; it fair glowed.

The door opened. Peter started, as did the woman stepping out of the building. She wore a heavy shawl and had her hair tied up and appeared to be a servant. A charwoman, perhaps.

"Oh, pardon! You gave me a fright," she said, not unkindly. She laughed. "Merry Christmas, in keeping with the situation."

"A Merry Christmas," Peter replied.

The woman, too, was positively alight, but he saw behind her the trailing edges of wisps of darkness. The shadows had been on her, too, but just this moment thrown from her shoulders as if they were nothing more than a disintegrating shawl.

She stepped past him, and Peter nearly let her go, but the words were out before he could stop himself. "May I ask..?"

She turned, waiting.

"Are things...well...here?"

"Young master." The woman's smile only grew. "Things have never been so well as they are here. It's changed, I must say myself. It's... well, it's Christmas!" Then, with another "Merry Christmas!" from her lips, she was off. Peter eyed the closed door.

Changed, indeed.

Peter went home, wondering if change might also exist enough for him.

★

BY THE DAY after Christmas, it was confirmed. Tiny Tim had been right about the turkey, and more than that, Mr. Ebenezer Scrooge had not only seen fit to give his father more time to be with his family, but a raise in salary as well. Peter stood quietly back as his father exclaimed the virtues of this new Mr. Scrooge, and he watched the shadows flee every corner of their home.

It should have filled him with joy, Peter thought. It should have left him overflowing. But instead, Peter felt a weakness in the place behind his heart, a duller ache than he remembered. Why should it be so, he wanted to know, now there were no shadows in his home to worry about? Why should that leave him so troubled when all the troubles he'd seen for so long were finally banished?

Indeed, the world around Peter Cratchit lightened hour by hour. The darknesses he saw in full retreat. Routed so thoroughly, in fact, the only place even the sense of the umbra remained were those very ropes he felt within his own heart.

For his family, though, Peter managed to smile and laugh, skills he'd been honing since the first braids of sorrow had started to appear throughout the world.

Those same laughs and smiles he prepared to carry to his first day of his situation. Where before he'd felt a sense of pride and minor triumph of delay against a future so determined to take his brother Tim from him, now he had only uncertainty. Five shillings and sixpence didn't shift the world everywhere he looked, but rather Ebenezer Scrooge did. He had joined the Cratchit family for a dinner—Peter's mind still spun at how much brighter the man seemed from all previous glances—and by the end of it, Peter had been hard pressed to find even a shred of ill fortune lingering.

He'd even touched Tim's crutch, a thing he'd long ago learned never to do.

There had been *nothing*. In fact, there'd been a sense of *needlessness* of all things, that the crutch might soon be relegated to convenience rather than requirement, and then at some time beyond approaching with an unreal alacrity it would simply lose all necessity entirely.

And so, as he stood outside where he was to work, he wondered what he could possibly do, who he could possibly be, now the only thing to give him direction had shifted so suddenly and without his being of any usefulness or impact at all.

All that remains is myself. A person Peter Cratchitt had crafted no plans for, so busy had he been in battle in a war so suddenly and definitively ended.

Five shillings and sixpence. Perhaps he'd build on that. He looked at the place of business that would now be his place of employment, and then to either side at the adjacent buildings. One a chandler's storefront—a convenience for their own lighting needs, to be sure—and quite a bit further, being a carver's shop, he thought.

It was while he still stared in that direction, at the handsomely carved sign above the carver's shop, when a fresh darkness gathered at the corner and crouched like a cat, twisting with tension and anticipation and catching his attention wholly. Peter turned, his breath coming quickly. A woman began crossing the street, and beside her a cart was awaiting unloading at the warehouse across the street, which blocked her from plain view. Then, beyond, a horse and carriage approached and the angles contrived to be not just unfortunate, but calamitous.

Peter Cratchit cried out in warning even as he moved, but did not rely on being heard nor understood. Instead, he leapt, catching the woman by the arm, half-swinging and half-pulling her with him. They fell together backwards into dirty snow, and the horse and carriage passed them with room for but a barest breath between where she'd have been.

"I'm so sorry," Peter said once he realized their landing had soaked and soiled them both.

"No, no," the woman said, her voice shaking as they rose and she eyed him. "That was nearly my life. I've see you before, I believe."

Peter didn't recognize her, but he offered his hand. "Peter Cratchit, at your service."

"Indeed you were," she said, with a small laugh he thought might still be born of shock as much as humour. She was older than he'd first thought, though only now was it obvious. Still, her eyes were kind and her smile was easy. "And that settles where I've seen you. You're the new clerk."

Peter gestured to the building where he was to work, though he didn't follow. "There, yes."

"There." She nodded. "My husband's company. Come. I'll come in with you and explain why we're both so wet. I'd only meant to stop by to see my husband and son." She winked. "Now, I have a tale to tell."

Peter gestured for her to go first. The feline darkness scattered away from them, undone.

Undone by *him*.

Upon the woman's completion of telling the story, her husband—Peter's employer—embraced her despite the wet snow drenching her coat and dress, and kissed her forehead. "My Belle," he said, his heart obviously full of a deep love. "Never." He said it again, like it was a vow. "Never."

"I am unharmed and well," she said, though she did not let go of his hand. "Thanks to young Peter."

"I knew I'd made a good choice," the man said, and Peter blushed.

He was shown to his desk, and introduced to the man's eldest son, who would be his companion in the small office they would share. It was cozy, warmed by a fire. Peter thought of his father's office, and a small shiver ran through him, though his father said it had been much changed in his office of late.

"Are you warm enough?" the owner's son asked him.

"I am," Peter said. Faint shadows fled from the young man, ones Peter knew, had nothing to do with Ebenezer Scrooge. A future that had almost been, thanks to a horse and carriage, was instead never to be. And he'd done that. Peter himself. "Thank you. I was just thinking of...something else."

"Oh?" His companion asked it with genuine interest.

"I'm afraid I can be over-concerned with the future," Peter said.

"That seems wise to me."

"Does it?"

"The grasshopper and the ant," his companion said.

"Yes. In a way."

A moment drew out between them, and Peter found himself not looking away, even if they should both get back to their work.

"Join me for dinner," the man said.

Peter blinked, surprised. "I..." He wasn't sure what to say.

"By every account, you saved my mother's life today. It seems only fair I treat you to a simple dinner. Besides, you're a working man now, Peter Cratchit, and we working men might as well be friends."

Peter looked at him. Really looked. Despite the man's smile, and the brightness of his voice, something familiar lay between them. It took a moment to find a twisting dark behind his companion's heart. Worry. Fear. A hopelessness. A future only imagined alone, because...

Ah.

Because.

Except... *no.* Even as Peter watched with his eyes-that-weren't-eyes, tiny pieces of the knots behind this young man's heart began to fray and drift away.

Something familiar indeed.

"I would like that very much," Peter said, wondering.

Another fray. Peter saw his acceptance of a simple meal shift another fragment free. *Which means what, exactly?*

Of all things, Peter Cratchit's thoughts turned to Old Mr. Marley. He wasn't sure why, but the memory of him, so close to Mr. Scrooge even before his father had worked for him, suddenly struck as clear as day, even though he'd but met him only once.

Peter shook his head. Over-concerned with the future. But it did occur to him to wonder what Mr. Scrooge might have been like had Mr. Marley remained alive longer. What would this world be like had Mr. Marley perhaps had the chance to see the shadows Scrooge could have undone, and what that might have meant for both of the men going forward?

Peter dipped his pen into the inkwell. He should start. The sums on the paper in front of him would keep his mind's attention from all these imaginings, and that was a good thing.

Besides, there was no way to know, of course, and what a curious thing to consider. Perhaps just a strange and random thought. Mind, graveyards, door knockers, charwomen... It had been a strange and random week, all told.

He looked at the other clerk and caught him looking back at him.

"I do look forward to being friends," Peter said.

His new companion smiled.

They got to work.

THE DOORS
OF PENLYON

Tom Danby listened at the door, his fingertips not touching the handle nor wood, not daring the the temptations such contact with reality might cause him to consider. Penlyon Place was cool and dark around him, warmed only by fireplaces and the misery of all those under its proud roof, and he had not slept much in the last nights.

In all his life, Tom Danby had never hated a door as much as he hated this one right now. Doors had been his friends since he'd come into his own strange and certainly unmonied inheritance, and he was used to doors as companions, if not outright collaborators.

He'd once heard someone say, "No door is closed to Mr. Danby, as he seems to have a way of opening them all." They'd intended it as a mild jest at his station, he assumed, and how many people so much higher and far more solvent seemed to take him in. For Mr. Danby, errant bachelor, needed rarely worry about having a permanent address of his own. He stayed with personages, moving from one place to another, one invitation to the next, and generally found himself to be welcome everywhere.

It wasn't why Tom Danby loved doors, of course. But his own reasons were by necessity a secret, and had nothing to do with something as banal as social status, a fine bed, or access to a decent cook.

Rather, it came down to his peculiar nature. Doors in the hand of one such as Tom Danby, for it should matter to point out Tom Danby was not alone in his peculiarity with doorways, were not *just* doors.

No. Similarly, conversations were not just conversations. Not if Tom Danby put his mind to it.

At a look, Tom Danby might not garner a second glance, and he certainly gave no hint of this peculiarity. He was not displeasing, nor was he handsome, though he maintained a neatness that greatly compensated him overall. He had grey eyes no one would mistake for blue, brown hair that was beginning to silver as he approached fifty, and he stood of middling height with slenderness of build.

If pressed for a reason as to why those grander people enjoyed the company of Mr. Danby, they would all agree he possessed good spirits, had grand—if often odd—ideas, and that somehow, merely being around Mr. Danby elevated one's mood.

Tom let out a breath, exhaling slowly, and closing his eyes. He hadn't elevated anything at all here in Penlyon Place, and now...

Moppet. God. What had he done?

He could hear the little girl breathing. It was an unhealthy sound, and though he tried to take comfort in the existence of her breath at all, there was a gurgle to it, and it strained as though a wolf sat upon her chest.

Dr. South had spoken with Sir John Penlyon and Tom Danby. Danby had hoped he'd echo the words of kind Dr. Nichols, the local doctor, of how children often did well against maladies of the lungs, instead, Dr. South—London's best in the care of children—had made comment to the unusual nature of Moppet and...

This is all your fault, you contemptible fool.

On some level, Tom Danby had enough grace to understand his lack of control over the whims of disease and infection, but it held at best a cold comfort in the moment. This child—who was more than anyone but he in this grand manor currently knew—lay on the edge of death, and she was only here on his whim.

If Adela had not mentioned children. If Tom had not seen the thinnest wedge he might use. If Sir John Penlyon hadn't been ever so slightly open to the thought.

If Tom hadn't *inspired*.

But he had. He'd used his peculiarity with words and set them all on this course.

He'd been working the words, sitting comfortably by the fire. Listening, as always, to Adela and Sir John as they spoke. Adela's attempts to berate Sir John for his lack of joy in the season had finally turned to her recollections of her childhood Christmases, and how much more wonderful Christmas had always seemed as a child.

"Ah, there you've hit the mark, Adela. Christmas is a splendid institution in a house where there are children," Sir John had said. "Christmas can hardly be made too much of where there are children in question."

Tom didn't dare rouse from his position, but the thrill of the conversation ran through him. He could feel these moments with that peculiar otherness he'd had since his twenties, so he pressed those words in his mind and aimed them squarely at Sir John, nudging at the normally closed and bolted doors in his mind. The mind's doors, too, were friends to those of Tom Danby's ilk, and frankly, the sort of doors Danby preferred. People spent a lot of time closing the doors inside them.

Tom Danby took great pleasure in opening them when opportunity presented.

Yes, he'd smiled with triumph as Sir John Penlyon waxed poetic about the spirit of the season being all about children.

It felt enough to Tom. And so, feeling the change in the room and Sir John both, Tom Danby outlined the most ridiculous plan. He would, for Adela and Sir John, *hire* some children to make their Christmas as enjoyable as one had ever been.

Adela's amusement had shattered into outright disbelief when Sir John readily agreed. He had even written Tom a check, which was a good thing, as the plan already forming in Tom Danby's head would require at least a quartet of train tickets.

Yes, many rooms had found their doors locked tight throughout Sir John Penlyon's life, and it was time for Tom Danby to air them out.

He'd been so damned sure of himself. It was such a simple arrangement to make, and the children in question had always adored Uncle Tom, even without knowing exactly why he'd known their mother. Taking the train with them had been more pleasant than he'd imagined—it had been a while since Tom Danby had bothered with the railways, given his peculiarity—but there were rules to these sorts of things among his sort.

There were *rules*.

Tom's hand shook, barely room for a breath between his fingertips and the wooden door.

★

"DR. SOUTH," TOM pitched his voice low, not wishing to catch the attention of Sir John or Adela, both of whom had now retired to what had become a purgatory in the sitting room. He'd not seen Laddie or Lassie this morning, and he briefly wondered how Moppet's elder siblings were handling her illness, but the thought was quick and easily nudged aside. The two children had an admittedly dusty room full of toys in what had been the Penlyon nursery, and last he'd seen of them, the boy was reading and the girl played with four dolls she noted were queens when he'd last spoken with them, as she had discovered four doll-sized crowns. He'd left them to it, knowing the servants would ensure they were fed and settled and most importantly, Lassie and Laddie were *well*, and well children could always be thought of later.

The ill, on the other hand, demanded attention, and so this whispered discussion between Tom and the good doctor.

Dr. South nodded and stepped just a little farther into the front hall, gesturing. Tom understood. There, they would be able to have a quiet conversation without bothering the others. Tom Danby's estimation of the doctor rose no small amount in the moment.

He was taller than Tom, perhaps a few years younger, and handsome in a gentle way, though his long travels to Penlyon and near lack of sleep thereafter had left deep smudges under his dark eyes.

Face to face with him, Tom shored up some courage from what little remained and asked what he needed to ask.

"Is there anything—from near or far—that might help the situation?" Tom said.

A small line appeared between Dr. South's eyebrows. His lips parted, and he drew in the slightest breath, but then he closed them again. The line deepened.

"Doctor," Tom pressed, and now, spurred on by that simplest tell from the doctor, reached out and took the doctor's forearm in hand. "It was in the way you spoke of what *you* could do, rather than a grander sense of everything that *might* be done. I've no doubt of your skill, nor your compassion, but if indeed there's something you didn't mention given the hopelessness of, say, geography, please—it it exists, *anything*, do tell me." Tom Danby swallowed. "Even if the solution is elsewhere."

Dr. South's countenance softened with compassion, and once again Tom was struck by how gentle the man seemed. When he spoke, his voice remained whisper soft, as though he feared it might slip beneath a door and stray to the ears of the heartbroken who waited, and be mistaken for hope.

"If I had every tool at my disposal, I would try a treatment in particular, yes," Dr. South said. "But some things do not travel well, so even were I to send for them and able to bring them in from London, by the time they arrived..." He did not finish the sentence.

The unsaid was well clear enough. The timetable would have such a treatment arrive after it would be of no use.

"Still," Tom said. "If I might indulge the question? I understand you, I promise, and I would never be so cruel as to offer Sir John or Adela something that could never be."

Dr. South hesitated.

Please, Tom thought, leaning the thought in the doctor's direction, having already noticed the doctor's mind did not close many doors with finality. *The truth costs nothing*.

He *inspired* the doctor.

Dr. South finally spoke, outlining what he might have done if Moppet had been in London with him, and he had at his fingertips all that science might offer to aid in her recovery.

Tom listened carefully, asking only a question or two in the face of Dr. South's eloquent explanations. When Tom thanked him, Dr. South's hands both twitched, as though they intended a glad handshake or simple touch. A small flush had risen on his cheeks, and it helped him cross the line to handsome after all.

"You musn't tell them," he said. "There's no way..." Once again, he let his sentence fade.

"Of course not," Tom agreed readily. "But I thank you. Truly."

His own hands felt empty in the moment. Tom Danby knew his own cheeks were alight.

Dr. South bid him a good evening, his voice softer still, going to a greatly earned sleep. He assured Tom the nurse would rouse him were anything to change, but otherwise, the doctor repeated clearly, there was nothing anyone could do but pray, sleep, and hope.

Tom forced a smile and agreement both, but knew better.

★

TOM DANBY LISTENED to Moppet's struggling breaths for a few seconds more, then pressed his fingertips against the door handle, allowing his peculiarity full reign the moment the connection was made.

All the world's doors waited, as they always did.

Tom turned the handle.

AFTER A DREADFUL breakfast, Tom waited for Dr. South outside Moppet's door. The doctor closed the door quietly behind him, and they walked together towards his leave-taking.

"May I ask..." the doctor said, then hesitated, aborting the sentence.

"I brought the three children here to enliven the season," Tom said. "Their mother is on her way."

"That's good." He swallowed. "I had heard Sir John had... lost his own daughters. His eldest to illness, and his youngest to... chance."

"Yes." Tom looked at the gentle doctor, and their gazes met long enough for each to confirm everything the other already knew.

At the door, they were joined by Sir John and Adela.

Dr. South eyed them all.

"The outlook is brighter today than it was last night," he said. "But I mustn't promise too much. We are not out of the woods yet. Please let me have an occasional telegram to say how she is going on. She is a dear little child—most winning." This he seemed to aim at Sir John, though he glanced at Tom again thereafter. "I have seen the loveliest children who did not interest me half so much as that quaint little face of hers, with the large forehead and the dark deep-set eyes." Another pause, one with weight and another glance at Tom. "I hope her mother will be here today."

And with that, the London doctor left.

WHILE TOM DANBY had never been to the very hospital where Dr. South worked, he'd been to London on the regular, and to Tom's peculiarity, that was more than enough. He chose a block he'd frequented often, stepping out from the front door and eyeing the street just long enough to get his bearings before heading towards his destination.

From there, his business became as simple as anything else he'd managed by door.

He recalled the doctor's soft voice, remembering every word as he selected the things he needed, and only as he turned to leave the chill of the room with its bottles and containers did he pause, hand raised but not quite touching the door.

The others. The full range of his brothers and sisters of the doors, especially the keepers. This went against the rules because it left the door to discovery. It left the door they guarded most vigilantly of all unlocked.

Then again, with luck it was wholly possible no others would even ask. He'd the cover of the night to raise his chances of being undetected. There were more than a few others like him in the city but if they were asleep they'd be far less likely to sense him coming or going. It wasn't a surety though. It was always day *somewhere*, which meant others of his kind might feel him passing by, but then and there, in the full measure of all the consequences, Tom Danby didn't care.

If this gamble paid off in only that one most important regard and cost him everything in another, he'd pay that price.

He touched the door. Beneath his fingers, he could feel the pulse of others like himself. Peculiar muses, awakened to the pathways between all doors sometime in their twenties, as he had been. Beyond that, he could feel the everywhere of his own personal pathways—every door he'd ever passed through, every room or building he'd ever entered or left. Every door went to every other door, if someone like Tom Danby turned the handle.

Big Ben began to chime the hour.

The very best of science in hand, Tom Danby stepped through the door from the hospital in London and exited the door to Moppet's room in Penlyon Place, a swirl of night air mixing with the warmer air inside the manor in a twist of mist gone between blinks.

Sir John's clock finished chiming.

Tom Danby turned around, opened the door to Moppet's room as quietly as he could, and went inside to speak to the nurse of some last-minute adjustments.

NOT LONG AFTER Moppet's sudden turn for the better, Tom Danby received a telegram from Dr. South. He read it twice, and told Sir John and Adela and Moppet and—of course—Moppet's mother of the doctor's relief at her recovery. Only one of many a small moment lost along the much grander one unfolding, of course, but it felt important to Tom to include the doctor, even just by his word, given the situation.

Word from the doctor, when there'd been no word from the other muses, had also struck Tom as mildly ironic. His luck, he supposed, had always tended to a footnoted positive, rather than a simple, uncomplicated good. Those who could feel him come and go through their own connection to everywhere had turned out not to notice anything amiss. A positive he could not deny he'd hoped for.

Dr. South's request, on the other hand…

The end of the doctor's telegram Tom Danby did not share with the others. For it concluded with: *Do stop by when next you are in London.* One *could* have read the words as a polite request were one to use a casual eye, but by the fourth or fifth reading, Tom found himself rather sure the words were intended as an imperative.

And so the very morning Tom Danby took his leave of Sir John, already calculating how long it would reasonably take to get from Penlyon Place to his next accepted invitation and finding himself with over a week to his own devices, Tom took the opportunity to grasp the door at the train station local to Penlyon Place and return to Dr. South's very hospital in his more direct—peculiar—route.

At it so happened, the doctor was free to see him, and Tom Danby was soon restored to his presence.

They regarded each other—dark eyes meeting grey—for a few breaths.

"There is a manifest kept," Dr. South said, instead of any polite greeting Danby might have expected.

"A manifest?" Tom said.

"Of medicines." Dr. South gestured to the chair across from his desk, sitting behind it once Danby sat.

"Ah," Tom said.

Dr. South regarded him again. "I'm pleased she recovered."

A genuine smile lighted his face. "So are we all."

"And her mother?"

"Arrived," Tom said, then added, meaningfully. "And stayed. All is quite restored at Penlyon Place."

Dr. South's smile did nice things to his eyes. "You know, I've asked around about you," he said, looking down at his desk top and smoothing away some invisible bit of dust.

"Oh dear," Tom said. "One hesitates to hear more. I'm sure someone rose to the challenge of disclosing to you of my itinerant ways."

"Indeed," the doctor said, though gently enough to remove any sting. "But, it seems, you are invited wherever you go."

"As you invited me yourself," Tom said, countering with his best smile in return and pulling out the telegram.

Dr. South paused, eyeing it with a small turn of his lips. The overall look on the doctor's face was triumphant, and Tom realized his mistake too late to take it back.

"Yes," the doctor said. "A telegram I sent *yesterday*. And here you are. The very day after."

Tom waited. He didn't really have any response he could make. His own eagerness to attend the doctor's company held the blame.

"The manifest…" Dr. South swallowed. "The night we spoke. The *same* night. By the morning recount…"

Tom realized he found the good doctor's habit of letting sentences fade more than a little endearing. Tom imagined the doctor found many people felt obliged to fill in the gap.

Tom himself, however, did not.

Dr. South let the silence hang a moment longer. "If I asked the nurse who treated Moppet, or the local man, Dr. Nichols, about what treatments were suggested in my name, I can't help but feel I'd have a mystery on my hands."

Well and truly caught, Tom could only blow out a breath. "I believe you are correct."

Dr. South's laugh was as soft as his voice. "And if I were to investigate the trains from Penlyon Place to London—a trip I took myself, one significantly more than a day to achieve when I left at first light—you are, I think, not going to satisfy even my mildest curiosity over discrepancies to your arrival time, are you, Mr. Danby?"

"Please, call me Tom." Tom said. "But let me ask you a question in return. If a mystery turns out for the best—or even a holiday miracle, let's call it—it might be worth leaving it to stand as such, would it not, doctor?"

"Charles," Dr. South said. "If you're going to offer me not so much as a crumb to explain…" He waved a hand in the air, as if to encompass everything around him. "You can at least call me Charles."

"Charles, then," Tom said. He rose. "I appreciate it."

The doctor laughed again, rising himself. "I'm sure you do." He shook his head, then eyed the clock. "Have you had dinner, Tom?"

Tom shook his head. "No. Not yet."

"Well," Charles said, the lightest of flushes crossing his cheeks. "If you would like, you may consider yourself invited. I know a place nearby. If you won't give me any crumbs, they'll give me a whole meal."

"As you say." Tom Danby smiled. "And I'm never one to turn down an invitation."

A DAY
(OR TWO) AGO

WHEN I WAS quite young, I lived a day twice.

It happened to be on the first Christmas I can remember. I woke to find a beautiful carved wooden horse in the stocking hung at the end of my little bed. I was still in the nursery rather than a bedroom of my own, though both my brothers had moved on, and it was mine in its entirety. Beneath the carved horse was the usual: an orange, a handkerchief, the typical delights, but that horse had a glow to it. It wasn't something seen as much as felt, golden in a way one remembered more than experienced. I picked it up, and even though I needed to use the privy, I held myself back and sat with the toy in my bed, looking at the horse. I could have sworn it contained a light of its own.

The rest of that Christmas was poor. My father and mother and elder brothers woke shortly after, and when we gathered for our morning meal, my brothers declared their stockings had been empty, and I saw a look of something like fear in the eyes of my parents, so I tucked the carved wooden horse into the pocket of my robe and said nothing at all.

Something had gone very wrong, and though I was young, I was not so young to not know when to stay quiet. I said nothing about my own stocking, and I clutched the horse all the tighter when I saw our family tree stood solemn and alone in the corner of the great room. It remained colorful and decorated, but beneath it lay but one parcel.

I dashed away to the nursery and was quick enough to hide the small bounty from my stocking and that beautiful horse in a dollhouse never used by any of my brothers nor myself. I remained still short of breath from my efforts when the door opened, and my mother appeared with the single parcel from beneath the tree.

"It's for you," she said.

We opened it alone together, while downstairs I heard my father's rising angry voice speaking with the servants, and my brothers, too, echoing his tones of fear and dismay.

The toy inside the package was a beautiful sleigh, and it, too, seemed to have a glow about it. I picked it up, delighted, and my mother gasped. When I looked at her, I could see a reflection of myself in her eyes, one far brighter than should be possible given the low lamplight in the room.

I, too, glowed.

And she could see it.

I spent that strange Christmas in the nursery. My mother closed the door, denied even my brothers from entering the room, and told me she'd bring me my lunch and my dinner. The rest of that day is hazy. At times, people yelled outside, though it was a faint sound given the distance between our manor and the village. I played with my horse and the sleigh, which was exquisite in detail, and ate my orange. I wiped my chin with the fresh handkerchief, feeling quite the man.

And I looked in the small round mirror in the nursery, and marveled at my golden glow.

When the dim sun had crossed the sky and it snowed once again, I crawled back into my bed, and pulled the covers up to my chin, and just as I drifted off, I heard the faint ringing of tiny bells.

WHEN I WAS quite young, I lived a day twice.

The second first Christmas I remember, I woke to find the same beautiful carved wooden horse in the stocking someone had rehung at the end of my little bed, though I'd not heard anyone come into the nursery. More, beneath the carved horse were the same presents as before: another orange, an identical handkerchief, all the typical delights repeated. I regarded the horse, which had the same glow, then turned to the little table beside my bed where I would have sworn I had left that very horse the night before, but it was not there. I picked it up, and even though once again I needed to use the privy, I held myself back and sat with the toy in my bed in my little room beside the stairs, stared at the horse, and wondered.

This time, the rest of that Christmas was festive. My father and mother and elder brothers woke shortly after, and while we gathered for our morning meal, my brothers exclaimed over what they'd found in their stockings, and my parents indulged their excitement. I had tucked the carved wooden horse into the pocket of my robe, but when this morning, this same morning, unfolded so differently, I pulled it free. Everyone at the table agreed it was quite the fine horse, except for my mother, who frowned at me as though she couldn't quite recall something. She said nothing at all, though she smiled a smile that seemed real enough to my young eyes.

Years later, she'd mention in passing as we put the horse on a high shelf in the nursery for some future child that the first time she'd seen the toy, she'd had the strongest moment of déjà vu of her life.

But that morning, all I knew for certain was that something strange was happening, and though I was young, I was not so young to not know when to stay quiet. I said nothing about the oddly barren Christmas I'd already enjoyed, and I clutched the horse all the tighter when I saw our family tree stood brightly in the corner of the great room, colorful and decorated, the space beneath full of parcels.

Again, I saw a shadow pass across my mother's face, and as was custom in my family, she was the first to pull a present from beneath the tree. She looked at it, read the tag, and turned to me.

"It's for you," she said, handing it over with the smallest hesitation.

The toy inside was the same beautiful sleigh, and it also seemed to have a glow about it. I hesitated, not wanting to pick it up while my mother watched, but her attention was fixed on the sleigh itself, not me. Again, her face seemed clouded by some feeling I was too young to understand. I picked up the sleigh and met her gaze. My reflection in her eyes was as it always had been, though I knew I had not imagined the glow in the sleigh or the horse.

More importantly, this time my mother hadn't noticed.

I wasn't glowing—at least, not to anyone else's eyes—nor was I to be shut away for the day.

Around us, my brothers opened packages and cheered, my father as well. He handed something to my mother, and the moment between us was gone.

I spent that second Christmas with my family, as always. The servants were there for our meals, but my father let them to their own devices for the rest of the day, and even taught my brothers and I how to set a proper fire. In truth, the rest of that day is hazy. Mostly, I played with my horse and the sleigh, which was exquisite in detail, and when I ate my orange, I was aware of how every curl of the skin would unpeel. When I wiped my chin with the fresh handkerchief, this time I did not feel like a man, but rather marveled at the shape the juices left on the cloth, entirely and exactly the same.

That night, when I looked in the small round mirror in the nursery, there was no glow, but I put a hand to my chest, and knew the light wasn't gone, but was somewhere inside me. I checked the end of my bed, but the stocking had been pulled down. I put the horse and the sleigh on the bedside table with care, noting exactly where they stood.

When the dim sun had crossed the sky and it snowed once again, I crawled back into my bed, and pulled the covers up to my chin, I drifted off still waiting for the faint ringing of tiny bells.

But this time, the night remained silent.

TWO DECADES LATER, on a first morning of the year's return of the sleighs, after a breakfast with my parents, my brothers, my eldest brother's wife, and my niece, the family scattered and went about their business while I considered my latest tale.

Most of the village looked forward to the arrival of the quartet of open sleighs, and every year my father offered space in our stables for the care and keeping of the horses, as we only kept a trio of horses for ourselves—four if you counted Bob, which only I did, and we had ample room remaining.

Every year, I tried to take the time to visit Old Mr. Pierpont, who already seemed to have been getting on in years back when I'd first toddled around unsteadily. By the time I was grown, I delighted in sneaking him some brandy from my father's best stock. He'd tell me silly stories of his horse breeding business, especially the often truly astounding quirks of people who hired him—most of which I assumed were nonfictional, as they made too little sense to be anything but real—and I would read to him from whatever my latest work might be. He had a penchant for my holiday tales, which were always a favorite of my own, and so we got along famously.

His loss the previous summer had left me feeling bereft on this most recent yuletide, and I'd yet to go to the stables to meet his replacement even though they'd arrived the evening before. Someone had told my mother the new hand was an orphan Old Mr. Pierpont had both trained and to whom he had left his business, owing to Old Mr. Pierpont being unwed and having no sons of his own.

While growing up, my elder brothers failed to see the allure of the old man, though they enjoyed the sleigh rides. My eldest brother, John, now married and living in the city, brought his wife Mary back on their first Christmas together, and I honestly believe he did it to take her on such a sleigh ride. She had come back breathless and pink-cheeked and all the more in love with him than he deserved, but if one cared to count, the birth of my first niece in September seemed a sincere enough review of their enjoying their time together.

That particular detail did not make it to "September's Child," the children's story I penned the season after with a character named for my niece, but my publisher loved it nonetheless, and the story sold better than could be expected, no doubt due to the cloying sentimentality other people seemed to feel for children, especially when their fictional antics led to the happiness of equally fictional adults.

My middle brother, James, wasn't kinder so much as ambivalent to my existence, but once my eldest brother had moved out and moved on, it seemed to occur to James were I somehow to manage to marry and leave the manor before him, that he would end up inheriting the worst aspects of the place. It would be he left with the duties and "privileges" of making appearances and guiding our small town.

Thus began his attempts in earnest to find someone suitable for the position of his wife.

I mention this, because once his goal became clear in the village, something rather astounding began to happen to me, in that women began speaking to me. Especially while James was away finishing his most recent round of schooling, I found myself in conversation with many a woman. I don't mean matrons with children who wished to tell me how much little Suzette enjoyed "Candle and Robin" or my first collected volume of holiday fables, but rather the daughters of prominent town men who were, as yet, unmatched and wished to rectify the situation with haste.

I couldn't say it was unwelcome—one can't say these things, however strongly one feels them, but the most clever and, therefore, woefully overqualified to be with my middle brother—was Miss Fanny Bright, who was both daughter of the village banker, and Parson Brown's niece. She was also a nurse, which my mother declared shockingly self-determinative, but that would pass once she had a child of her own.

Again, I must stress how much I felt Miss Fanny Bright would only be the worse for pairing with James, her self-determinative nature being one of her highest qualities, to my mind.

It was, however, a quality that didn't make for particularly enjoyable company. On a morning walk along the manor grounds, I saw her approaching, thus I took it upon myself to step into the stables in high hopes that she had not yet seen me.

This was how I met the new handler of the sleigh rides, as he happened to be putting a harness on a particularly beautiful bay. The harness itself was also a thing of beauty, finely tooled and festooned with a series of bells, which jingled as he affixed them to the horse.

"Hello," he said.

For my part, the words I had no trouble putting on paper and selling in no less than a dozen countries around the globe fled my mind completely in that moment. He was taller than I, which granted is no feat in and of itself, and broader, for which the same caveat must be applied, but where I had the near-black hair and eyes of my grandfather's South European lineage, this new stableman had the kind of russet hair that could appear browner or redder depending on the light and was most welcome in the best of novels.

"I'll be right with you," he said, and then he led the horse outside to where the last two sleighs remained. A couple I'd not noticed given the prompt nature of my decision to enter the stables exclaimed over the bay, which the stableman took no time at all in setting to place. Presently, the couple were under a blanket, the man took the reins, and the bay took them off at a good clip.

Fortunately, my mind had rediscovered words by then.

"You are Mr. Pierpont's protégé," I said, once he returned. "I'm sorry for your loss."

"Henry Wilson." He dipped his head for a brief moment. "Thank you. You're the youngest master?" He nodded toward the manor proper. "The author?"

"Samuel Brunswick. And, I am. At your service," I said, wondering if I was about to be summarily dismissed as so many did. Instead, we regarded each other in a silence quite comfortable.

Until Miss Fanny Bright broke it.

"There you are, Samuel!"

I turned, and it was with greatly schooled countenance I managed a simple, "Miss Bright."

"Just the man I wished to find," she said, displaying her usual ability to read between my few words, which is to say, understanding fully but possessing a complete lack of willingness to be dismissed. Truly, she was a force of nature, and one I would admire if she were not so adamant to use me to get to James.

"Well," I said tonelessly. "I am found."

"And a sleigh, too. Such a kindness of you to entertain me."

"To...?" Despite seeking a polite method of egress, I came up empty. "I suppose it is." I turned to the stableman, then eyed the remaining horses the man had brought. To a beast, they were suitably majestic creatures I could never, ever ride. I liked to hire cabs if I needed to travel nearby, and for my infrequent meetings in the city I took the train.

"I could harness Bob," Henry the stableman said, showing far more understanding of what I wasn't saying than Miss Fanny Bright had ever done.

Bob was technically my horse, poor thing. Lean, perhaps a bit lank, and yet my favorite of the stable precisely because he wasn't the broadest beast. More woeful than willful, whatever misfortune had brought him to my mother's attention had likely saved him from a short and unhappy life elsewhere and graced him with the easiest of careers in the annals of horsedom: my personal steed.

"That would be wonderful. Thank you," I said, quite concerned that Bob would be able to budge the sleigh at all.

"So," Miss Fanny Bright said, not even bothering to wait until we were in the sleigh in question. "How is James doing? Is he back from school?"

She knew he was, I assumed, but I spoke of my brother's studies while the stableman pulled out the last of his sleigh harnesses and set Bob to rights. Bedecked in the belled straps, Bob nearly cut a fine figure, and I swear he seemed a hair's breadth from chipper as he was led to the final sleigh. I helped Miss Fanny Bright settle herself and climbed in beside her, trying to leave as significant space between us as possible in the open sleigh. She drew a blanket across us both, sliding closer to me and making another inquiry as to my brother's plans. Had he decided upon a career? Whatever I answered seemed to placate her—I must confess something about the bells on the harness had caught my attention, reminding me of a particularly odd Christmas, years ago. It wasn't until Henry the stableman handed me the reins that I remembered my deep miscalculation.

"Ah," I said, holding the reins as one might hold a rare python from another continent. I did not ride, and while this was not riding, it was not dissimilar, either.

"Shall we?" Miss Fanny Bright said.

I conjured as much cheer as possible, tipped my head to the stableman, and gave the reins a good shake.

Bob snorted, shook his head, and then grudgingly began to move. Progress best described as glacial made our leaving less than eventful, but upon realizing that this was not, in fact, a joke, Bob seemed to put more leg into it. The manor fell behind us, and while I tried my best to concentrate both on Miss Bright's detailed inquest and puzzling out the appropriate methods of guiding Bob, it was a losing battle. I tried to imitate what I'd seen others do in both regards, but I knew I wasn't providing enough charm for Miss Fanny Bright, and Bob decided to drift from the wide-open field toward the more passable road despite my urgings.

The sound of the bells, however, was lovely.

A glimmer of something golden caught my eye, and I turned, allowing my attention to wander from Miss Fanny Bright and Bob both. It was the bells, I imagined, as it was often laughter or music that brought these glimpses of spirits to me. It struck me then that the sound of sleigh bells was the equal of laughter and music entwined.

I should note that while I call them spirits, I'm not sure of their nature at all. They move as spirits might, figures that seem unfettered by such banalities as gravity or wind, but they are often delightfully more or less than human. This time, I could just barely discern the trio of spritely figures dancing with each other, the palest of gold against the snowy field. Each seemed to spin the next in an ongoing tradeoff, and, as always, these tiny glimpses of merry and bright creatures ignited a muse.

Three fairies dancing in the snow. It could be a tale of the little twists of snow that the wind cast about like dust devils. And three was such a magical notion, really, in so many tales of folklore and faith alike.

They were beautiful, and they made the whole distressing pattern of the morning so worthwhile. Honestly, they were delightful.

At least, they were right up until Bob pulled the sleigh rather directly against a large drift, and I learned that Miss Fanny Bright's relentless calculations of patience and cheer were not, it turned out, endless. Being tipped onto the snow snuffed both rather deftly.

I walked Bob back to the stables, once I'd managed to disentangle him from the now-sideways sleigh. Miss Fanny Bright opted to escort herself back to the village, and I opted to show concern and make appropriate noises of apology, both of which I hoped were enough to avoid too much damage to our family name.

"Honestly, Bob, the sooner my brother picks a bride, the better," I said. "Though I still maintain Miss Fanny Bright deserves someone capable of matching her wit." I considered. "Although, I imagine those such men are few and far between. Perhaps she has decided to settle for a man with a square jaw?"

Bob nickered his noncommittal reply but followed along amiably enough, seemingly having made his point with the drift. In truth, despite the cold and wet remaining from my tumble, I didn't much mind his company or the walk. He'd at least had the grace to tip us into soft snow, and he had never been going at much more than a trot. It could have been worse.

Also, my discussion of square jaws had reminded me of a particular jaw that waited at the end of this walk, one covered with a short beard that might be brown in some settings, but definitely seemed red by the light of day.

The bells on Bob's harness continued to chime as we made our way back, and though there were no more spirits, it was such a pure, clear sound I found myself closing my eyes at times just to listen, trusting Bob to stay the course. When we finally made it back to the manor stables, and I held on to my shreds of dignity while explaining the situation to Henry, I stroked Bob along and beneath the harness and was surprised when a single bell came loose in my hand.

Henry took a different horse to go collect the sleigh, while the manor's man gave Bob a brush down and put him back in his stall. It did not escape my notice Henry felt himself the match of tipping the sleigh back on its runners by himself.

Truthfully, I shared in his confidence and rather enjoyed imagining it playing out.

That night in my bed, I held up the bell I'd palmed. Still cold to the touch, like it had been trapped in a winter's moment, I might have sworn it reflected more light than was present in the room. I shook it, and the issued ring was crystalline and oddly distant.

My eyes grew heavy, and I closed them.

AT BREAKFAST, MY eldest brother and his wife declared they would continue their tradition of being the first to rent a sleigh, and as no one else corrected them, I said nothing. I'd woken with an odd sense about me, but a familiar one. Today, it seemed, was a day I should strive for the least notice I might garner. A lightness of my spirit, this kind of awareness of myself was both wondrous and unsettling. My middle brother spoke of his plans next, and by the time the breakfast was over, I had barely stopped myself from speaking their every word with them. I'd had this breakfast before. Yesterday.

Which, it seemed, was also today.

I only interrupted when things were drawing to a close.

"Say," I said, with a mild clearing of throat. "Did you have plans with Miss Fanny Bright today?" I asked of my middle brother.

The noise he made was less than a word but rather eloquent in its own way. My parents reminded my brother of her breeding and standing, and my brother aimed malice my way, and I decided to return to my attempts to vanish.

Though I knew it would by no means settle my nerves, once my family scattered and went about their business, I went straight to my study and regarded my notes for my latest tale. Sure enough, everything was as it had been the prior morning, which was—it seemed—this morning as well.

For a moment, I considered rescribing the words I'd lost in a sense, but as I recalled the events of the day both ahead and behind me, I remembered what was to come, and decided discretion would be the better of valor, and made it my mission to avoid Miss Fanny Bright completely.

As such, I was there to see both my eldest brother, his wife, and my niece glide away with the first sleigh, and my middle brother climb onto the next. The couple who would come to take the third were as yet unseen, so I knew I had time, and I slipped into the stables.

"Hello," Henry said.

Given I knew what to expect, one would suppose that I would find myself suitably girded and prepared for the impact of the russet-haired handler and his gentle eyes.

One would be incorrect.

My mind had lost language completely. Again. Luckily, I had the words I'd already used at hand.

"You are Mr. Pierpont's protégé," I said, clearing my throat. "Henry, is it not? I'm sorry for your loss."

"Thank you," he said. To my ears, his tone was different than I recalled from the previous today. Perhaps it was because we were alone? But no, we'd been alone before, too, had we not?

"You're the young master?" he said, pointing toward the manor proper. "The author?"

"Samuel Brunswick. And, I am. At your service," I said, this time more confidently, knowing I wouldn't be dismissed out of hand as so many men tended to do. Instead, I knew a comfortable interlude of silence would follow, and one would not be misguided to say I revelled in it.

In fact, I let the companionable quiet draw out longer than perhaps I should, for I noticed a familiar couple walking through the manor gates and realized the clock was running forward as always, and it wouldn't be long before Miss Fanny Bright made her appearance. I turned and clearly telegraphed my anxieties to Henry.

"Did you wish to take a sleigh ride?" the russet-haired Henry asked.

I wanted nothing of the sort.

"Yes," I said, and he pulled the bay from its stable. But instead of the finely tooled harness I'd seen him place on the horse in the last version of this day, he chose the fourth harness again, which wasn't quite so fine, but still lovely. I wondered at this, but there was little time to inquire, as the other couple had arrived, and I was eager to make my escape.

Under the blanket, reins in hand, I took a deep breath, shook the straps and tutted, and the bay had us dashing through the snow at a pace I will admit stole my breath away from me.

The bells were once again the sound of laughter and music both, which meant at least one of us was having a delightful time. By the time I passed through the manor gates—wholly not in command of either our destination nor the speed at which we were approaching whatever that destination might eventually be—I was quite sure the bay had decided this was his solitary chance at freedom forever, and I'd never been seen nor heard from again.

Likely my publisher would even choose to print dreadfully non-illustrated versions for my stories for folios, and claim it my last request, the villains.

Even the hills weren't slowing the beast down. And while the bells were conjuring pale golden whimsies to either side of me, I had neither time nor inclination to look at them, as no muse was worth this terror or my imminent demise.

Finally, I realized I had but one option to me, and that was to make it perfectly clear to this beast who was in charge. I braced myself, rose to a slight crouch from which I imagined it might be easier to recover, and with as mighty a pull as I could manage on the reins, intoned the deepest "woah!" my throat would issue.

The bay stopped dead and threw me from the sleigh, where I landed on my back and stared up at the sky for a few moments of sheer joy in no longer being at the horse's mercy before the dampness reminded me I lay in snow.

Just as I'd decided I would begin to rise at any moment now—perhaps once I'd caught my breath—the shadow of James loomed over me, and I saw him bring his own sleigh and horse blithely alongside me just long enough to laugh.

It was in that moment I decided a life under Miss Fanny Bright's order might be the best thing to ever happen to my middle brother.

I rose, eyed the sleigh, and decided I'd rather lead the bay back on foot than climb back aboard. The bay seemed well content to be led, though, and while it was a good long trudge back to the manor yard, we came to an understanding and had a rather heated debate about the merits of showing kindness to those who are not as strong as oneself in which I think I was clearly the victor.

I even stroked the large bay, which was when a single bell came free from his harness.

Henry the stableman was dealing with James's horse when I returned, so I left the bay tied up to take his turn, thanked him briefly from out of direct view, and then went inside to request a hot bath and to change. By the time the long evening was done, I'd rewritten the words back into my latest story, the very ones I'd lost from the morning before, received notice that I'd missed Miss Fanny Bright's visit by mere minutes that morning—such a pity—and as I lay back in my bed, I once again drew out the bell. There was no light but what little of the moon snuck around my bed curtains, but even this seemed magnified by the small silver thing.

I shook it and closed my eyes.

AT BREAKFAST, I waited for my eldest brother and his wife to declare they would continue their tradition of being the first to rent a sleigh, and no sooner than the words spoken than I leaned forward and drew the attention of all at the table.

All eyes turned to me, a panoply of confusion, worry, interest, and hope from my blood kin and in-laws, as my asking for their attention had a tendency to run counter to what they considered the smooth operation of our standing.

"Miss Fanny Bright will be dropping by this morning," I said, applying a jam to toast to keep my hands busy and provide me with a place to aim a confidence I didn't wear easily. "Knowing you were back, James, I asked if she might drop by. You two should take a sleigh as well."

All eyes turned to James next, especially those of my mother. He opened his mouth, but then took note of our mother's gaze and—more importantly— the rather willful turn of her lips. Instead of whatever invective he might have considered, my middle brother replied simply with, "Thank you."

That his intonation would have been better suited to a different variety of imperative, no one seemed fit to notice.

That settled, I reclaimed the lightness of spirit I'd felt the previous today, and this time, as the conversations unfolded around me, I took a light joy in polite interjections that matched wits what the various men of the table had intended to say. For the women—my mother and my sister-in-law both—I offered only an interested ear, drawing out questions and having, all told, one of the most delightful breakfasts of my life.

Practice making perfect, and all that.

"Do enjoy your ride," I said, offering it to my brother with all sincerely as I left the table.

The noise he made was less than a word and spurred my mother to remind my brother of Miss Fanny Bright's breeding and standing.

Freed from the need to flee the manor, I went back to my papers and found them as unfinished as they'd been the prior two todays, but when I picked up my pencil, I found I didn't want to restore the words for a third and, one hoped, final time.

I tapped a finger against the papers, then gave in to a particularly russet shade of temptation.

"Hello," he said, the moment I crossed the threshold of the stables. I had just enough time to watch my brother and Miss Fanny Price and the powerful bay leave ahead of my arrival, and then he was there, the same amiable smile and remarkable jaw as always.

Having had two prior attempts to live up to my nature as a worker of words, I faced the impact of the russet-haired handler and his gentle eyes with eloquence befitting my station.

"Ah. Yes. Hello. To you. Good."

Perhaps I could have Bob stave in my skull with a well-timed kick. But no. I went back to the tried and true.

"You are Mr. Pierpont's protégé," I said, curling my hands in the pockets of my greatcoat. "Henry, correct? I'm sorry for your loss. I enjoyed Mr. Pierpont's stories immensely."

"Thank you," he said, and this time I was sure his voice gentler than before. "You're the young master?" he said, a warm smile adding all the more to his charm. "The author?"

"Samuel Brunswick. And, I am. At your service," I said, leaning into what I knew would be a comfortable silence. It did repeat, but even the most comfortable silence must end, and after I found myself meeting his gaze one too many times, I glanced through at the final remaining sleigh.

"Did you want to ride?"

The laugh that escaped me restored his smile. "I think I've had enough of sleigh rides of late."

"You have?" He put a hand to his chest, as though I'd wounded him, then colored slightly when he saw my delight in the gesture. A ruddy blush on a russet-haired gentleman was a particularly winning combination, and I stored away the note for a future line or two.

"I am, as they say, ill-suited for it. I have it on experience."

"But when was that?"

"A day or two ago," I said. "Or both. It didn't end well. I think, perhaps, I'm not made for sleighing."

"Ah." It was clear he knew full well I'd not been hitched up to any sleigh rides yesterday or the day before, but he seemed content enough to allow me my folly. Still, the delight it brought to his face was worth him thinking me playing at the fool. Perhaps he thought this of all my family, and who would blame him, really?

We laughed, and I opened my mouth to continue in jest, but lost all words upon turning back to him and seeing—or, rather, it was once more of a sense of feeling rather than sight—a certain tell-tale golden glow. I couldn't catch where the light had come from before it was gone.

"Are you all right?" he said. As always, he spoke amiably, but this time, I had enough sense to really look at him. What he said could be assumed politeness, yes, but the cast of his shoulders, the tilt of his head...

Had he been looking, too? Was that possible?

"I know you likely have more than enough of your time spoken for," I said, unsure of the words I was going to say even while I said them. "But is there any chance I could borrow not just this last sleigh, but your skill in the use of it?"

"If we say I am teaching you," Henry said, "it would even be within my role."

I considered that. "As long as we only say it. Between you and me, I have no desire to learn, and even less skill to work with."

He dipped his head, but it didn't hide the amused twist of his lips. He drew the fourth harness out, and I almost suggested Bob until he stuck his head out of his stall in a way that made it clear he was more than content to be exactly where he was. I scratched him while Henry harnessed up the last of the horses he'd brought with him and led it outside to the sleigh.

"Your brothers seem to enjoy their riding," Henry said, fastening some buckle or other. I climbed in the sleigh and made room, quite aware of just how little of it there was, really.

"My brothers enjoy taking the lead in all things."

"I think the lady who left with Master James might be more likely to have the lead there," Henry said, and though I'd already decided upon a ruddy, russet hero for my next tale, at that point I decided a series was more in order. A trilogy. No, at least a quintet.

"If I were to write a tale with a horse breeder," I said. "Would you be willing to rise to my endless ignorance of the subject?"

Having settled the last of the buckles, he tilted his head up to reply. "I'm not sure there's much story there, but I'd be happy to try."

Unable to both flush and speak at the same time, I fell silent while he climbed aboard. I pulled the lap blanket over both of us with hands determined to be anything but steady, and he took the reins in hand. "Ready?"

"Seems best to go it while we're young."

That made him laugh again. "You're a funny one, Master Samuel."

He whistled before I could reply, and what had been a terrifying speed the today before at my own lack of control was instead breathtaking in a delightful way. The manor gate fell behind us in a moment, and then we were dashing, the snow spraying it behind us, the bells ringing in time with the hoofbeats of the horse.

Gold appeared among the white of the snowy fields.

I turned, watching the pale twists—birdlike, this time—as they danced and wove ahead of us, as though caught in a gravity of the horse itself, sparkling as they flitted just out of reach. I took in a deep breath, thinking of a tale of birds in winter. Robins, perhaps. I turned to ask Henry if he had a favorite bird, and saw him looking up and ahead, a similar smile on his face, delight in his eyes, and golden light reflecting there.

He saw. He actually *saw*.

When he turned my way, I was still staring, and that flush returned to his face.

"Penny for your thoughts?" he said, voice just shy of a low rumble.

"I am remembering something," I said. "Something odd that happened to me as a boy."

"One of your stories?" he asked, and when I tilted my head, he shrugged as though I'd caught him out. "Mr. Pierpont had them all. I read them to him."

"Oh," I said. "No. This isn't a fiction. Or, at least, when I was young, I was convinced of it. I lived a day twice. It was the first Christmas I remember."

His gentle eyes widened, and I caught my own reflection in them. The golden glow, though, now came not from the merry spirits still glittering around us, but from around me.

"It's not a story I've written down," I said. "So, if you know the tale, it's not because you've read it. There'd only be one way to know it, really."

Henry returned his gaze forward, and with his guidance, the horse seemed content to let us glide behind him, crossing the field toward the hills. The bells jingled, and all around us, merry spirits bloomed, much brighter than I'd ever seen them before.

"It wasn't the first Christmas I remember," Henry said. His own spirit grew bright. A golden light around him, reddening his russet beard. "But then, I think I'm a few years older than you. It's the only Christmas that happened to me twice, though."

We took turns with our tales, surrounded by those bright, merry spirits, then spoke of other things less grand and important. We circled all the hills, crossed the fields, and paused twice by the river in comfortable silences, and then we allowed the horse a rest while we partook of a silence of a different sort.

That evening, when my brother James and Miss Fanny Bright announced their engagement, it drew all the attention in the room, which was fine, as I didn't need anyone to note my breathlessness nor my pink cheeks. But all agreed my notion of a series of tales about man and horse would likely be appealing to a broad variety of readers.

That night, there was no bell in my hand, but with thoughts of a russet-bearded hero in mind—not to mention many necessary "consultations"—when I closed my eyes I had never been happier to bid farewell of a magical day.

Likely it aided to know I had so many more to come.

THE FUTURE
IN FLAME

THE FIRST GLIMPSE I caught of the future in flame happened when was still a young boy. Old enough to help my mother in the kitchen with the simplest tasks—though decidedly *not* old enough to be trusted with anything complicated, given how easily my mind wandered—I was often left to the stirring or the peeling or arranging the cutlery around our table, a particular favourite.

We had a large fireplace, and I would often sit in front of it with whatever task had been given to me, which on that day was to peel potatoes, and allow the heat to wash over me while I worked. I often made a game of it, trying to get the whole peel off in a single, thin curl. And I considered some of the tales I'd heard of how young women might toss the peel over their shoulder and it would arrange itself into a symbol as it landed, denoting the man they were to wed.

Somewhere between those thoughts—the act of throwing a peel, the notion of prophecy, the confusing, unreliable concept the future seemed to me—the fire snapped, I looked up, and *saw*.

As though the flames themselves were a window, the edges rimed with smoke instead of frost, I regarded two men, one pale skinned, lean and tall and barely possessing a beard, and the other a burlier, stockier sort, with bronze-brown skin, and an enviable beard growth indeed. They seemed to live somewhere grand.

Behind them, I saw an odd room, with a large table covered in a snow-white cloth, laid out with many table settings and lit with so many candles and...

Were they dancing?

With *each other*?

Despite their surroundings, neither was dressed finely but rather in what appeared to be work clothes—heavy aprons over plain shirts and breeches—and, yes, they were dancing. I watched as the thicker of the two spun the taller, leaner man, and for the first time, this slender man's features came into clear view through the odd window-effect of the fire in the fireplace and...

I gasped, and with a flare of heat, the fire was once again just a fire.

"Everything all right, pet?" My mother, in the kitchen, must have heard me.

"Yes," I said, with an instinct I couldn't quite name to hold what had just happened close to my own, now rapidly tripping heart.

The man in the fireplace had my eyebrow. I'd split it open a winter ago after a fall on slick ice cut my forehead. The brow never rejoined. The white mark of the scar was the first thing people noticed now. My father said it granted me a rough character. My brothers were less polite about it, though I secretly believed my eldest brother reluctantly thought it made me look quite dashing, like one of the heroes in the Brunswick tales of adventure he enjoyed.

They all worked with my father making candles, all proud workers with colza, braiding wicks and crafting candles as near to smokeless as one could imagine. I would start there soon myself, perhaps as early as the new year.

"Are you done peeling, then?" My mother had entered the room. She eyed me, and the slightest frown drew a line between her eyes. "You're flushed. Have you been sitting too close to the fire?"

"No," I said. I lifted the two bowls, one full of peelings, one full of newly bare potatoes. "I'm done."

"Bring them in, then, pet," she said.

I did, though I glanced back at the fire as I left. It remained a fire. Whatever window I had seen through, for the moment at least, had closed.

MY MOUSTACHE WOULD never quite reach the hair that grew on my chin, and what fluff formed beneath my sideburns or along my jaw was best not spoken of, even in jest. But a moustache I did manage, and a tidied mark of hair beneath my mouth on my chin. It did little to compensate for a face most politely described "interesting," but at least I escaped the gangling awkwardness of my youth and found skill in my fingers and hands to work wax freely, as well as the more regular work of molds and dipping.

My eldest brother left my father's business to be a Bow Street Runner—he'd always had a head for adventure and justice, and believed this his path to both. And while my middle brother was a decent, hard-working sort, he didn't have the head for the numbers the way I did, nor any real joy in the work.

That I would inherit the shop was a foregone conclusion to my whole family, alongside the unspoken promise that I would keep my remaining brother employed—and thus solvent—for his future as a husband and father. His inheritance was perhaps more practical than mine: the features from our parents blended in his face to something quite handsome, and so as he had a job, never drank to excess, and always smelled pleasant thanks to the waxes we shaped, he had a fair share of attention among the eligible women in the city and was soon engaged.

Since it afforded me an anonymity to have a brother so handsome, I didn't even begrudge it of him, as by this point, my *nature* the flames had shown me in that one encounter of my youth by the hearth had started to assert itself in earnest.

I did not dream of dancing with fine ladies, but rather I dreamed of bearded men. The dreams had come on with increasing insistence and detail.

As did my way with fire itself.

This latter began simply enough by burning a candle to check the efficacy of my tight braid of a self-trimming wick. My thoughts focused on how long it might burn, but as I watched the candle burn, the small flame seemed to *open*. One moment it was a bright flame, the next it was as though it didn't exist, and in the space where the flame had been, I instead saw my father's face, his eyes closing, and a long, slow exhale that was not followed by another inhalation.

The window was small—a candle's flame—but I found I could move about the candle, so long as I kept my eyes on the spot where the flame should be, and look through it like a keyhole of a door, were one to keep their face at the hole as the door swung open.

He was in bed, beside my mother, and there was snow on the windowsill, and his glasses on the dresser and...

The window closed. I blinked a few times, trying to restore what strange opening I'd been able to peer through, but it had vanished, leaving only the bright flame, and a braided wick performing as it should.

As deaths go, a peaceful passing in slumber cannot likely be improved upon, and thanks to the candle's warning, I had nearly three weeks' time to say all the things a son might wish he'd said to a kind father but held off in other circumstances.

After he passed, the business became mine, and in time, I took a room of my own while my middle brother and his new wife joined my mother in our family home, starting their family there.

In my room, no one questioned if I peered into the fire, and so I gained practice.

THE SECOND TIME I saw the bearded dancing man was in a pub. I'd taken the habit of eating a meal out after closing the shop at the end of the week, rather than with my mother and my middle brother's family. On one of those evenings, some friends who also owned shops along the same street as I introduced me to a carver and sculptor new to the city but already possessed of some fame for his work.

He would be opening a store two doors down from me, where the childless furniture maker was to retire.

Though he was introduced to me as Atlas, I knew it was the man I saw through the fireplace window of my youth. He was broad and had certainly earned his nickname, but his beard had not yet reached the magnificent state I recalled in my glimpse.

It was strange to see him, and even stranger, I caught a similar shock in his dark brown eyes.

"It is good to meet you, Atlas, was it?" I said, to cover our awkwardness in the eyes of the other clerks and store owners.

"It was," he said, recovering. His voice was softer than I'd thought to expect, and we shook hands. A rush of warmth ran down my arm, and what returned was cool and of a different nature entirely, though not uncomfortable. "You're the chandler?"

"I am." We let go. Both of us glanced down at our hands, as though the sensation of my warmth exchanged for his cool calm had been apparent to him as well.

That was the sum of our conversation that first night. I was too taken aback to have finally met this man I'd seen so many years ago in my fireplace, and he, I would later learn during a pillow confession, had been similarly tongue-tied for a different, though similar, reason.

As a young orphan, Atlas had been accosted one day by a man as he passed what he called "a shop of mirror, glass, and silver." The man took Atlas inside, and asked him to name with only one word what he sought, and the man would show him where he might find it.

"Why would you help me?" Atlas had asked.

"Because you can help others. Your hands can bring life to what you make, I think."

Atlas, who didn't understand, only shook his head, but the man waved it off. "It will come," the man said. "Now. Your word, Atticus?"

Given he hadn't told the man his name, Atlas should have been scared. But he wasn't. Instead, he said his word.

This man had repeated the word for Atlas—*home*—spoken over a flat, silver mirror, and Atlas had seen not a place in the glass placed before him, but a face.

Mine, as it turned out.

My split eyebrow of particular note to him, Atlas had thereafter looked at every man's eyebrows, wondering when he might find the person who, it seemed, might finally grant him a sense of home.

That first night, however, we did little more than glance at each other furtively, though I certainly dreamed of him that night, and the next, and the next. His beard, especially, favoured heavily in my thoughts, as I wondered at the texture it might have against my skin.

THREE DAYS LATER, I left my middle brother the reins of the store and brought a package of candles two doors down to the newly opened carver's shop, which bore Atlas's name on a beautifully smoothed wooden sign. The bell rang when I pushed open the door, and Atlas himself came out from the back room, wiping his hands on a rag, in an apron I'd seen before, though it currently looked less worn.

"I brought you candles," I said, feeling both foolish and excited to be in his store with him. "As a welcome gift." The words landed clumsily, but at least my skill with wax outstripped my tongue. I handed him the package, and he opened it.

"Thank you," he said, pulling one of the long tapers free and smiling at the colour, which went from the pure white at the wick to a deep golden brown at the base.

Most of my stock and trade was made in simple and useful utility. But making candles as beautiful as they were useful brought me joy, even if they rarely sold beyond a wedding or during the holidays.

"I have just the holder," he said, and he placed the candle back into the box with a reverence that made my skin shiver—ridiculous, as he had not touched *me*, after all, but there it was—and he stepped once more into the rear of the store.

I took the moment to look around at his wares. He seemed to deal primarily in woods and stone, and the carved items were a mix of utility—walking sticks, stools, tables, candleholders—and beauty, such as frames and bowls and even some carved figurines, a few of which were dyed and painted, but most with the beauty of their own woodgrain left standing.

He returned, and I turned from a bowl full of wooden soldier Christmas ornaments to see he'd brought out a flared candlestick of a dark wood, with carved designs of robins around the flared base, brushed with only the faintest of red dyes on their breasts. He once again picked up the candle, and placed it into the holder and—

Two things happened at once.

The first was all of a flare of heat that washed through me, much like when I shook his hand in the pub, though this time it was not a mere warmth but something akin to the heat of an open flame, and it lanced out from my chest, crossing the distance to where Atlas stood, no sooner gone than a responding coolness rushed forth from him that soothed my overheated skin in kind.

The second, though, there would be no way to deny. The tapered candle lit itself as sure as if a match had been held to it, and from its flame, golden shapes emerged and flitted through the room. By the time I recovered from the dual sensation of heat-and-cool, I could see the creatures that danced from surface to surface.

Robins. Robins made entirely of light.

I swallowed and turned to Atlas, sure I would see recrimination or fear or—worst of all—fury in the man's eyes, but instead, there was only wonder.

"I've seen you before," I said. "When I was a child. A vision in an open flame."

Atlas's slow smile grew even as the robins made of light faded, their soft twit-tweets and the patter of their feet tapping around us quieter and quieter until, with a last glimmer, they were gone.

His beard, I would learn that night, was indeed very soft against my skin.

★

OVER EVENING MEALS and clandestine nights, we learned each other's gifts, and they both seemed determined to grow since we were together. Finding the future in flame became almost second nature to me, and whatever thought I might have while I stared into fire steered the vision's direction. But more than that, now I could bring the flame itself and spark the life-giving heat elsewhere if I drew it from myself *just so*. When dipping or molding or braiding wicks, I found I could weave or shape purpose into the tapers.

This candle would bring hope. That candle would bring luck. Another, peace after loss.

Atlas showed me his creations, small birds carved of wood which, if he crafted of a size he could close his large rough hands around entirely, would thereafter, when he opened his wonderful fingers, simply fly away from his open palm, as alive and real as any bird hatched from an egg.

"Do they come back?" I asked, one evening when we lay together in his bed, which was by need larger than mine, in a small home above his shop. "Do they return to what they were, become wood again?"

"None I've ever seen," he said. He could bring to life birds, mice, and anything tiny he could carve and hold inside his two closed hands. Fantastical things, too: elves and fairies, some of which would speak to him and even stay and keep him company a while before they felt a need to be elsewhere. They would thank him for crafting them and granting them spirit before they'd head out to wherever they felt pulled to be—the woods or an orphanage, or—he delighted in telling me of a pair of elves in particular, ones he'd carved from applewood—even a shoe-maker's shop.

Even his larger carvings held spirit in much the same way my candles now seemed to embody. Things he couldn't close his hands around, couldn't bring completely to life, had qualities worked into them just the same.

A wash basin carved with mermaids cleaned away unearned shame as well as dirt. A walking stick with an eagle's face lightened the step of its owner. Candlesticks decorated with suns and moons and stars brightened any candle they held—and were the candle one of mine, to near *incandescence*.

Joy lived in us, and through it, our businesses prospered all the more. Customers would speak to us of their lives, and we could gently suggest a candle or a carving best suited to lightening their sorrows, and on some level, the connection was made.

When the rooming house became available, my mother and my brothers all questioned how I could possibly run such a place and still maintain the Chandler business, even with Atlas also throwing his broad shoulders half into the joint venture. But I'd sent my gaze through the fireplace with my thoughts aligned with the needs of the business and found a pair of women, a cook and a former housemaid, both of whom were ready to retire from the grand house where they served. Like Atlas and myself, they secretly kept their time together, and they would run the place, as well as live there, where they would have more freedom to be together than ever before.

I cast my gaze through the flame-windows for those who would rent rooms as well, and it was not long before The Candle and Robin had the half-dozen rooms filled: a teacher and his dockworker friend; two seamstresses who worked both in a dressmaker's shop and for the theatre's costumes; and two medical students who would one day, the fire showed me, save many lives, one on a battlefield and the other at a hospital.

We would often join them for meals, and one New Year's Eve night, when the table was set, and we'd arrived but not yet changed, I remarked upon the beauty of the table our cook had set, and the warmth that radiated from the great iron stove with shining brass fixtures. From upstairs we could hear the medical student playing his fiddle, and the seamstresses were singing, and Atlas pulled me in and danced me around the room.

I felt myself watching. It was a curious sensation, but not an unpleasant one, and then, as though through a new muscle once flexed a motion had been learned, I felt *another* pair of eyes, and ceased the dance.

"Someone…" I frowned, unsure.

"What's wrong?" Atlas said.

I couldn't find words akin to the sensation of… A view? A glimpse? A gaze, but like my own, but *different*. Smaller. Certainly not a fireplace and perhaps not even a candle. No, the window that had fallen upon me had been…

What had it been?

I realized.

"I need a match," I said.

★

I STRUCK A match.

She had no shoes.

Snow fell, a night full of cold and wind, and the girl wore no shoes.

It took every effort to turn my eyes away from her poor feet, to try and see where she was, where she might be going, but the window of a match was so narrow.

The child wore an apron, and in the pockets...

Matches. Boxes of matches. She held them out to people as they passed, but none so much as glanced down at her, and though she asked if they might need matches, they did not reply and—

The match burned out.

The *frustration* of it left me at loose ends, and it was only Atlas's hand upon my shoulder that stopped me from running out into the night to any and all streets, to no avail.

"Try the fireplace," he said, and he had the right of it. I'd seen her now, and with the fireplace I could find her future, and so I sat, brought the child's near-hopeless face, her cheeks so red, her head so cruelly bare as snow fell, her feet, her poor, poor feet, and turned to the fire.

The window opened.

At first, all it offered was a corner formed by two houses. The frustration returned, but then, nearly lost in the corner, leaning against the wall, there sat the little girl with the once-red cheeks, her mouth oddly smiling, frozen to death. A pale sun rose, casting a wan light on the tiny figure. The body, stiff and cold, held a bundle of matches, the whole of which was almost burned.

"No!"

I rose from the chair, stepping back, and the window closed. She was like me, this child. I knew it. I had felt her gaze on us just now, and *this* was to be her future?

No.

"Love?" Atlas took my shoulders in his strong hands, facing me, dark eyes holding my gaze and the gentle strength of him once again restored my thoughts.

"Sunlight," I said. "There was sunlight on her body."

"You saw a death, then?" Atlas said, drawing me into a tight embrace.

"Yes," I said, allowing myself only one breath in his arms. "But the fire shows me the future." I pulled away. "It is the present we need concern ourselves with now. Whoever is meant to care for her does not. A little girl, Atlas, a near-broken little girl, barefoot and no hat on a night like tonight—and I will not *allow* it." I shook my head, once again losing the words I needed. "It... *offends*, love. It offends."

"What do you need from me?" he asked. I had never loved him more than in that moment.

"We need to find her," I said. "But—"

My voice was stolen by the same sense of presence. "She's looking again," I said. "She is like me, she *sees* through the fire..." I turned around in a slow circle, until my gaze landed on the table, where the pure white cloth was spread, and the shining dinner service. Where soon cook's roast goose would steam gloriously, stuffed with apples and prunes.

I looked back through the small window her match made and forced myself to look past her frail little form, to the buildings behind her, but they might have been any building on any street, any corner.

The window closed again. I cried out, as near to physical pain was the helplessness I felt.

"You feel her?" Atlas said.

I could only nod.

"Come," he said, taking my hand.

IN THE BACK of his store, Atlas moved about with purpose, and I stood shaking with worry. Luckily, it was only a few blocks from The Candle and Robin, but now we were here, and my urgency and fear had risen as I was idle while he had purpose.

"Here," Atlas said finally, placing the candleholder with the robins on his workbench. The one with the gold-hued candle I'd gifted him, still mostly intact. The one we'd named our rooming house for.

He wrapped his big hands around the base, covering the carvings of the robins and nodded to me.

I exhaled, and with my exhalation, released every bit of the heat and flame inside me I could spare, my thoughts on that little girl selling matches in the street.

The candle bloomed, the light flaring so brightly it rivalled a summer sun, and I heard my love whispering, a soft request he repeated three times before he lifted his hands.

The eight robins were creatures of brilliant, blazing gold, and they circled the room. Atlas held out his hands, and they landed.

"Please," he said, repeating his words for the fourth time. "Take us to her."

They flew from his palms into the store, trailing motes of golden-white light, their sharp twittering cries full of intent, shooting stars given wings and voices.

We followed.

One by one, the robins winked out, and as each vanished with a final, sad twitter, I ached with the realization the magic we shared might not be enough. We tromped through the snow, running until our breaths barely had chance to catch in our chest before we needed another, and another robin vanished, and another, swallowed up by the cold and the dark...

Until finally, the last, beautiful golden robin twittered once and drove between two buildings, flaring before vanishing entirely.

Please, I thought, aiming a prayer to where I was not sure, as I had no beliefs worth merit. I stumbled into the corner formed by the two buildings and...

There she was.

I saw her inhale, crumpled in the snow, and with her exhalation she said, "Gran... take me with you..." and in her hand, a bundle of matches smouldered, on the edge of going out.

"No." I cried the word, for her exhalation was not followed by another breath, and I could feel the very heat of her, the *being* of her, begin to flee...

I conjured the heat and flame I possessed and pressed it into the little body in the snow, and she breathed again.

"You've done it," Atlas said beside me, but I shook my head.

"I am doing it," I said. "What life she has is borrowed." Knowledge I barely understood was slipping through my fingers even as I tried to grip it. "There is death here, a death I saw, a fate with nowhere to go, her light..."

But still I fed the warmth in my heart toward her. I *could* grant her more moments. Minutes, perhaps.

So I would.

"Hold on to her, love, as long as you can," Atlas's soft voice held hope, but I couldn't look away from the child and maintain the flow of all that I had. "Just as long as you can," he said, his voice now farther ahead of me, and to my left.

I longed to turn and see what he was doing, but the threads of heat and light I fed into the child were starting to dim, and I could feel a numbness and chill in my toes, my fingertips.

I could not do this forever. Her life, the braided wick of it, was woven like any other I might have fashioned in my shop: self-trimming, and little left of it.

When I began to shiver, I risked a glance as I knew time was running short.

Beside me, Atlas had sculpted another girl from the snow and ice and frost itself. His gifted hands—now red and burning with the cold—had caught every curve of her, right down to the smile she bore from whatever last vision she'd glimpsed through her matches.

"Now, my love," he said.

I understood. He could not grant life to something so large, only things that fit between his palms, but this sculpture? This thing he'd made?

He'd sculpted it to never have life.

From the little match girl, I unbraided the wick of her life. My hands moved in front of me, as though working with strands physical, not of spirit, but the method remained the same. Those strands I pulled to the left now, and entangled into the body my Atlas had made of ice and snow and frost instead.

Before my eyes, ice became bone, and snow flesh, and frost skin—but no life remained there for her.

In front of me, however, the weakest single breath.

"Hurry," I said, and Atlas pulled the girl into his arms, wrapping her in his coat, and leading the way back to The Candle and Robin as fast as we might run in our nearly broken state.

NOT LONG INTO New Year's Day I learned a little match-selling girl was found frozen in the corner of the two buildings. The next morning, from customers at my chandler shop, I heard the same refrain so often it might become a new carol to be sung every season: "She wanted to warm herself, poor thing." Then, from my eldest brother, the Bow Street Runner, I learned of her father, a cruel and angry man who showed little remorse.

It made the course we must set all the clearer.

She recovered in the kitchen of The Candle and Robin, the warmest room in the building, under the care of the two gentle students of medicine, and with the hearty food of the cook. We introduced her as our own: the niece of my Atlas, left orphaned but now in our care, and though none of the eight under the roof of our rooming house believed us, all did the courtesy of pretending.

Indeed, one of the medical students procured for us the "proof" we needed of her birth.

She believes she saw Heaven and her grandmother, though she herself said her grandmother had never been so grand nor beautiful.

She didn't intend to see the future.

That much, the people of the city had right: she only wanted to warm herself.

We will keep her warm. Besides, it will take time, no doubt, to explain to her what she can do, though at least I've my own experiences to guide her. For, like me, I know the little match girl can see the future in flame, and like me I believe she caught a glimpse through a match-flame window not of her late grandmother, but rather of someone she will herself one day be.

And as for the "Heaven" she saw?

Well.

I think her descriptions of tables and chairs and food and grand trees full of candles sounds much like the Christmases we celebrate here at The Candle and Robin. Heaven enough for me.

And, I expect, a tradition she will continue long after I and my Atlas have gone.

NOT THE
MARRYING KIND

I - Dick Larrabee

I'M TOLD IT was on a Christmas Eve and a Saturday night that Mrs. Larrabee—who, it is important to note, was my step-mother, having married my father, the minister, after the death of my mother—came up with her notion of putting her talents toward a Christmas card.

It's also important to note in fairness, and I do wish to be fair wherever I can in this telling, given how unfairly most had treated us, that Mrs. Larrabee was a fairly lovely woman. She certainly brought cheer to our home after my mother died, and I wouldn't be exaggerating to say it was the first time that emotion had joined the Larrabee household. My birth mother hadn't much room for joy.

No, she'd kept most of the space in our home for godliness, which was more-or-less a synonym for castigation and correction and disappointment, really.

Specifically, disappointment in *me*.

When you grow up feeling you can do no right, it's not a far step to deciding you might as well do wrong. Not to excuse most of my behaviour, of course, but I was a young boy with a minister for a father, a joyless critic for a mother until I was six, and the eyes of the entire town watching me for the slightest misstep, especially in the twelve years before the arrival of the woman who would become the second Mrs. Larrabee.

But all that was years ago, and the night in question I wish to describe was more about my stepmother than my mother or my father, and began with her declaration of two plans.

"Luther," my stepmother said, "I'm going to run down to Letty's."

That was her first plan, and it involved visiting Letty—Letitia—because the twins, Letitia's niece and nephew, seemed to be coming down with something, and my step-mother knew full well Letitia Gilman, despite the help of Miss Clarissa Perry, the town's childless baby-rearing expert, was often of a maudlin nature and might need a dose of Reba Larrabee's joy to make it through the night.

My father, I imagine, made noises of assent, and perhaps even genuine ones, if I credit him a positive mood for the evening.

Which I can do, having not witnessed it firsthand, but as I am already trying to be fair, it seems not too much further a step to decide to also be kind to the people of this town.

"And oh! Luther, I have some fresh ideas for Christmas cards and I am going to try my luck with them," Mrs. Larrabee said, which was her second plan.

It might sound near flighty for a minister's wife to suggest she intended to pen a Christmas card, but my stepmother's verses had been picked up in the newspapers a few times now, and she did have a way with words that was both pleasant and pious, alongside a rather *authentic* intent to follow through on any promises inherent in the platitudes.

My father suggested she speak to Letty about the second plan, this Christmas card notion, because Letty's half-brother David—most notably and notoriously to all in the small town as the father of the twins in his half-sister's care—had once been involved in some sort of picture business in the city, and Letty might know where to send a potential card for publication.

Ah, David.

If I'm to continue with fairness and kindness in mind, it's perhaps not the right time to speak of David Gilman beyond those two things: his twins being raised by his half-sister, his presence being elsewhere.

It's perhaps also my habit simply not to speak of David Gilman. My father's Lord knew that wasn't a problem anyone else in our town had. Old Maria Popham, who I'd once heard most accurately described as 'the town's professional pessimist' thought nothing of reminding anyone who'd listen how David Gilman had done his half-sister wrong and didn't seem to own a shred of guilt besides. Her husband, Ossian—everyone called him called Osh—who rarely allowed his wife's cruel observances much time before countering with a softer touch on any topic with a notable exception of me, the minister's son, didn't rise to David Gilman's defence, either. It was like that throughout the whole town, I knew. If there was a race run on bad reputations through the centre of town, I'm not sure if David or myself— the scandalous Dick Larrabee—would take the ribbon, but once the winner was announced, I would certainly know where to wager my money on a runner-up.

Indeed, even my stepmother found little good to say of David Gilman.

My father, though, often cautioned those who would simply brush off David completely as a lost cause. In fact, I'm told he did so in my name, remembering how, for quite a few years, Dick, Letty, and I ran in the same circles as friends, before...

Well.

I want to say it again: *ah, David.*

Never mind. I promise, more on him later.

For now, when my stepmother arrived at Letty Gilman's home, she saw a sight that inspired her.

Letitia Boynton's one-storey grey cottage wasn't much. Behind it, a clump of tall cedar trees for background, and in front, bare branches of elms laden now with snow. And at the parlour window, a single candlestick with lit candle illuminated the view of Letty Gilman sitting at the window, which was open despite the winter night.

The rest of the parlour was lit only by a hearth-fire, bright enough to show the portrait of Letty's mother over the mantel. The angle of my step-mother's approach allowed one more view: past the edge of the fireplace, through a half-open door, the flames granted just enough light to halo the heads of two sleeping children, snuggled together, their blond tangled curls flowing over one pillow in the bed that took up nearly the whole of their tiny bedroom.

Letty waited in her chair by the open window, wrapped in an old red-brown homespun cape. And it did look like she was waiting—her chin in hand, head turned. To hear my stepmother tell it, she was a creature designed entirely of waiting, hoping, and something so very much full of *longing* that in that moment, Reba Larrabee, second wife of the minister of the small town I'd left as soon as I could, knew what she wanted to draw and paint on her Christmas card.

II - David Gilman

I SWEAR I never intended my half-sister to bear my burdens, nor had I ever intended to live down to the expectations of everyone in our home town, but sometimes I think my entire life could be served up by those three words—"I never intended"— and a sour smile beside.

You know how you can get off on the wrong foot with someone, and you never quite seem to find your balance again in their presence? That was me, but not just with some*one*, with the whole damn town itself, and the world beyond, if I care to admit it. I misstepped at birth, and then every stumbling stagger thereafter only seemed to make it worse for me, my father, my half-sister, and everyone I touched.

A smarter man would have stopped touching people, no? I suppose I can put some of that down to being a boy and having a lot more hope then than later in life, but I tried, tripping up over and over again until, in the end, I don't believe a single soul in that town could have honestly said they weren't glad to see me go.

Not even my half sister, Letty, or…

Or anyone else.

The night my sister had banked the fire warm enough she didn't mind an open window in winter, and Mrs. Reba Larrabee came to visit her, Letty admitted to having put that candle there for me.

There! I can hear your words. *It's not true no one wanted you back in your home, and you've just admitted it!*

Well, *yes*—but also *no*. I can't blame Letty for wanting her half-brother to return, what with what I'd left behind, but it's what I'd left behind that made her want me to return, you see, no abiding love or welcome. Had I been the one walking in the snow that night and coming across Letty in her wrap at her table, waiting, a candle in the window, the light of the cottage's parted door offering a place to stop in welcome, with the portrait of our mother so visible, I might have stopped, true. But then I would have caught a glimpse beyond that table, that woman in the wrap, that portrait, and seen…

Two children.

Twins.

Well. As I said, I stepped wrong from the start with everyone in that town, and my sister was by no means excepted from the list. And so it was a good thing it wasn't me walking past that night, but rather Mrs. Reba Larrabee, who stopped to speak with my half sister, and—of all things—ask her permission to draw and paint that very scene as her attempt to publish a Christmas card.

Poor Letty. In the face of one as joyous and—I'll sound crass and bitter for this, but there's no other way to state it—*relentless* as Mrs. Reba Larrabee, it's no wonder she gave her permission.

I have no trouble imagining their conversation. Imagining conversations is, in fact, a cursed gift of mine: to replay what was said or done and to imagine not a *single* misstep? Many an evening I should have slept well was instead taken up by my knack of playing those games with myself: *What David Gilman should have done.* Especially when it came to Dick Larrabee.

"Your house looks so quaint, backed by those dark cedars," my imagined Mrs. Reba Larrabee would exclaim.

"Oh, but—"

"And with the moon and snow making everything shimmer so, Letty?" Mrs. Reba Larrabee continues, because surely Letty simply didn't understand.

"Reba, I—" Letty's second attempt.

"And the firelight through the open door danced so, Letty!" I imagine Mrs. Reba Larrabee using her hands to speak, as she so often did. Gestures sweeping away all concerns Letty might have had.

"Well, that's—" A third attempt, aborted.

"And your charming Hessian soldier andirons, your mother's lovely face..."

"My mother?" Defences crumbling now in the face of such a reference to our mother.

"In the portrait! And oh, oh, Letty, behind it all, the children sleeping like angels resting, and then you, Letty!"

"Me? But I—"

"You! Wrapped in your cape waiting vigil for someone. It's so perfect!"

And here, Letty would simply have nothing left but to agree.

No, not a soul alive could withstand the targeted joy of Mrs. Reba Larrabee, and Letty relied on her for company and conversation, and so much more, what with me not providing any of those things with any regularity, and so Letty agreed to it, I'm sure in no small part because Mrs. Larrabee suggested it only proper they split any earnings.

A poem of Mrs. Larrabee's own crafting was intended to go with this picture of Letty with her face turned away in vigil, the twins sleeping, our mother's portrait, and the light and the snow and the candle in the window:

My door is on the latch tonight,
The hearth fire is aglow.
I seem to hear swift passing feet,
The Christ Child in the snow.
My heart is open wide tonight
For stranger, kith or kin.
I would not bar a single door
Where Love might enter in!

If you have any doubts of Mrs. Larrabee's honest and pious character, I figure those words will settle it, even if you're of the misstepping sort as myself and can't help but hear the words of the poem in your mind's voice with a cadence of scorn.

The thing was, though, Letty hadn't lit that candle for Christ's boy, or a stranger, or any friend or acquaintance. No, Letty Gilman had left that candle for kin—me, though I don't deserve the word—out of desperation or anger or well-earned bitterness, as it was three years to the day since those twins had been born, and it had been three months since I'd written, and before that half a year, both with a five dollar bill, and neither adequate.

Cracking her cottage door ajar, opening the window, stoking the fire, revealing the twins through their bedroom door, all of it was a kind of prayer, really. A prayer for the arrival of her awful, selfish, life-destroying half-brother.

And such a typical prayer for my half-sister Letty: unspoken.

And, I suppose, even more typical for her?

Unanswered.

III - Dick Larrabee

AH, DAVID.

I suppose to understand David, it's best we start with his sister, Letitia, and work our way forward. Letty Boynton's father had been the village doctor, though she'd never recalled much of him and what she thought she recalled had been made up from stories others had told her so often she simply believed she remembered.

Her mother had remarried an older man, John Gilman, who was a curious mix of respected country lawyer while completely incompetent at nearly anything else. One assumes the marriage might have started out of sheer pity for the man, but it flourished into love, and Letty's mother and Letty's stepfather had brought kindness and joy, and three years later David himself, but it seemed to be purchased at a heavy price.

First, John Gilman declined in health, and Letty and her mother were often left to care for him.

Then, when Letty was but eighteen, her mother died, and in all ways that truly mattered, it was Letty left to care for everyone, including the fifteen year-old David.

And, the final blow, John Gilman's death.

Ah, David.

I'm not sure I can do David's verve justice. He had a way of leaping at life—true, without looking—which was infectious. He was handsome, possessed of dark hair, dark eyes, and a winsome smile as good as any logical argument ever was for convincing others to partake of a particular path. His mind was sharp, and he picked up new ideas easily. He was, despite being four years younger than myself, as constant my companion as Letty herself, and no matter our intent to have our own fun with no bother to others, somehow we bothered others in a fashion most constant.

And as the elder of us—not to mention being the minister's boy—the blame landed squarely on my shoulders in the eyes of most of the town.

I won't put all that down to David, of course. Letty was too young to run a household, I was too angry at a town full of people determined to see me with as unfriendly a gaze as my own mother's had been, and I absolutely played my part, both in temperament and action, to earn the foundation of my reputation.

But the town built storeys upon that foundation with unbridled enthusiasm every time they so much as aimed their gaze at Letty and David or myself, and they seemed to like to do little else. My father's sermons, that bloody Deacon Todd... all I endured, before I chose otherwise, wasn't intentionally the fault of myself or Letty or David, but somehow the blame was most often on me.

And in a small town, anything known by one is soon noticed and known by all. There needn't even be much maliciousness in it, though I'd posit a healthy dose of that flavour was indeed added by Maria Popham and Deacon Todd. It simply *becomes* acknowledged. Truth or nuance have no place in a small town.

That David, one would have said, with a slow shake of head.

Ah, yes, but what can you expect? another would say, matching the slow shake of head. *After all, Dick.*

Indeed. Their heads shake in unison. *And he the minister's son.*

It diminished David, it quieted Letty, and it furied me. And then...

Ah, David.

If it hadn't been Deacon Todd, would it have been someone else? I'm never sure if it was his version of events which had been passed to Mrs. Maria Popham, who, in turn, shared it around the town beneath a guise of *genuine concern.* I couldn't believe Mrs. Popham's talk ever meant to be her version of a pious sort of kindness, nor if Deacon Todd simply hadn't seen things as they'd been, but with my name on everyone's lips and David's sudden departure, I'd been a thread ready to unravel as it was.

Father tried to be patient, again; my stepmother entreated me to be the person she'd seen me be with others with my father. Letty bent her head to the role of family matriarch and so rarely showed happiness unless in our company, and even then, I think Letty knew there was little time left.

I did try, for Letty as much as David, even absent as he was. They were...

Well. Everyone has a reason for enduring, no? Though I think I did no one a favour.

Then Deacon Todd had opened his mouth in a public prayer on my behalf—making a mockery of me and my father's parish both—and I could bear no more.

My mother had left me a small house and farm, if no warm memories, love, or nostalgia, and by this time, I'd finished my college education. It was assumed I would stay in the town, earn my keep, live in that home, and perhaps even work that farm or hire others to do so. But the moment I was offered a share in a good business—most notably in a city twelve miles away—I rented it all away and left.

First, though, I let the anger stoked so long quite free. I raised my voice to my father, condemned the town, parish, and all its people, and I won't lie and say I took no joy in it. The face of my fury exhausted my father's patience, and he returned condemnation in kind.

And so, I left.

I left this town. I left Deacon Todd, and Mrs. Maria Popham, and my father, and my step-mother. I left Letty Boynton, and...

Everyone who'd already left me.

After I, the notorious Dick Larrabee, had all but twain the parish in half and left this town in total disarray—at least to hear Mrs. Maria Popham tell it—the town then witnessed Letty's despondence until some time later, when they saw the return of David Gilman from Boston.

David's return must have seemed divine vindication for Deacon Todd and Mrs. Popham, given the state in which he returned. I'm sure both believed David Gilman's situation all they needed to declare the ruin of the man, for his return came without his verve, with his head bowed. It was soon said, whether true or not, that his time in Boston had done him no good and much ill, and he rarely lifted his dark eyes from the ground. He had no money and no job, but to the town's further talk, he'd asked his sister for board in their childhood home.

But not for himself.

No, David Gilman left again, but in his place he'd left Eva.

She was David's pregnant wife, near her time of birth, and she was rumoured to be colder than the bitter winter itself.

Raven-haired and darker than even David, Eva was by all accounts sour, bitter, and ill. Letty did her best to rally as I'm sure only Letty could—always the caretaker, always before her time—and if not for Miss Clarissa Perry, the town's childless expert in the bringing-up of babies, the house itself would have been woefully unprepared for the birth of a child, as David Gilman had left meagre funds behind and nothing in the way of a crib or of swaddling.

Eva held no joy and much anger in its place, and Letty could not understand it. They even quarreled. I cannot imagine Letty so aggrieved to quarrel with an ill, pregnant sister-in-law, so Eva must have been beyond the pale. But in the end, when nothing seemed to lift Eva from the darkness and the time grew ever closer for the birth, even the town doctor took Letty aside to tell her a truth perhaps too harsh but no less true.

He believed it was up to Eva herself to find peace, but she might not choose to do so. The child might help, and would be their last hope of it, he believed.

This all happened after I'd left. I don't remind you as to excuse my part in it, but so that, perhaps, you'll do David the favour this town never did, and not judge him before the story is finished.

It occurs to me I'd promised to tell you about David, and all I've done is tell you about myself and Letty and Eva and even Mrs. Maria Popham and Deacon Todd and my father. It's unfair, and as typical of the town, frankly—eyes on him turned to judgement on me; thoughts of him turned to talk of me.

I'll have to try again.

IV - David Gilman

IT'S A COWARD who misses the birth of his children, and a rogue who doesn't provide for them, and I can't deny many times in my life I have lived as both. When I did make it back to the only cottage where I'd ever felt at home, I found only my sister and the twins, Eva buried, and I had but a pittance to offer as the results of my efforts.

"When we showed her the bairns," Letty said to me then, "she *shrieked*, David. A noise without love nor joy. The way she shrieked, David, you'd think the babes the worst of all creation. I... I admit to having uncharitable thoughts about her, and about twins, if we're to tell truths. Doctor Lee, he said the very sight of them seemed to turn her away from life, and she did turn away, David. She simply stopped living."

It wasn't hard to see what Eva had seen in those children, even wriggling and pink and the way of babies so recently born, and all my effort, my attempt to make something right of it all simply froze and crumbled around me, and I knew with an utter certainty that this wasn't just stepping wrong in life. This wasn't one of my usual misplacement of a foot, or a word loosed with too little thought beforehand. I hadn't misstepped.

I had begun a ruinous path I couldn't turn back from.

But I couldn't take those children with me, either.

And—God judge me, for it *is* true—I could barely look at them, for they were the most unwelcome reminder of the life I needed to return to, and as quickly as possible were they to survive.

And so, with no fatherly pride and—in truth, again, God judge me—more insult than goodwill, I left them with my sister, and I returned to Boston.

As I've said, I have always seemed to have the perfectly imperfect knack of placing my first foot wrong, and then spending my life in an increasingly difficult dance to put my steps back into alignment with those around me. It's a losing battle, a fool's errand, and a pattern repeated no matter how far I went from my home, this attempt to regain some balance. Most people know the sensation of a misstep, if only in the literal sense, but I'd wager the vast majority of those of us who live and breathe have experienced that yawning chasm of a moment between acting wrong and seeing the recognition of that act in the eyes of everyone gathered.

Humiliation is what I'm speaking of, I suppose. Speaking the wrong word. Shaking the wrong hand while speaking the wrong name. Knowing that no matter how sharp your mind might be, the simple act of navigating an aimless and weightless conversation will no doubt leave you verbally sprawled on the floor in front of those gathered, exposed in some way as *wrong*.

It was that and more I returned to at my work in Boston. That was where I'd placed my foot wrong in the first step on the journey to where I was now.

There is a sort of person for whom misstepping is never a concern. Though it brought him no great peace in his youth, Dick Larrabee was one such as that. He knew his mind, knew his business, knew his words, and knew his direction. Those people are a map and compass to those like me, a way to see the world we might never navigate on our own, but at least acknowledge exists for others. They see those of us who stumble around, trip over our own self, and offer a hand and find something to like in our harum-scarum ways. In the company of one such as Dick Larrabee, my life never did seem quite as off the rails at it would otherwise be.

And so I, of course, ruined it.

There is also a third sort of person who seems much the same as the map and compass sort, but is not, and this is where the true misfortune began for me. This third sort is also there to offer a hand and find something to like in the harum-scarum way, but it is not to lift us so much as to know they could lead us anywhere they want, which in and of itself is enjoyable to them, and that there will be no consequence to them for wherever they might leave us.

Sir Alfred Crenshaw—call me "Freddy"—was that to me, and more fool I, I didn't realize it in time to stop… Well, any of it.

So, as I left Letty with a barely mumbled, "I hope the children will be good," and they screamed and wailed in the back room in an obvious unified declaration to be anything but, I could barely hold my head upright, as my only hope to have a way to offer my dear sister any aid in the raising of those twins was to return to Freddy Crenshaw, and continue working for him as though none of this had happened.

Clarissa Perry, a childless woman who nonetheless was an expert in the bringing-up of babies, had already offered her aid, and in the face of one such as Clarissa Perry, what more could I add?

Only money. And for money, I needed work.

And for work, I needed Freddy Crenshaw's firm.

He had not a blond hair out of place despite the curls, not a crack in his smile and a simple, softly spoken, "Welcome back, David," upon my return. He simply nodded to my desk, and I took my spot feeling as off balance and unsuited to living any sort of life at that desk as ever, not that I could fathom a life with a sense of suitability.

"The wife?" he said, waiting until I'd sat, as though to underline my lower position in comparison to his, and he could cast his soft blue eyes downward to match. Such dispassion in the words. *The wife.* Not even *your wife.* Eva an object to him, not even a person.

How had I never seen how he looked at those around him in that way, you might wonder. But the truth is, Freddy could look at you and make you feel seen when he wanted to.

But only when he wanted to.

"She..." I had to swallow after a word, as so often, and I saw the little curl of his lips. *Yes,* that curl said. *You know your place, I know mine, and we shall move past this ugly business and return to what was, at my leisure and for my pleasure.* "Died," I managed.

I watched, and when that smile did not alter in the slightest, and his voice didn't change in the least when he replied, "Condolences, David," I knew that even my own stumbling self would never take this man's offered hand again.

Never.

Never had come too late, was cold comfort, and when Sir Alfred Crenshaw realized he didn't need to simply reapply the pleasant facade he'd first used to gain my friendship, loyalty, and—yes—intimate company, he instead made work impossible, assigning tasks I had no hope of completing, and ultimately, at the end of three miserable years I endured for the sake of those twins and my sister, ending my employment and leaving me with no way to offer even the ten pound pittances I'd been sending back to Letty.

My lodgings went next, as I tried to find new income, and if some part of me considered acting on what it would take to regain my employment with Sir Alfred Crenshaw, I can at least speak this much of my character: in the cold at night especially, the temptation *would* come, but I never gave in.

I would never give in again.

And so it was I went hand-to-mouth, scraping by as I could, and though I should have written Letty, every attempt at a letter began so wrong I could not recover.

Dear Letty, I am afraid I have lost my job—
Dear Letty, I am afraid I must find new employment—
Dear Letty, I am afraid—

I worked when I could, tried to gather scraps into a whole, and when I closed my eyes, I hoped I wouldn't see the falsely smiling face of Freddy Crenshaw.

Then, my health, too, fled. I had no choice but to retire the publishing position I'd been able to procure for myself and adjourn to St. Joseph's, where I learned some piece of me was badly wrong and would need to come out.

I inhaled the gas and thought, *How will they ever know which wrong and badly gone piece to take?*

The rest was silence.

V – Dick Larrabee

T'WAS NEARLY Christmas the year I saw David Gilman again, for the first time since he'd fled our town and everyone in it, and I could scarcely have come up with a less comfortable notion than making my way through the North Station in Boston, stepping into the train car at one end, and finding myself face-to-face with a slender Ghost of Christmas Past regarding me with as much shock as I no doubt had upon my own countenance.

He'd entered the car from the other end, so our eyes caught across the middle.

"Dick Larrabee, upon my word!" David's voice was soft, and wan, and it seemed to me he looked like a man made fragile over the years.

"Dave Gilman, by all that's great!" I could hear the forced cheer in my own voice and had the oddest sensation of being unsure of my balance and words both. To whit, I turned. "Here, let's turn over a seat for our baggage and sit together."

I did so, David's smaller cases much less grand than my own, but tucked together, and then we sat.

"Going home, I suppose?" I said to him. An inanity for sure, for where else could he be going on this train, at this time of year, on course for exactly that place and a few others he'd have even less interest in? But the question gave me time to look at him, to really look, and...

Wan. Fragile. Pale. He'd always had a trace of scrappiness to him, had Dave, but now it looked like most of the fight had been taken from him. And the way he looked back at me? I was not so foolish as to believe there would be a freedom of delight at seeing me, nor even perhaps should I have expected even a smile, but the way he *assessed* me with his dark eyes was so thoroughly beyond the worst I might have imagined.

The dark eyes of David Gilman wondered, *Are you still a threat?*

"Yes," he said, and it took me a breath to remember the question I'd asked of him. "I'm going home"—here his voice caught on the word—"for a couple of days. It's such a journey." This last was accompanied by that wan smile of his. "A one-horse village that a man can't get to but once in a generation."

"It's an awful hole." I found myself agreeing, though at the same time, I wondered of David's scarcity of time there. I knew of his wife, her death, of his children. Even far removed, word occasionally traveled to me, and none of those words were kind to David Gilman, even now. "I didn't get that town out of my system for years," I said, then flinched as I heard how the words might be taken.

David, though, simply nodded, gently. "Married?" he said.

He would ask that. He should. It was well his right.

"No," I said, swallowing, and I will not dissemble to say meeting his gaze on that crowded train was anything less than a Herculean task in that moment. "Rather think I'm not the marrying kind," I said. Aware of our surroundings and those dark eyes of his both, I couldn't hold my tongue. "Though the fact is I've had no time for love affairs—too busy." I wanted this conversation to end, but I didn't know how. "Let's see. You have…" I wanted to swallow the words as soon as I'd said them, knowing they weren't kind, but I couldn't quite stop the flow. "You have a child, haven't you?"

Why did I say such a thing? Why even *a child* when I knew it was two?

But all he did was nod again, in that pale way of his. "Yes," David said. "Though Letty has seen to all that business for me since my wife died."

Some silence fell, and this time I was determined to let it. I didn't know how to navigate with this new David, who didn't seem to leap at life the way he'd once done.

"Wonder if there have been many changes in the village?" David said, after a time.

I dismissed that with what I hoped was a laugh far more humour than bitterness. As though old Mrs. Popham would deign to die and make the world a happier place, nor Deacon Todd, when he could instead preserve his high opinion of himself—and for the first time, I caught a glimpse of spark in David's eyes. "But it's possible I've a trace of animosity colouring my thoughts on the subject."

"That's true enough, I'd wager," he said.

This time, when the silence fell, I couldn't stop myself.

"How——" I almost asked him plain, *How are you?*, but lost my nerve. "How's business with you, David?"

"Only so-so," David said. "I've had the devil's own luck lately." He went on to tell me how he hadn't found a position to suit—and certainly none to live on—and while he had some hope of a new connection he'd recently made in publishing, he seemed almost afraid to speak of it, as though words might break the hope in some way.

Then he let out a soft breath. "I'm just out of hospital."

At my jolt of surprise, he explained again. He'd had not one, but two operations. He joked, though I could see effort in the humour, that they'd missed the right target on their first account, and as such he'd spent two months there recovering from not one operation, but two. Finally, his dark eyes found mine again, his story finished.

"That's hard luck," I said, then found myself offering a précis of my own life. I chose to purposefully note that my own luck had only changed in the last few months, though I'd certainly not begun in as tenuous a position as he'd just described, in hope that he'd maybe see things *could* change.

Then, I recalled how things could indeed change for the worse, as well. "No trouble at home calls you back?" I asked. "I hope Letty is all right?" I watched him carefully, wondering if this new David would admit anything of the truth if she wasn't.

"Oh, no. Everything's serene, so far as I know." He admitted to being a poor correspondent—more so when he had no bright news to share—and then finished with another soft breath. "I suppose I'm just here to surprise Letty."

I looked at David again, and I began to think I didn't like this new version of him, who was cool and calm and seemed to be bracing for an impact of some kind. As a child, Dave had been a shadow and a companion and a friend, and...

David caught me looking, and I daresay he caught the turn of my thoughts as well, something he'd had skill at in our youth as well, and—more importantly—courage.

Ah, David. There you are.

He looked away first, and I wondered what else had happened before he'd brought that unaccountable wife home and foisted her and her babies on Letty. Back then, I'd allowed myself to be rather turned on him—which wasn't fair, and I think I knew that even then. Now, to look at him, it wasn't as easy to find the young man he'd been those years ago, especially now he was so pale and thin-chested.

Though his mouth was the same: soft and pretty. David had a good face, too, straight and clean, with honest eyes and a likeable smile when he let it out.

It flickered now, there-and-gone-again, when he turned back and found me still looking at him.

"And you, Dick? Your father's still living?" David glanced out the window into the dark and snow. "I haven't kept up with our town."

I assured him the minister was hale and hearty.

"Do you visit every Christmas?" David said.

Admitting it was my first seemed to surprise him, but he chuckled.

"That's about my case, too." He hung his head a little, and my fingers twitched with the desire to lift his chin, which... No. But how they twitched.

Instead, I laughed. "I was a hot-headed fool when I said goodbye." I laughed again. "Well, I never did say goodbye, even. I gave the town my fury, and I left. It's taken me all this time to lose that temper, and even so, I never thought I'd return, but then..."

"Then?" David said.

"There's—there's rather an odd coincidence, really," I said. "That's what's brought me here, I suppose."

"Coincidence?" David said, and for the first time, the full wide smile of the Dave I knew returned. "I can beat yours, I'm sure." Even his cadence was back to that of his youth, of daring me, asking me to rise to his challenge and knowing he'd meet me there.

I bit my lip. "How so?"

Then the most remarkable thing. He reached into his jacket and he pulled out a Christmas card. "Do you see that?" he said. "It was my late mother that drew me back."

I'm afraid I didn't look long, because the word coincidence didn't do it justice, in fact. He held a Christmas card and called it his reason for returning, and I reached into my own coat to pull out the very same thing—the Christmas card responsible for my taking this trip. It had the same cut, the same paper, and though the two designs were not the same card, they were the same artist, style, and even their subject matter, I realized.

David's card showed the same cottage as my card, one I'd have recognized as David Gilman's childhood cottage at a glance, but his card pulled in tight to the view, with a door open and his sister—I recognized her wrap and her hair and

110

her ear—head turned away, two children sleeping in a room beyond, a fire in the mantle and the portrait of David Gilman's mother above the fireplace. My own card was of the cottage as well, though farther back, though once again there was the impression of a woman in the window that could only be Letty to my mind.

And the verse.

My heart is open wide tonight
For stranger, kith or kin
I would not bar a single door
Where Love might enter in!

"It was that portrait of my mother," David said, tapping where it hung above the fireplace. "That's what drew me back, though the whole of the picture was the charm. And Letty, though I didn't recognize her right off, I'm sad to admit." He delighted in pointing out each part of the image—the andirons, the sitting room, the door ajar, and I listened to him, just as delighted to hear such life in his voice. "When I'd studied the card five minutes, I bought a ticket and started for home."

"It's prettier than mine, I think," I said, comparing the two images, though they were both quaint and lovely.

"What really affected me, though," David said, "was the verse. I liked that open door. It meant welcome, no matter how little you'd deserved it."

He took another breath, and I realized he wasn't as sure of this welcome.

"Where'd you get your card?" I asked, if only to chase that look away from his eyes, and to stop myself from wanting to do something about it myself. He'd married. He'd had children. He'd left town, and I knew why.

I'd *been* why.

"A nurse brought it to me in the hospital just because she took a fancy to it." David laughed with some darker humour. "She thought I might like it, and instead it sent me into a relapse."

"No!"

"Yes. I guess Nora will confine herself to beef tea now," he said, with another wry chuckle. "But it was worth it, I think." He looked at my card again. "Where'd you get yours?"

"Nothing so dramatic. I picked it up on a dentist's mantelpiece when I was waiting for an appointment." I'd been idling my way round the room, hands in my pockets to keep from boredom, when I saw the card standing up against an hourglass. The colour had caught my eye, and then… "I took it to the window," I said, shaking my head in remembered bafflement. "It certainly was Letty's house. The door's open you see and there's somebody in the window. I knew it was Letty, but how could any card publisher have found the way to our town?" I opened it, and read the verses, which were less religious and more popular.

Now here's a Christmas greeting
To the "folks back home."
It comes to you across the space,
Dear folks back home!
I've searched the wide world over,
But no matter where I roam,
No friends are like the old friends,
No folks like those back home!

David nodded, looking back at his card as though the thought of the cards having made quite the journey to find us hadn't occurred to him. Maybe it hadn't.

I tapped the corner of his card. "Then I discovered my stepmother's initials snarled up in the holly, and I remembered that she was always painting and illustrating."

David breathed. "I've always liked your mother's verses. She always had a knack of being pious without cramming piety down your throat."

I had to agree there, and I did. Not like my mother at all, was Mrs. Reba Larrabee.

"Life is odd," David said, putting the card back in his pocket. His dark eyes had returned to me. "A strange, queer job," he added, and then his lips parted as though he had more words for me, but none came. He closed his lips, and I would have done anything for them to open of his own accord. But they didn't.

"You're right," I said. "A job. And one we can't shirk, isn't it?"

David glanced away, and once again it occurred to me I'd said something that might have sounded like a judgment on his character. "Still, those cards brought us back here. A sort of magic, aren't they?" I eyed my own card, then slipped it back into my pocket, only to realize the next station was our town. "Jiminy! Is it the next station?"

No. No, no, no. I needed more time with David, I needed to talk of a thing, not all around it, and I needed—

What?

"Yes, here we are," David said, with that trace of grim humour that seemed to be with him most of the time now. "Seven o'clock and the train *only* thirty-five minutes late."

Had he been aching to be done with me? I couldn't tell. It occurred to me, far too late, that this whole conversation might have been painful to him, and that, more than anything else, spurred me on to try again.

"Never mind!" I said, as bright as he'd been grey. "They'll have tucked away the food, but it won't be so far gone—just in the pantry. They'll bring them back out again, and mince pies too. And cheese." I winked at him, tapping my pocket where my card rested again. "*The folks back home* will be there."

"They won't be at home, Dick," David said, and the way he said my name brought that twitch back to my fingers. "We're so late. If nothing has changed—and it never did, not here—they'll be at the Christmas Eve festival. In the church." The last three words he were so soft he might not have spoken them.

The train had pulled into the station, and we gathered our cases, stepping off the platform. He was right, of course, about where everyone would be, but I didn't like the maudlin way he'd spoken of it.

"Maybe they can have me for Santa Claus then," I joked. I flagged down one of the two sleighs available, and the driver drew it up beside us. "I'll be the merriest Saint Nicholas in the town."

That earned me an odd look from David, but then we both fell silent at the view around us which was, as he'd said, unchanged. Yet with the peculiar charm of a white Christmas, it somehow seemed bright and new, nor even as cold as it should be, given the late hour and the snow.

"Look at the ice on the river," I said, remembering how we'd skated together in the past. "What skating... and the moon." She was full and shining and that was why the world was so bright, I realized.

When I turned to him, he was looking up at the moon and smiling, and it seemed to me there was surprise in that smile, like he'd never expected anything of a delight to be had in this town.

I opened my mouth, but then the baggage handler was tossing my other packages out from the train with the casualness of someone long accustomed to knowing just how far and with as little effort as possible one could accomplish a passable job. I started to load them into the sleigh.

"Are you spending the winter?" David said, watching the parcels add up around me. A slyness in his tone and eyes both delighted me as much as the teasing itself. He stood just a step away, though the lean of his body made it clear he was about to depart.

I didn't want him to.

"Presents, if I'm in time for the tree," I said. "I'm going to give those blue-nosed, frost-bitten little youngsters something to remember!" I drew as much of the vaunted Saint Nicholas's tone into my words, proclaiming it with deep and resonant cheer, and that made David's head shake in wonder. "You know, Dave, I feel I could shake hands with Deacon Todd."

That made him laugh, and it was such a sweet sound of mirth I cannot tell it.

"Better you than I. Well, Merry Christmas to you, Dick," he said. "I'm going to walk—"

"No," I said, shaking my head. "Help me pack these onto the sleigh, and I'll at least drop you mid-way." I turned my voice to a casualness I had to force with will, but he agreed readily enough, and soon we were in the back of the sleigh together, side-to-side, the driver ahead of us and a bright moon above and all for the magic of two Christmas cards.

I faced him, resolute, and found the dark eyes of David Gilman were already facing me.

VI - David Gilman

I WANTED TO explain. I wanted to open my mouth and let every word of these last three years—and more beyond—spill out until Dick Larrabee quit aiming that look of pity in my direction, but I couldn't help but wonder if every word I had would still end up leaving him in that same place regardless.

We'd only have a few minutes before the old signboard marking the path to the town centre in one direction would appear, and then I'd be off the sleigh and heading down a different route.

And Dick Larrabee was looking at me, and my words were as frozen in my throat as if the lap blanket covering us both wasn't there, and the heat from Dick's body beside mine wasn't there.

Both were, yet frozen I was.

"I—" I began softly, as he said, "Well—" in his usual voice.

"No," he said. "You."

"There's a lot to say," I said, finding I couldn't withstand his expression. I adjusted my gaze downward. "And I needs say it, but there is someone owed the truth more than you, Dick, and I won't rob her of that dignity." I took one more shaking breath, watching my previous words skitter away like clouds in the night air. "I intend to tell her all of it, Dick."

There. It was said, and if it was a decision I'd not been successful in making ever since I'd seen that Christmas card, ever since the very idea it might be possible to walk through Letty's door and be *welcome* had taken such root in my mind, it was made now.

Only fair to warn Dick, as his unwilling part in it would also be known, and as sorrowful as I was for that, I needed this. Needed that door unbarred, even just for a single holiday.

I already knew I wouldn't stay. Not after, but for a while, this town—or, no, that *cottage*—might once again be a home for a spell.

Beneath the lap blanket, Dick took my and in his and squeezed in urgency, and I could not choose if he meant a warning, an acceptance, or even a comfort, so I raised my gaze and found him regarding me with none of them at all—instead with something akin to concern, or perhaps just a compassion that might share a room with it.

"After your wife died," he said. "I thought of you unkindly. I am sorry for that."

"After my wife died," I said. "So did I." He was still holding my hand beneath the blanket, and I curled my own fingers around his and afforded him a squeeze in return. "You should know more about her, about all of it, and I wish there were time and the privacy, but I owe those both first to Letty, too."

Indeed, the sleigh was slowing. We'd reached our intersection, where his path went to the town and church and people beyond, and mine to a small cottage where I hoped I might find that door unbarred after all.

I let go and jumped down from the sleigh.

"Merry Christmas again, Dick." I waved.

"Same to you, Dave," Dick said, then leaning forward, blurted out a stream of words so quickly and so oddly I barely had time to take the measure of them. "I'll come myself to say it to Letty the first minute I see smoke coming from your chimney in the morning, okay?" His eyes met mine, and he kept going. "Tell her you met me, will you? And this visit, this visit is partly for her as well, but my father had to have his turn first." He paused again, and I knew he was thinking about all the things I intended to tell Letty, and his part in it. "And Dave? She'll understand. Make sure you tell her about the cards, and perhaps we—"

"If you're coming tomorrow," I said. "Tell her the rest yourself, will you?" I gave him no time to answer, and in truth hadn't wanted to hear more about what might be coming in regard to Dick Larrabee's thoughts for my sister. Instead, breaking into a run with my cases in hand, I headed down the path that would lead me to Letty's door.

By the time I'd reached the path to the cottage itself, my run had faded into something closer to a march, and my heart was pounding as much from the anticipation of what might lie ahead as the effort. And then I came round the final bend and...

The snow covered the earth as though it had intended to imitate Dick's card, yet as I drew closer, I saw it was more the scene of the card I'd squirrelled away in my own pocket that was before me: a candle burned in the window of the parlour, sending a shaft of light across the snow like a mat of gold upon the cold. Firelight danced from the hearth, and—just as in the card—the front door was opened enough to reveal the slice of the inside, including my sister, who sat at the table, her wrap around her shoulders and sat at the table.

I'd later learn she hadn't gone to the church festival because Clarissa Perry's niece had a part to play in the festivities, and thus wanted to fulfil familial duties rather than sit for Letty, but in that moment, my heart simply leapt that she was here, she was at home, and I was but steps away and...

And she might bar that door yet.

I approached, remembering the words on the heavy paper beside my heart.

My door is on the latch tonight,
The hearth-fire is aglow.
I seem to hear swift passing feet,
The Christ Child in the snow.
My heart is open wide tonight
For stranger, kith, or kin;
I would not bar a single door
Where Love might enter in!

Stranger, kith, or kin. I'd more claim to the first than the latter, but I crunched my way forward through the snow, as far as the gate, before my nerve failed me so much I had to stop, and then—knowing she'd hear me from where she was, and my footsteps if nothing else—I raised my voice to her.

"Don't be frightened, Letty," I said, though I was the one struck with fear, truth be told. "It's David." A breath drifted from my lips as a cloud, and then, I made my plea. "Can I come in? I haven't any right to, except that it's Christmas Eve."

The door, already ajar, opened wide, and there she stood.

"Come in, David," she said, and her voice was as hoarse with emotion as mine. "Come in."

You'd think we'd have so much to say to each other, and she especially to me, but instead we hugged and held and made little noises of something that might have been crying but was also somehow laughter, and we stood a long while in this way, until finally we pulled back to take each other in, and I imagine I came out the worse for that inspection than she did.

She gripped my hands, and I squeezed back just as tight. Both our cheeks wet, both our lips turned up in smiles, and her brown eyes were so full of forgiving warmth for me I nearly lost all my resolve to tell her the truth of things.

But no. The door was not barred yet, and if it were thereafter? Well, that was as it might be, but it would be for things I'd done, at least.

"Come," she said, and with a little tug, she led me to the door behind which two children lay deep asleep, their blond curls spread across the pillow, and their hands entwined with each other even in the depths of dream.

I waited for what had come over me the first time I'd seen them to return, bracing myself for it, in fact, but no. Perhaps time, perhaps distance, perhaps...

Oh, who knew, really? Who could ever know?

I cried then, again, and let those tears take as much of the bitterness from my heart as I thought possible. Then, wiping away the worst of it, I returned to find Letty at the table, by the fire, her eyes searching mine with so much hope I couldn't wait a moment longer. I *needed* to explain.

"As God is my witness, Letty, there's been something you couldn't have known up until this moment," I said, and though she gestured to the other chair, I didn't dare sit. "I tried, but I never thought of them as my children, not before, and now..." I was telling it out of order, but I couldn't stop myself. "They were never wanted, is the thing, and I've never given you enough for them, Letty. What they are is owed to you, Letty. I've done nothing for them, not really. It's been you and no one else, and…"

"It was easy enough to love them, David, though I'll make no claim on the ease of raising them, as you know. But they do take after our mother, you know," Letty said, but then she stopped, as she must have seen something on my face. "David?"

"If they take after her, it is from your temperament, for my wife's children have no relation to her."

I saw her eyes darken, and raised my hand to halt her train of thought before it could leave the station down a rail it might never return from.

"Please, Letty, let me tell it all, because it's bad enough, but not at all likely where you're taking it."

She nodded slowly.

"You see, Letty, I married Eva when it became clear the man who should have been standing by her had no intention—had *never* the intention—to take that place. My name seemed better than no name at all and scandal besides."

"But why?" she said. "She held no love for you, I could see that plain even before she said as much, and you no love for her. If her situation wasn't yours, then… *why?*"

"There's some who'd say that since she's in her grave and can't tell her side, that I shouldn't give you mine," I said, and when she leaned forward, I raised my hand. "But I want to, Letty, and I hope you'll hear it out?"

"Of course," she said, but not in an offhand way. Letty knew she was entering into a bargain she might not come out the better of, and in that moment, it struck me how much she'd changed. Though it should never have been her lot, motherhood suited her, and though the cottage was not nearly enough, it was comfortable and clean, and touches of love were everywhere. Stockings hung, plump with what I could only imagine, as she'd rarely any extra money beyond what I could so feebly offer, and in only a trickle. Letty Boynton was not broken, nor defeated.

I hoped this wouldn't tip those scales.

"When I say the man—Alfred, Sir Alfred Crenshaw his name is—had no intention, it's because he made it clear to both of us, you see, when she learned his attentions weren't for her alone, and I learned the same, which is—to say it plainly, Letty—that his attentions weren't for me, either. At least not as I'd assumed them to be."

I hadn't known it was possible for words to hold time still until I'd spoken, but they could, and they did.

Letty swallowed, but otherwise held still.

"I'm not the marrying kind," I said. The tiny nod of her head—and was I mistaken, or was there also a ghost of a smile in there, too?—bade me to continue. "But this man was my superior at the firm, and thus the source of any income I might have, and…"

"The Boston firm?" Letty said, as though scandalized this could happen in so good a place as Boston. Or maybe the scandal was that someone of good society could be such a cad? I wasn't sure.

"Yes," I said.

A tiny exhalation from her joined the creasing of her brow. "But you remained there for years. Nearly three years, even after…" Her gaze drifted to the small room where the children slept.

"That I could, at least, send you *something*."

"And he..?" she said, clearly unable to continue the question.

I answered what I thought the query might have been. "Would have liked to continue as before, even after I'd seen him cast Eva aside, and after I'd married her. Even then, he thought so little of me…" I had to pause. "When I told him Eva had died, he offered condolences for *my* loss," I said. "And when it was clear I had no intention of…" I swallowed, skipping past words I couldn't utter, not to my sister. "He ended my career, though it took him a few years, and it seemed word traveled all through Boston's firms that I was not a clever man, nor a very good worker."

"Vile," she said, the word almost spat.

But not, it seemed, at *me*.

"And the bairns?" she said, shaking her head.

"I never told him. He knew there should have been a child—never two—but I believe when he offered his condolences, he thought it was not just the mother who'd perished." I exhaled. "I never set him to right on his assumptions."

"I've spent these years wishing their father would return," Letty said, shaking her head. "And now I learn that would have been the cruelest injustice. Such a man."

She did not seem to have the same disposition towards me, though, and so I finally took the seat across from her, and when she tipped her chin, ready for the rest of it, I continued.

"When they were born," I said. "I looked at those babies, and all I could see was him. Letty, I won't lie—not any more, and not for his behalf least of all—but I... loved him, or, I suppose as near as anyone could love someone given his temperament was so false to everyone else. Those children seemed as retribution and reminder had come together as living things. Their screams were condemnation of my nature, of my lies, of trying to fix what was wrong with me by exchanging those false vows with Eva for a future neither of us really wanted, and then..." I lifted my shoulders. "And then I fled. Again."

Letty regarded me for a good while now, and I forced myself not to hide. I let my feelings show, plain and clear, something I'd only done twice before, and both times to my chagrin.

"They were never retribution, David," she said. "I'd rather think they were compensation."

I couldn't stop the tiniest of scoffs, and she placed her hand over mine on the table.

"No, do listen." She took a breath. "I ought to have written to you of how clever and kind and beautiful they were, but you never asked, and I have too much pride." She shook her head. "I had it in my mind that a man should *want* to be a father to his own flesh and blood, even if they were dull and unthinking and ugly. That's what I believe. But I didn't know."

"You have done none of the wrong here, Letty," I said, hearing the pain in her voice. "I'm the one who's been frozen and numb, making whatever ends meet I could, forcing my heart closed—I think that's what drove me into the hospital these last two months."

"David!" Letty said. "Hospital? For two months? And you didn't send word?"

"You're not the only one with pride," I reminded her, and she scoffed the same noise back at me I'd loosed at her. "It was far. And I was ill so suddenly. They operated twice, and I was all but useless most of the time."

"Oh, poor, poor Buddy!" she said, and her use of my childhood nickname, one brought out to tend scraped knees or bloodied elbows, was a balm. "Did you have good care?"

I couldn't have asked for a better opening. She would have had every right to have ended this conversation three times over already, to bar her door with me on the other side of it, but here she was, listening, asking, and already knowing so much of me.

"I had more than good care, I had Ruth Bentley. She was the nurse who brought me back to life, really, and made me see what a useless creature I was being."

Letty's eyes flicked then, and I suppose she heard something in my voice. I could almost see another puff of smoke from her train of thought, but again on the wrong rail.

"No," I said, holding up one hand. "Not like that, though in a fashion. A long illness is a time you're forced to look at yourself—there's scarce else to do—and I was never one to walk where I could stumble, was I? I spoke, in my fevers, of regrets and losses and the bairns, and Eva, and..." I paused, not quite ready for that final piece. "And Miss Bentley saw me clear enough."

"That you're..." Letty's blush rose. "Not the marrying kind?"

She truly was grasping this clearer and easier than I'd expected.

"That," I agreed. "But in part, because Miss Bentley herself is not the marrying kind."

"Oh. Oh, I see," Letty said, and she glanced at the wood in the fire, then back at me. "I see."

Was a smile? I couldn't tell.

"Through her, I've met others. In fact, I've met a Mr. Brunswick, who writes, and he's found me a position in publishing come the new year." And with that, everything that chance meeting with Miss Bentley brought my way came tumbling out for Letty—a place to live, a new position, friends who didn't see me as a ruin and a pauper, but rather someone in need of bracing up, that I might take another run at the battle of life. They were good people, these friends, and they looked out for each other as sure as kin would.

"They're stronger than me," I confessed. "But I draw comfort in that, being who I am. And it was Miss Ruth Bentley and Mrs. Reba Larrabee who sent me on this path home—though neither intended it, I'm sure."

"Reba?" Letty shook her head. "I'm afraid I don't follow."

"When I was laid up, even weaker than I am now, Miss Bentley brought me a Christmas card." I pulled the card out of my pocket, and Letty's eyes grew bright and wide to see it. "It was such a shock to see this place I fainted dead away, and had a relapse."

"You did no such thing!"

"I did." And now it was in the past, I could laugh, the way one often could at misfortunes quite worrisome at the time. "When I was better, though, that card drew all the story from me. Alfred Crenshaw, Eva, the children, you, father, mother, this town…" I'd been delaying too long, and needed to place the last piece clear on the table. "Dick Larrabee."

Letty had always been a sharp-eyed woman, and her attention no doubt caught on my voice.

"After you were away so suddenly, those years ago," Letty said. "He wasn't but soon after gone himself."

"I'm sorry for that," I said. "I know you and he were close."

Letty, with that there-and-gone-again smile, this time I was *sure* of it, didn't turn away.

"He's back too," I said. "And thanks to another card of Reba Larrabee, with a similar view of this one, but from farther away."

"*The folks back home?*" Letty said.

"The very one," I said, surprised she could quote the verse in the card.

"So, one of Reba's cards—the one the publisher thought wouldn't sell—found you, and the other—which Reba herself thought trite and popular—brought the minister's son back. How good!"

"I hope it is," I said, wondering at the genuine delight in her voice a bit. "He said he'd be by in the morning, and that his visit wasn't only for his father, but in part for you as well, and I can't know his mind, Letty, but he was fit as any a man whose life has turned in the right ways."

"Dear David," she said, taking my hand on top of the table again. "I look forward to exchanging cheer with him." Then, finally, that smile which had so played hide and seek throughout their talk by the fire returned, and this time didn't flee. "But I daresay we both know better than to think Dick Larrabee the marrying kind."

I swallowed. My heart was unaccountably light and glad, and there's no doubt she could tell.

"Now, David," she said. "About the children."

"Once I have position and income, I will send for them—"

Letty scoffed again. "Will you? And is *that* to be my Christmas gift?" Her tone was light enough that I realized my misstep without complete mortification, only a partial one. She *loved* those children. To take them from her would be cruel indeed. And yet, what was I to do?

"I cannot stay," I said, because that much was very much the truth. My tenuous new position—and my life, with those people who were as much kin as

Letty herself—were elsewhere. What else could I offer? "I will send money. As often as I can."

"And you will *visit*," she said. "I won't lie and claim the money unwelcome or unnecessary, but it's your company I'd like the most, even if it will send the town to talking that your children stay here while you don't."

"I'll confess, I don't see much of a solution there," I said. "Though it seems to me the town likes having me as its chosen villain, really."

"And I the martyr," Letty said.

"I don't want to leave you without help," I said.

"Well," Letty said, and this time, her eyes darted to the table, the fireplace, and anywhere but my own gaze. "Miss Clarissa Perry is quite often a help, David. And has been. For years."

"I see," I said, then, with a hide-and-seek smile of my own, I inquired, "She's still unmarried, then?"

"Oh," Letty said, waving a hand. "I don't think she's the marrying type, David."

VII - Dick Larrabee

I STOPPED AT home long enough to discover the key remained under the doormat—unthinkable to a city man such as myself, but to my fortune nonetheless—and the place deserted, as would always be the case on Christmas Eve. I sent the sleigh away, as t'was easy enough to make my way to the church on foot given the path my father had long-cleared and long-walked. I found myself a mince pie and some cider applesauce and washed both down with tea heated on a stove unchanged in a house unchanged for years.

I took the path, David's words still inside my ears. *You should know more about her, about all of it, and I wish there were time and the privacy, but I owe those both first to Letty, too.* Was it fair to hold a grudge this long, for a slight he'd had every right to make—if one could call living one's own life a slight at all, which one couldn't. Not really.

Ah, David.

It was fitting to be thinking of grudges as I came upon the church at nearly eight o'clock, as by chance my approach coincided with the opening of the door and the appearance of Deacon Todd's wife, and I daresay I gave her half a fright with my greeting.

"Dick Larrabee? Was your folks lookin' for you?" The poor woman was astounded. "They ain't breathed a word to none of us."

I assured her my visit was a surprise, and to my amusement she asked me to wait a spell, as the younger children were doing their recitations, and Lord knew even the slightest interruption would bring that house of cards down right quick.

So we stood in the snow, and she watched me, then turned her head and called for the man I'd least liked to have seen in the world, her husband the deacon, explaining he was behind their "stage," helping poor John Trimble to feel well enough to play Santa, which involved a mustard plaster, some cajoling, and—it seemed to me—no success to be had regardless, given how dour and unpleasant a man John Trimble might be in the best of days.

Deacon Todd, though, left his charge long enough to take sight of me.

"Here's Dick Larrabee come back, Isaac," Mrs. Todd said.

Deacon Todd stayed atop the highest step, the better to aim that grey face of judgement down at me, and if I'd expected no quarter, I was not to be surprised.

"Well," the man said, "Found your way home? Just soon enough, I suppose, if you want to see your father while he's still alive."

I'd come with such a desire to make good by my father, but so very much of why I had that task at hand lay at the foot of his grizzled, grey excuse of piety, and I found my words to David playing back, mocking me now: *You know, Dave, I feel I could shake hands with Deacon Todd.*

"If it hadn't been for you—and all those like you—I'd not have left in the first place," I told him, and my voice came out with heat, but not fury, and with the assurance of a man grown and settled, rather than the younger Dick Larrabee who'd been so wholly humiliated by this man.

Not one to eat his words, he attempted a defence of his opinions and actions both, sparing details now as he had then, as likely out of care for his wife as anything else. But I found myself able to stare the old man down, and as he railed about my playing cards, my poor reflection on my father, and his contemptuously muttered "worse" to tie it all together in a pious ribbon, I simply waited him out, and when he fell silent, I lifted a single shoulder in careless disconcern of his thoughts.

"I never did a thing I'm ashamed of but one," I said, and when his eyes flashed, I shook my head. "No, not your *worse*, neither. Only the way I spoke to my father before I left, and the fuel to those words came from you, Isaac Todd, and your deciding to humiliate me in the eyes of everyone with that public prayer for my immortal soul." I took a breath when his lips turned a grim line, but it was his wife who came to my rescue.

"There," she said. "I've told you time and again you did Dick wrong in that way exactly!"

"Prayin' ain't a deadly sin," he said, saying more than that, of course, but aimed at me in words his wife couldn't hear.

"Prayer ain't a weapon, either," I said. "Yet you wielded it as such." From beyond, in the brittle silence that followed, we heard a deep, mournful groan.

"John Trimble?" Mrs. Todd said, as much changing the subject as of concern, I thought.

"He'll make it," Deacon Todd said firmly, but that groan repeated, and I exchanged a look with Mrs. Todd.

"Dick," she said, with a soft note of pleading.

"I'll do it for you," I said. "And for my father, as well." I eyed Deacon Todd. "And the children. But not for anyone else."

And so I was the Santa Claus who finished off the Christmas festival in the orthodox church of our town, and if I hadn't been wearing a false beard, a costume, and a pillow for a belly, I'm not sure as I'd have had the courage to go through with it, what with being surrounded by those who'd heard Deacon Todd pray to heaven to save my soul from eternal damnation for a sin he'd never named.

Every pillar of the church was here, and every person free to attend, and I confess I was of two minds about the whole thing. One, these people would never have invited me in had they known who I was, and two, I would show them such a joyous Santa they'd never be able to recant a welcome on grounds of wrongdoing on my part.

Truly, I wasn't spiteful. I did want those children to have some laughter and pleasantness, and there was true happiness in the giving out of all I'd brought— that, too, took them all aback, and I could see such puzzlement in their faces. I had simple dolls for the girls, tin trumpets for the boys, and to each one tied with a ribbon a copy of that very Christmas card that had brought me here—*to the folks back home*—and more beyond that. Simple linen handkerchiefs for the adults, too, and that was a genuine surprise.

I'd gifted everyone in the church with two exceptions, and those I'd snuck into the bottom of the sack, knowing they'd be the final ones. A lace scarf I placed around Mrs. Reba Larrabee's shoulders, and then a fine beaver collar to hand to my father, my hands shaking so much I nearly dropped the thing.

He looked at me, then, and I think he saw my eyes, or perhaps beyond the beard and silly hat, but either way, I heard him say "my son," beneath his breath, and so, as it was done, and the children were already on their way out the doors and I could pull my father a step or two back behind the curtained area where I'd dressed, I did so, then pulled the hat and beard away.

"Father," I said, hoping it said enough, that word.

Enough of the adults were there to see, and even if they'd not been, Mrs. Reba Larrabee had, and that would be enough to share the story of how John Trimble hadn't had a complete change of disposition at all, but rather Dick Larrabee had returned, and it was he who'd brought such cheer and presence to the festival.

And I found I didn't care in the slightest what they thought. This gesture, those gifts, even the way I'd spoken to Deacon Todd meant little.

"My son," my father said again, and behind him I saw Mrs. Larrabee raise her handkerchief to her eyes. "You look well," he said.

"I am. I came to apologize, first."

My father nodded, and that nod, with fresh tears present in his eyes, was all the absolution I needed.

"It's a shame Letty isn't here," Mrs. Larrabee said. "Clarissa Perry came to watch her niece's recitation, so Letty had to stay with the children. More's the pity, the recitation didn't go to plan, and I'm afraid Clarissa Perry had to take the girl back to her parents, so distraught was she, so it might have been better had Clarissa and her niece both skipped the festival."

"She's at home, now?" I said. "Letty?"

"I expect so," Mrs. Larrabee said. "I'm sure she would have liked to see you, though."

It was late, but knowing David Gilman would have had his chance to speak already set a burn in the centre of my chest.

"I'll meet you both back at the house," I said. "And I'll try not to be too long."

My father's lips curled up in the faintest of humours. "Not years, this time?"

I couldn't help but laugh. "No, before sunrise, at the worst."

I hugged them both and then set off for Letty Boynton's cottage.

IX - David Gilman

A KNOCK AT the door startled us both from our mutual confessions, and Letty rose, folding herself tighter in her wrap and rising with an effortlessness I thought had come from the unburdening. She opened the door with a delighted smile.

"Clarissa!" she said, and I turned to see it was, indeed, Miss Perry at the door, looking somewhere between amused and chagrined, but there was no mistaking the delight in her eyes for my dear sister.

"The night I've had, lo—" she began, and then she looked past Letty to me, and all that delight and amusement and chagrin fell away as though coated in coal black dust.

Miss Clarissa Petty, it appeared, had no favour to bestow upon me, Christmas or nay. But who could blame her? I, the rogue who left Letty Boynton with his own whelps, who never so much as visited, who sent triflings and...

And still I smiled, for I knew where that aborted word she'd almost spoken was to end.

"I'll leave you two a spell to talk," I said, drawing my coat around my shoulders—there weren't many other options but to vacate the cottage itself, given the twins still slept in the back room—and such a frosted gaze did Miss Perry aim my way as I passed her and tipped my hat I don't think I could describe.

Outside again, under the bright moon and somehow not cold despite the winter night, I took a few steps away from the door as to not hear any words through the cracked window, though I'd already heard a few choice ones from Clarissa Perry, who, it seemed, was not just an expert in the bringing-up of babies but also in a rather crass vernacular.

I had such fatigue. It had been so since the operations, and this had been a long day of trains and confessions and emotion. I wouldn't rush the conversation behind me, but I would welcome its closure.

Still, I smiled. And when I turned to look back at that cottage, I saw the view from the card, albeit now the door was closed, but I knew at least my sister welcomed me. *Bless the card*, I thought. *Bless the card.*

"David?"

At the voice, I turned, and despite knowing full well the time of night, I aimed a glance at the horizon, wondering if the sun should be rising and I'd somehow misplaced hours upon hours. But no, the moon was high, the stars were out, and Dick Larrabee stood not five paces away from me.

"Dick?" I said. "It's not the morning."

"No, it's not, but I was at the church—I was Santa Claus, if you'll believe it—and I may not have made full peace with my father as yet, but the foundation was laid, only then..." His words created clouds in front of his fine features. "Only then I knew I needed be here, to do the same."

Oh no. I glanced back at the cottage. I could barely hold myself upright, I was so tired, and behind me, in that building... "The thing is, Dick, Letty isn't free to talk just this moment, and—"

"Not her, David," Dick Larrabee said, and he'd closed those five paces now, face-to-face with me. "Not her."

Right. Well. I knew this was to come, and I'd braced for it, though I'd hoped for a night's sleep first. "I apologize, Dick," I said. "For my—" Words fled like mice in a pantry to the sound of a sudden step, and I snatched out at the first tail I might catch. "—unwarranted declarations and attentions both."

"But that's just it, David," Dick Larrabee's gaze had always had a way of shoring me up, even when I felt the ground beneath me tilt and sway, and it did so now. "I don't think you know the whole of it. That shove, Dave, wasn't what you think."

Shove. All the shoring in the world couldn't have kept my eyes open at the word. My declaration, my tentative closing of the distance between us, a single, terrified kiss upon the lips of Dick Larrabee, minister's son, and then—

Then his hands at my shoulders, pushing me away.

Shove. Such a simple word for what sent me running from him, from Letty, from this whole town.

"David," Dick said, and I forced my eyes open to wait for the next words from him, however devastating they might be. He'd come here in part for Letty, he'd said, and woe on the horizon that might be, if his intentions were—

"Deacon Todd," Dick Larrabee said.

"Wh-what?" I quite lost myself to a swoon and nearly my balance, too, as I physically stumbled at the words I could have expected not at all less than any others at all. *Deacon Todd?*

Dick caught me again, holding me up by my shoulders.

"He was watching me. That afternoon. When you were so brave to say all the things you'd kept hidden, and then when I said nothing in return, braver still

128

to…" He lifted his hands from my shoulder and, pulling off his glove, he touched my lips with one fingertip.

"If he'd seen us, then…" Dick said, shaking his head. "He saw *me*, clearly enough, but you behind a tree meant, I think, that he mistook you for your sister or some other girl and thought me a defiler of an innocent."

A rogue laugh escaped me. I had never cut a particularly manly figure, but that descriptor was far-fetched. "I hardly think *innocent* has been a word ascribed to me before, Dick."

"I tried to get to you, I did, but you'd left," Dick said. "And then he led a prayer for me, that man, in front of the whole orthodox church…" Dick shook his head. "My pride and my fury got the better of me and… I imagine you know the rest."

I did, though now I knew the start of it.

"When you married," Dick said, swallowing and looking down. "I suppose I saw it in as poor a light as I could muster, really."

"Oh, but Dick," I said, shaking my head. "There's more to that tale than you know, and—"

"Please, Dave." The weight of his hand, now on my shoulder, was the only thing keeping me from floating off into the stars above us. "Let me try to say it all, would you? You've been the brave one, not me, and I'd like to even the balance."

How I managed to silence my tongue I don't know, but I did.

He took a deep breath. "Your declarations and attentions were never unwarranted, Dave Gilman. And I would like it very much for you to know that, even if the time is wrong and past in all other measures." He took another breath, in fortification of bravery, I quite thought. "And I should be as honest with your sister, who—I must admit—I allowed, along with the whole town, to think there might be more than our friendship, which I do treasure."

"You'll have to wait a spell," I said, unable to stop another of those laughs—how long had it been since I'd laughed like this?

"Wait," Dick said, as though he'd just realized where we were. "You're outside, on Christmas Eve, and you'll pardon me for saying so but you look ready to faint dead away, Dave. Surely she didn't bar the door?"

"Oh, oh no, Dick, we've spoken, and I've told her all—more than I've told you, which we need to even out—but you see, I think it might take time for Letty to engender some of the forgiveness she's sent my way in the heart of Miss Clarissa Perry, who is right now no doubt reminding her of how I've spun her life in orbit of those twins these last three years and more." I managed a wan smile. "I'm out here to give Letty time for the attempt, though I agree I'd rather it be sooner than later I was back by the fire."

"Oh," Dick said, with an odd frown. "How queer Miss Perry should drop by tonight, though."

"Dick," I said carefully. "I rather think Miss Perry's visits are never unwarranted."

The widening of his eyes, and the curl of his lips came first, then a laugh of his own, which he smothered with one hand.

"I see. Oh! I see! You know, I told Deacon Todd I had but one regret," Dick said. "And that was how I'd spoken to my father. But I think I have at least one more." His hands returned to my shoulders, and he held me firm.

"I would like to tell you all about Eva, and someone else, a man who was the ruin of her, and nearly of me, and—" I watched his eyes, which widened once again the more I spoke. "—the father of those children. But it's a long story to tell, and I've told it once tonight already. I am quite out of breath, I'm afraid."

He might have felt the shiver in my shoulders or seen the paleness in my countenance, but he pulled me up against his chest and wrapped his arms around behind me.

"Take a little warmth then, Dave," he said. "Take a little warmth." He chuckled into my hair. "Miss Clarissa Perry, then?"

"You must act pleased *and* surprised, Dick," I said, realizing yet another misstep. "If it's told you."

"I promise," Dick said, pulling back enough to examine my face. "I'm about to knock on the door, truth be told. You need to go inside."

"Another minute or two," I said. "I'd rather their conversation be done before I do."

"Well," Dick said. "If we must wait for that, then I'll take it in trade to not wait for anything else."

"I'm sorry?" I said, for my tired mind didn't follow where his thoughts might be going.

At least, not until he returned a kiss I'd left many years in his possession. My heart opened wide at that kiss, and this man, no stranger, nor kith or kin, entered well enough. It was as simple as it could be, and I knew there'd be complications in the dawn enough for both of us, but in that moment, I allowed myself what I hoped might be the grandest misstep of my life, to love Dick Larrabee and have him love me.

The rest? That was for tomorrow.

At the end of the kiss, quite breathless, Dick Larrabee lowered his forehead to mine, pressed one hand against my chest, and said, "Bless the card."

I laughed again, knowing that sentiment quite well myself.

Bless the card, indeed.

MOST OF '81

December, 1981

DESPITE THE SCENT of the cooking food—a favourite part of his favourite holiday—and a determined effort to reclaim this night in some way, Christopher found himself wincing as that awful Christmas medley started playing on the radio.

Again.

"Bah humbug," Christopher said to himself, rolling his eyes at his own frustration, but he fiddled with the dial until the holiday music—which of course he kept finding on multiple stations—was finally replaced with something he could stand.

Blondie, explaining he couldn't outrun a gun-wielding alien about to shoot him and eat his head, seemed a much better choice, frankly.

What a year.

Closing his eyes and rocking his chin along to Blondie, Christopher tried to gather some sense of purpose or energy beyond "get to the end of the day." He took a breath, snorting to himself, and pushed off from the wall. If he could skip Christmas this year, he would. Hell, he was doing a pretty close facsimile as it was.

Today had sucked. The whole month had sucked. Fuck, everything about this entire goddamn year had sucked…

Well.

Christopher smiled.

Most of '81.

February, 1981

"So, THE LESSON here is I am shit at skiing," Christopher said, pushing open the door to the ski shop and tying not to limp too badly.

"You almost had it by the end of the day," Patty said, tugging her pom-pommed toque off her head and grinning at him. Her short dark hair was barely ruffled, which was better than Christopher could say about his own spikes, all but destroyed by his hat.

Standing beside Patty, Ariel made a choking, laughing sound of derision, but didn't overtly argue with her girlfriend, which was honestly a rare moment of kindness from the butch, and one he intended to take in stride.

Man, his ass hurt.

"Uh huh," he said. "How about we hit somewhere with alcohol? Numb my pain?" He aimed his best *please-can-we-stop-being-butch-lesbians-now?* gaze their way.

"Black Russians it is," Ariel said.

"Delightful," Christopher said. Spinning away from the two of them to try and find a mirror so he could fix his spikes, he collided bodily with someone who'd apparently decided to take the same narrow aisle between the puffy ski jackets.

Someone cute. Tall, good shoulders, and short blond hair done with stylish, wavy volume, and killer brown eyes.

Hopefully not intending to kill Christopher, at least.

"Sorry," Christopher said, holding up his hands and deepening his voice to the most normal-dude register he could manage (not a forte) before spotting what he was almost completely sure was a welcome smile from Blondie Brown Eyes.

Christopher relaxed a notch.

"You're good," the man said, his smile revealing the most wonderfully crooked eyetooth Christopher had ever seen. The rest of his teeth were all perfect little soldiers, with just the one nudged back, and somehow it worked magic for his smile.

134

"I haven't been good all day," Christopher said. "My friends are trying to teach me to ski." He aimed a thumb at Patty and Ariel, and if that wouldn't be enough to tip off Blondie Brown Eyes he was family, nothing would. "I've been falling on my ass all day."

"Maybe you need more practice," he said, revealing the cutest eyetooth once again.

"Please don't tell them that," Christopher said putting his hands together, like he was begging. "I just convinced them to go to drinks."

"Where you heading?" he asked, and okay, that was a great question because it sounded an awful lot like maybe Blondie Brown Eyes was intending to meet him there.

"I... don't know," he said. "Any suggestions?"

"Don!" a voice called, and Blondie Brown Eyes turned to glance at a pair of men on the other side of the room. If they weren't family, Christopher would eat his toque. The hair, the moustaches—these boys were *not* being subtle, and given how nearly identical they looked, Christopher decided to err on the side of optimism and believe they were together, leaving Blondie Brown Eyes free to be single until the point at which Christopher captured his heart.

Or, y'know, his attention for an evening.

Or an hour.

He could work with an hour.

"Here," Blondie Brown Eyes said, sliding his hand into his pocket and pulling out a matchbook, and, after patting his jeans, a short pencil. He flipped open the lid of the matchbook, and wrote something down. Then he held out the matchbook towards Christopher in two fingers.

"I have to go," he said.

"That's awful," Christopher said, taking the matchbook.

Blondie Brown Eyes smiled, and then he was gone.

Christopher opened the matchbook. In it, underneath the name Don, was a phone number.

"Did you just pick up a trick in a ski shop?"

Christopher turned. He hadn't heard either Patty or Ariel approaching, but they were both behind him now, aiming big grins his way.

"Maybe," Christopher said, sliding the matchbook into his pocket. Maybe his months-long dry spell was over. Maybe despite a January man-drought, 1981 would be his year after all.

"Back to the hotel and change before drinks?" Ariel said.

"Please!" Christopher said. He kind of assumed he wasn't going to bump into Don at whichever bar they went to, but if it did happen, he was going to restore his spikes first.

In their room, however, the plastic cube light on the telephone was blinking.

"We have a message," Christopher said. Patty dialled down to the desk while Christopher surveyed the damage in the bathroom mirror. It was a miracle his post-toque hair hadn't scared Don away completely, he decided.

When he was restored to his best self, he looked through the shirts he'd brought, settling on his tightest option while he listened as Patty hung up and then, to his surprise, picked up the phone and started dialing again.

"Jonas wants us to call him," Patty said, sounding worried. "He left a message saying it was a family emergency." She finished dialing and waited.

Jonas didn't have a family. Well, he had *them*, obviously, which was the same as Christopher, but…

"Jonas?" Patty said, a few seconds later.

Christopher could hear Jonas's panicky, rising voice, even from here. He looked at Ariel, and she stepped close to Patty, sliding one arm around her girlfriend in support.

"What?" Patty said. "Oh God. Okay. Okay." Listening to her talk made Christopher want to scream, but he waited. Finally, she said. "We'll leave right away."

They would?

Patty hung up.

"What is it?" Christopher said, not able to hold it back any more.

"Cops raided the bathhouses. Like, all of them," Patty said. Her eyes were wide behind her glasses. "Jonas said they arrested everyone. He was working at the hotline when he found out."

"Let's go," Ariel said.

Christopher started packing.

It wasn't until they got back to Toronto he even remembered the matchbook in his pocket, but between helping to get nearly a dozen friends he knew out of jail, protesting, marching, and sitting-in, he was a little busy for the next two weeks trying not to get the hell beaten out of him by the asshole cops, alongside thousands of others—actual *thousands* of angry fags and dykes like him—filling Toronto's streets with their rage.

It wasn't just about the so-called "Operation Soap" anymore, or the day-to-day reality, no…

It was *everything*.

December, 1981

BLONDIE ENDED, AND when another Christmas song took her place, Christopher gave up and shut off the radio. He'd put on a record if he wanted music he could trust not to add more chill to his small bachelor apartment. The silence allowed the low howl of the winter wind outside into his kitchenette, a harshness that had him considering getting started early on the libation portion of the evening.

Don't drink alone, Christopher, it's never a good idea. The advice sounded like Ariel's voice in his head, and given she was a nurse and saw her fair share of the fallout of people drinking alone, he supposed it was good advice. He wondered how she was doing. Both she and Patty were at their family Christmases by now, no doubt counting the seconds until they could make a tactical withdrawal and get back to each other.

Though, in Patty's case, at least her mother cooked a mean turkey.

Speaking of.

He took a moment to check on the food and the trio of pots on the stovetop, then left the kitchenette to sit on the edge of his futon and consider his two-foot Christmas tree, which he and Jonas and Patty had decorated with popcorn strings. Beside the tree to one side was the painfully retro Christmas card Ariel had found at a second-hand shop with the hokey "folks back home" poem inside it. Ariel had used a black marker to change "folks" to "fucks," which made them all guffaw and secured it a place in his small box of holiday decorations forever. To the other side of the tree stood the dark wooden candlestick with the flared base covered in carved robins. That one his grandmother had left him in her will, and he'd always thought of as Christmassy for some reason.

Seeing the tree, card, and candlestick, he *almost* felt a little spark of holiday joy.

Maybe he should light the candle? Christopher swore any candle he lit in that candlestick was brighter than it had any right to be, and always made him think things could be better, no matter where his mood had begun.

Then he saw the calendar beyond his meagre tabletop ode to the holidays, where despite it being late in the year, he'd stopped crossing off the days after the big black X through December 1st, weeks ago now.

December 1st had more or less tanked the month for him.

No, not just the month. The year.

"Fuck you," he said, tossing a finger at the calendar, its picture of sparkling, snow-covered winter conifers, pretty streak of northern lights, and every asshole in the Ontario Legislature who'd raised their voice in a "nay" and turned what could have been something actually good, something helpful and necessary and, hell, what had the potential to have been one of the best fucking days of the whole awful fucking year into…

This.

They won't protect us. We'll have to protect ourselves, like always.

God, Christmas Eve and he already just wanted this winter over with.

March, 1981

AN ANGLED RAIN his umbrella did little to deflect soaked Christopher from the waist down as he attempted to cross the street and get under an overhang—any overhang—on his slushy, wet trek down Yonge.

Spotting a brief respite beside the stairwell up to Glad Day, Christopher managed to hop over a puddle and collide bodily with someone doing exactly the same thing from another angle.

"Shit, sorry!" Christopher said, his umbrella going one way while he grabbed out with his free hand for the railing in an attempt not to either fall down or knock the other person over.

"Damnit, shit!" the other man said, more or less doing the same, though he'd had no umbrella and instead used one hand on the railing and one grabbing at the front of Christopher's jacket, which was honestly the only thing that kept Christopher upright.

After a moment to let his heart stop pounding and a quick swipe at his eyes to get the rain out, he looked up, ready to apologize more meaningfully and…

"Don?" Christopher said, recognizing the dark brown eyes and the crooked eyetooth. Also the whole face, which was just as handsome as it had been, what, two months ago?

"Yes?" The recognition wasn't mutual, which stung, until those brown eyes widened. "Oh. Oh, hi!" The view of the smile, crooked-tooth-included, was all the more enjoyable for the minor delay.

It *was* him.

"You didn't call," Don said.

"No, I didn't," Christopher said, holding up his free hand. "But it was an accident."

"Sorry?" Don's smile grew amused now, like he couldn't wait to hear how that made sense.

"The raids," Christopher said, seeing the moment Don realized what he was referring to.

"Oh shit," Don said. "You got arrested?"

"Oh, no, the raids were when we were skiing, but we needed to get back right away," Christopher said. "Somewhere between getting our friends out of jail and hitting the streets..." He aimed what he hoped was a winning smile Don's way. "That matchbook? Went up in smoke. I think maybe one of the times I got arrested at a sit in, but I'm not sure."

"Well, now I have to forgive you," Don said. He licked his lips, which were still wet with the rain and also made Christopher want to lick Don's lips.

As well as other parts of him.

"Are you in Toronto long?" Don said.

What? Christopher frowned. "I live here."

"Oh, I thought you lived in Quebec, because..." He gestured out into the rain, which Christopher took a moment to parse into *We met in Quebec, skiing.* Was Don French? He did have a slight accent, and the way he spoke...

"No, we were just getting away together. Some friends, I mean." Christopher smiled. "So, if you want to give me your number again, I swear this time I'll actually use it. If it stops raining, we could even be dry."

"Wet isn't terrible," Don said, definitely flirting, and now Christopher definitely wanted to lick him. "But I am not free tonight, and tomorrow I head back."

"Back?"

"Montreal."

"You're from Montreal," Christopher said, finally getting why Don had asked the question.

"I am," Don said. "But I am back next month—April 11th. Saturday?"

Christopher winced. The date immediately pinged. "That's my night for the help line, but... Sunday?"

"I'm only here Saturday."

Well, damn.

They looked at each other. Don smiled, then pulled a pen from his pocket, as well as an only mostly-damp piece of paper. He wrote his name and number again—which this time Christopher noticed included an area code, which was *not* 416—and then tore the paper in half and handed his name, number, and the pen and other half of the paper to Christopher.

"Now you give me your number. Double our chances this time?"

Okay, Christopher was absolutely willing to double his chances with him if he continued to smile that smile and show off that damned sexy curl of his lip. Was it the tooth that did that to his smile, or was it just Don's whole "even sopping wet I'm desirable" thing?

Christopher didn't know. He didn't care. He wrote his name and number down, and after a brief glance at the torrents still coming down from above, Don nodded at the street. "I have to run. Keep in touch, Christopher."

Yeah, even the way he said Christopher's name was good.

"Yes," Christopher said.

Don made a run for it. Christopher lifted his umbrella and leaned out onto the street to get a good view of the wet jeans stuck to Don's ass like a second skin.

And of course, Don caught him looking when he looked back.

December, 1981

THE PHONE RANG.

Christopher got up, crossing the length of his apartment and lifting the receiver off the cradle. "Hello?"

"Oh, thank God you're home," came Ariel's voice, pitched low and whispery. "I'm going to need a rescue phone call in one hour. Deal?"

"Deal," he said, unable to stop himself from snorting out a little laugh. "Should I be your boss, all butch and growly? Or are you looking for something in a 'she's the best, if we had anyone else to call we would've' plea sort of thing?"

"I don't fucking care, just get me away from these people."

The call disconnected seconds later, and Christopher laughed again, checking the clock, then—not quite trusting himself—grabbing a scrap of paper and writing down a note to himself and popping it front and centre on his fridge with a magnet.

In one hour, he'd call Ariel's house, tell them he was so very sorry to interrupt their evening, but that their daughter was the next on the list for the on-call rotation and—*oh no*—she'd have to leave their family celebration.

He wondered if Patty had already initiated her evacuation attempt yet or not. Christopher was pretty sure Jonas was her lifeline this year. It was a good thing they both had fake hospital emergencies to fall back on.

Lesbian nurses for the win.

Christopher's gaze went back to the window, watching the snow blow by, and he closed his eyes, trying to remember what it was like to feel warm.

July, 1981

CHRISTOPHER STOOD IN his kitchen, closed his eyes, and tried to remember what it was like to feel cool.

It didn't work. Also, sweating hurt, and he was already down to just his underwear. Maybe he should open the fridge door? Did he even have any ice cream left? He took a deep breath, bracing himself for the discomfort, and crouched to check. Pain raced along his skin, but he managed to get into the fridge and located what remained of a small carton of ice cream.

One spoon later, and he was bracing himself once more for the journey back to his couch.

"You can do this," he said.

His phone rang.

"Noooo," he whined, looking at his ice cream and the spoon and the multiple steps it would take to get to the phone. But it could be work or the lifeline. He tried to be a big boy, put down the ice cream and his spoon, and stumbled his way to the phone with only one or two curses before lifting the receiver on the third ring.

"Hello?" he said.

"Hello," came a slightly accented, soft voice that was just a little teasing. "Do you like boats?"

"Don?" Christopher said, grinning in spite of the slices of pain criss-crossing his back from holding the phone to his ear. "Sorry, what? Boats?"

"Yes, it's me," Don said. "I am here in Toronto and we're taking my friend's boat around the islands—do you want to come? I know it's last minute, but I didn't know this was the plan until I got here."

Christopher turned until he could see his reflection in the hall mirror. The reflection regarded him in abject misery. Apart from visible strips on his upper thighs where his swim trunks had covered them, all of his exposed skin was bright red and angry.

Still, he considered saying yes until he turned away from the mirror and it sent another jolt of pain up his back.

"I... can't," Christopher said.

"Oh no," Don said. "You're working?" He sounded let down, but not too surprised. Every time they'd tried to meet up for months it had been like this—one or the other of them just couldn't make it work.

"No, I'm burned," Christopher said.

"Burned?"

"Sunburned. I went to the beach yesterday, actually. And I fell asleep." Christopher looped the phone cord around his finger, annoyed at himself all over again. "For hours."

"Oh no."

"Oh yes," Christopher said. "I am a lobster. A blistering lobster."

Don's muffled laugh didn't make him feel any better, but he caught himself smiling anyway.

"I'm sorry," Don said. "Next time?"

"I hope so," Christopher said, because he really did. Frankly, he needed a success of some sort, and as much fun as it was to touch base with Don over the phone and renew the spark that was definitely there between them, he'd much rather touch more than Don's damn base.

Indistinct voices rose in the background, as did the sound of traffic. Don must be on a pay phone. "I have to go," he said.

"Enjoy the boat," Christopher said.

"I would enjoy it more with lobster," Don said.

Christopher laughed, and Don hung up.

142

December, 1981

AN HOUR LATER, Christopher made the call. An older woman answered the phone, and when he asked for Ariel in his most professional, butchest tone, she didn't exactly reply with seasonal cheer.

"Ariel!" she yelled, not even bothering to cover the phone. "It's that damn hospital for you!" He heard muffled noises as the woman obviously read Ariel the riot act before passing her the phone. The receiver was pressed against the woman's sweater, given the scratching sound he was treated to, but it didn't quite drown out a quickly hissed "If you leave, your grandfather will be angry!"

"It's my job, mom," Ariel said, her voice growing clearer a moment later as she said. "Yes?"

"What are you wearing?" Christopher said.

"Oh no," Ariel said, with the absolutely falsest fake-let-down voice he'd ever heard.

"No one is going to believe that," Christopher said. "Try to put some actual sadness in your voice, honey. Like... Oh! I know. Picture this: I forgot to call you. The phone never rang. You are going to have to *stay there with your parents all night.*"

"That's horrible," Ariel said, and this time it held quite the emotional veracity. "But I understand."

In the background, Christopher could hear Ariel's mother already spinning up more anger over what she likely had intuited was the imminent exit of her daughter.

"Good luck," Christopher said. "If you have to, try throwing holy water at her."

"I'll do my best," Ariel said, in a deep, serious voice. "I'm on my way."

Christopher heard the "No!" in the background from Ariel's mother as the call disconnected. He put his own phone back on the cradle, smiling to himself. There. Good deed of the year done. Another Christmas miracle to unite the lesbian lovers in their own apartment for at least some of Christmas Eve.

Look at him: a regular gay Santa. Only without much magic of his own.

"Self-inflicted," he said. He'd turned down every invitation he'd received this year, not that he'd had a tonne. Jonas and some of the other guys from the lifeline had told him he'd be welcome, but the thought of socializing this year just felt...

What?

He eyed the calendar. The big X through December 1st.

Too much. That was the thing. Something about Christmas this year was just... too much. He didn't want the party lights, didn't want the dashing about—though the snow or otherwise—and as much as it made for a quiet apartment, he just wanted to relax on his own.

As of that phone call, his to-do list was officially done. He had dinner, he had his own company, and if he wanted to drink some Taster's Choice instead of getting tipsy that was his own business.

Yeah, so maybe gay Santa he was not.

Maybe he should put on a hat?

October, 1981

MAYBE CHRISTOPHER SHOULD have put on a hat.

The chill wind blasting down the Toronto street at him certainly made him think he'd picked the wrong costume for Hallowe'en, but he already had the devil horns from last year, and some red face paint, his tightest red shirt, and Jonas's black leather pants had made it complete.

At least he'd been smart enough to wear a black button-up over the red shirt, though he'd definitely shuck that once he got to Stages and—finally—got to dance with Don.

Arranging the evening had taken a colossal amount of effort, and more than a few favours owed at work and the lifeline, but whatever. It was worth it.

Assuming he didn't freeze to death.

He bumped into Jonas and Jonas's latest—was his name Mitchell or was this another one of Jonas's seemingly endless string of Michaels?—both of whom waved and dragged him through the doors before he could so much as say hello, and once they were up the stairs, the heat of Stages was wrapping itself all around them and the miserable chill of the walk over.

"I hate that you look better in those pants than I do," Jonas yelled, while Mitchell-or-Michael went to get them all drinks.

Christopher blew him a kiss, but his attention was aimed at the door. He knew

144

what costume Don was going to wear—Indiana Jones, which Christopher hoped included the mostly unbuttoned shirt—but so far, every hat he'd spotted belonged to a cowboy.

They clinked glasses, and then Mitchell-or-Michael downed his and dragged Jonas to the dance floor while Jonas laughed and tried to finish his own drink in time to drop the glass at the end of the bar.

Christopher smiled, feeling the same urge to just let go, but he'd wait for Don first.

After ten minutes, he was still riding an anticipatory high. After he finished his drink though, and another fifteen minutes had passed, the high was crashing, and his devil-may-care was starting to devil-might-not.

He got groped a few times, and a twinky angel with a tinfoil halo and very free roaming hands whispered some far-from-holy activities directly into Christopher's ear, but Christopher brushed him off as kindly as he could, still holding out for Indy. He danced with Jonas and Mitchell-or-Michael, and then by himself, and then when it became perfectly clear Don was not coming, he made a polite exit and pulled off his horns for the walk home.

Don called the next day. His car had broken down at the side of the highway, just outside of Montreal. He'd not even made it half the way to Toronto. His apology was genuine, and Christopher tried to be as gracious as he could about it.

"We'll try again," Don said.

"Sure," Christopher said, but he couldn't help but notice Don didn't have anything specific in the way of a time or date to offer, and neither did he.

Maybe he should have settled for the angel.

December, 1981

"FORGET IT," CHRISTOPHER said, after a swallow of coffee, staring at the tiny paper angel on the top of his little tabletop Christmas tree. Dwelling on Don was not going to make this particular holiday any more tolerable.

His stomach growled, and he put down his cup, kneeling down in front of his finicky oven to see the world's smallest turkey through the gritty glass. He was no chef, but it looked good, and he was looking forward to sitting down with turkey and mashed potatoes, gravy, stuffing, and, of course—

Christopher froze.

Wait.

He stared at his countertop, where he'd already set up a plate, as well as the trivet for the turkey pan and then back at the stovetop, where the three pots waited. He'd mashed the potatoes, made the gravy, and the carrots were done; all three were just there to stay warm now. But with a sinking sensation, he went to his cupboards, opening them and checking and...

"Oh damn," he said. He'd forgotten.

He crouched again, looking at the turkey. He had time. He looked up at the counter, not rising, considering. Did it matter?

His stomach growled again.

Fuck yes, it mattered.

If there was one thing about winter Christopher could do without, it was the boots and coat and scarf and mittens routine, but he threw them all back on and bundled up for the cold, late, trek to the closest grocery he was only half sure might still be open, but light streaming from the windows seemed to signify at least this one thing was going to go his way, and he stomped his boots at the entrance before heading right to the aisle in question, hoping they weren't out and...

There!

He grinned, triumphant, and picked up a can of cranberry sauce.

Christopher turned on his heel and headed back to the front of the store, where the line was only three people and took his position behind a tall, blond guy with nice shoulders and...

Hold on.

No way.

"*Don?*"

Tall, Blond, and Nice-Shoulders turned around so fast he nearly collided with Christopher, and it was, in fact, Don, crooked eyetooth making its usual glorious appearance as Don aimed a delighted smile Christopher's way.

"Christopher," he said. Okay, so that lightly accented voice was sort of the best thing ever, really. "Hello."

"Hello?" Christopher raised his hands, one empty, one gripping his cranberries. "You're in Toronto?"

It maybe came out a little accusatory.

"I am," Don said. "I was going to call you tomorrow. Just got here. I'm house-

sitting for my friend, the one with the boat. He had to go to New York, for a friend."
He shook his head, like the details weren't necessary, but then added, simply, "he's
sick." Christopher understood, and nodded to let Don know.

Christopher had heard the news out of New York, though the helpline,
mostly.

The sting of Don having come to Toronto without telling him faded to
nothing, and fizzled out.

"Anyway. I was housesitting anyway, so I decided to spend this one alone,"
Don said, and he sounded almost embarrassed by the admission. "This year has
been so crazy, I just needed a break."

"Me too. I'm sort of skipping Christmas this year," Christopher said,
completely understanding that particular sentiment. "But why here, here?"
Christopher waved at the store all around them.

"Oh, it's silly. I brought dinner with me—just turkey sandwiches—but I
forgot something." Don held up a can.

Cranberry sauce.

"You're kidding," Christopher said, showing off his own can.

Some pressure inside Christopher seemed to release at their laughter, and
those two cans of cranberry sauce seemed the singular most hilarious thing he'd
encountered all year. It seemed to strike Don the same way.

They howled.

Then the clerk cleared her throat because the people ahead of them were
already checked out, and so they wiped laugh-induced-tears and took their turns
buying their cans of cranberry sauce and shuffled back towards the front of the
store, still letting out puffy breaths of half-laughs whenever they looked at each
other as they returned to the windy, dark, and snowy outdoors.

"So, I may have been skipping Christmas this year, but I'm six blocks that way,
and I have something better than turkey sandwiches to offer you," Christopher
said, aiming a mittened thumb over his shoulder.

Don raised one eyebrow, that smile returning, and Christopher cleared his
throat, because he hadn't intended that double entendre. But frankly, he'd stand by it.

"So, you're saying maybe we don't skip Christmas?" Don said.

"Couldn't possibly," Christopher said. "Not this year."

Don glanced around, but they were alone on the street and snow and wind
was whipping in every direction, so when he leaned in for a kiss, Christopher rose

on his toes to meet him, and the moment they connected, the cold fell away all around him.

Magic.

Don's warm lip turned in a smile even as they broke apart, far too soon.

"I've been waiting all year to do that," Don said, with a little growl.

"Me too," Christopher said. "More please. Once we're out of the snow."

"Deal." Don laughed. "I really was going to call you tomorrow."

"After that? I really believe you." Christopher nodded.

Don grinned. "Just six blocks?"

"Just six blocks," Christopher said, leading the way.

FOLLY

DEATH LASTS A year.

For a whole year after a loss, everyone remembers it's a year of bad firsts. They call. They drop by. They ask if there's anything they can do. It's a kindness, and it's welcome. That first year, my three struggled through those bad firsts so fiercely I was glad of any help.

Their first birthdays without their parents.

Their first day of school without their parents.

Their first report cards brought home to me.

Their first colds where they didn't have their mom or their dad to tuck them in and make them feel better.

Only Uncle Huntington.

But the worst of the bad firsts had to be their first Christmas in our new apartment, instead of their house. Reminded of being orphans over and over again that first year left a mark on my three. I saw their hearts break every single bad first at a time, but nothing hurt them as much as Christmas did.

Santa couldn't bring them what they really wanted. Not even he could deliver my brother and his wife, so the whole day lost its magic.

We got through it, and I think that might be the best I can say. We got through it. Like a chore.

But for my mind, the *second* year is harder. In the second year, no one came to the door with a special thought on any of those days. No one thought, "this is the first year without their parents, poor things" because it wasn't.

Instead, the second year I felt like I had to *start* new things with my three, rather than holding them and comforting them in the face of the endings of what they'd had before.

Most of my life, I've been at peace with my little brain, but I've never felt so *unclever* as I did the second year. I missed my brother. I missed his wife.

A year is a long time; it's no time at all.

Same as two years, really. One Christmas, two Christmases. What's the difference? Just a few hundred days. Christmas, though, is designed to *feel* the same. The same ornaments, the same meals…

The third Christmas was closing in on us now, and tradition was on my mind. Traditions were what made things so difficult with my three. How can you have traditions when two out of your five were now gone? With a different person—and only an unclever uncle, at that—where before you had parents?

When Clark and I were young, our parents believed in four presents, a tradition from my mother's side, and one raised us with. A rhyme, which made it easy for me to remember, told us there would be four things beneath our tree for each of us.

Something to wear, something to read, something you want, something you need.

Four presents, but for Clark and I, especially when we were younger, it all came down to the third gift—that thing we *wanted*—and our wish it would be everything we hoped it to be.

My father's family traditions were our stockings and having our big dinner on Christmas Eve, where we also got what he called "a table gift," so in truth we didn't actually *only* get four presents, we had our stockings full of little things, a present for the dinner table, *and* the four gifts under the tree, but it my mother's third gift always took centre stage in our dreams, our letters to Santa when we were young, and our requests when we were older.

Clark's computer? My hockey gear? His telescope? My weights? All third gifts.

When it came to the books, I definitely took less to the yearly gift than Clark did, but our parents knew how to find me something I would read, most often biographies about people I admired, or books about physical training or how to cook and eat right once I started hockey, and eventually how to build things after I set aside my original dreams of being an athlete.

It's funny, but with my three the word "orphan" is always there on the tip of my tongue, but I never think of *myself* as an orphan, and I don't think Clark ever did, either. Clark and I were lucky, though. Clark had our folks long enough for them to see him get his degrees. I had our folks long enough for them to see me happy. I think they worried I'd never find anything I enjoyed as much as I enjoyed hockey, but the first time I showed them a house I'd help build, they knew I'd found my place in the world, as simple as it was—and continues—to be.

Maybe that's the real thing that makes an orphan an orphan. Not if you *have* parents or not, but how much of your life they got to *see* before they're gone.

"You okay, Hunt?"

The question pulled me back to the world, and I smiled at Gabe. Just like me, Gabe lived in one of the odd apartments above the storefronts that lined the Village. He'd stopped halfway down the narrow alley between the stores to ask me the question. He was a nice young man, dark-haired and always polite, and he lived with his boyfriend, Justin. A student, Gabe worked at Third Eye part-time. Probably he was coming home from work right now. His journey wasn't far; Third Eye was only a block down Bank Street.

His brown eyes looked just shy of worried, though, and I realized he'd probably asked me a question already. Or said hello.

"Sorry. Just in my head," I said, tapping my gloved hand against the side of my hood. Most people knew that about me: I could get in my own head sometimes, and there wouldn't be room left for much else.

Little brain and all that. He'd walked right up to me, and I hadn't so much as noticed he was there.

"Ah," Gabe said, chuckling. "Gotcha. Thank you, by the way." He gestured to the pathway I'd already shovelled between the buildings.

"Welcome," I said, and set back to shoveling once he took the rear door. I heard him start his journey to the third floor before the door closed. I looked after all the buildings on this side of the street for Marion when it snowed, She paid me, but I kept the money aside and donated it right back to her shelter and food bank—and I enjoyed the work. Shoveling snow in Ottawa can be hard, especially when it falls thick and wet, but even when it's heavy, I don't mind.

I know what I have to do, I know I can do it, and I know I'll get it done.
I've always liked things like that.

AN HOUR LATER I had the back walkways and through paths shovelled and salted, and I was back inside, pulling off my toque and coat and hanging them up on my hook by the door to the big apartment where I'd lived for the last two years. Once I blew the winter from my nose, I caught the smell of something warm and nice coming from farther inside.

I got my boots undone and followed the scent.

It led me to Micah, which shouldn't have surprised me.

"All done?" Micah said quietly, turning to look at me. He sat at the kitchen table, a book open in front of him, and a tin of dark brown cookies. Ginger. That's what I'd been smelling. They didn't look like gingerbread, though. They weren't shaped—he hadn't used a cookie cutter—just round cookies, and they seemed much thinner than gingerbread, with a kind of crackly look to them.

"All done," I said. "Thank you for looking after my three." Micah lived in the corner, one-bedroom apartment across from ours. Ours was the largest apartment Marion owned, and it took up one whole side of the hall. Micah's place had only one bedroom, but being on the corner gave him really good light, which he cared more about than space.

Micah is an illustrator, and his paintings are beautiful. The youngest of my three, Nellie, had connected with Micah in particular when she'd learned he had a job to do with books. The shared love of books between Micah and Nellie had quickly turned into a real friendship among my three and him. He was often happy to sit with them while I ran a quick errand, and it had become a habit for him to come over when I shoveled the walkways behind our block.

I truly appreciated him.

Also, I liked looking at him.

"They are never any trouble," Micah said, like he always did. "You'd already fed them and they'd had their baths. We baked." He gestured to the cookies. "And they went to bed without any fuss, once I invoked Santa, though I think Johnny was only humouring me for the girls."

"I'm pretty sure I have to have the talk with him soon," I said. I wasn't looking forward to it. I picked up a cookie and took a bite. I'd expected it to be crunchy, but it was soft inside. Molasses and cinnamon and ginger distracted me from thoughts of Johnny. I pointed to the rest of the cookie. "This is really good."

"Swiss ginger cookies. A recipe my nurse shared with me after my accident," Micah said. "You have to have a talk with Johnny?"

"Santa," I said. "Pretty soon—or maybe already—Johnny is going to realize, or get told, I figure."

"Ah," Micah said, leaning back in the chair. "Do you have a plan for that?"

"Well. My father told me Santa was real when you were little, but as you got older, you *become* Santa for the other little people around you." I smiled at the memory, and my father's voice explaining it to me as such an important responsibility, especially for my little brother. "He said becoming Santa was a big job for a big boy."

"That's sweet," Micah said. "I think Johnny will like that. He's a good big brother. Definitely better than mine."

"I hope so," I said, then frowned, because that didn't sound right. "I didn't mean—"

"I knew what you meant." He waved it off, then rubbed his bottom lip with his thumb, which made me notice his mouth.

I looked away and took another bite of the cookie. It might have been the best cookie I'd ever eaten. I realized this was the first baking that had happened in our kitchen this December. "I'm behind," I said. Our third Christmas, and I'd still not figured it all out.

"Beg your pardon?" Micah said. He always spoke like that, smart and proper-like. Another of the reasons Nellie loved him so much. He taught her words I'd never heard before, and how to use them, which delighted her.

"Their mom always baked cookies with them," I said. "I haven't fit it in yet. Or their letters to Santa, so I can make sure I find out their want for the year." I sighed. My boss Mick had five job sites on the go, and it had been non-stop for weeks. No one wanted construction running too far into December, not in their homes. Unfortunately, we'd had a run of finding problems we hadn't expected, which was always a risk in any renovation, but made for longer hours for all of us, even when Mick's stepson Ben stepped in and helped some, when he wasn't at college or working at his restaurant job. We were "all hands on deck" right now, which Mick always said when things got like this.

"You still have time," Micah said. "Don't forget you're one person, not two."

That made me laugh, though it wasn't *exactly* funny. It reminded me of how I'd been feeling very much like one Uncle Hunt, not a Mommy and a Daddy. "Believe me, I know."

"You're doing a wonderful job with them," Micah said. "Really."

"Thank you," I said. He was a very kind man. I held up the last bit of my cookie. "And your cookies are better than what we would have made, anyway." I popped it into my mouth.

"I'll give you the recipe," Micah said. He rose, picking up his book and his walking stick. "And I'll leave you to your evening."

I liked the way he always said that, even if my evenings tended to be exactly the same every night: feed my three, bathe my three, get my three to bed, and then get things ready for tomorrow before going to bed myself.

Not exciting, usually far from it. But I slept well most nights, even if some nights I needed to take care of myself before sleep would come. And maybe sometimes that included thinking about a particularly kind man who lived just across the hall.

I walked Micah to the door. He didn't have a jacket, but he leaned his stick against the wall and sat on the stool I left there for him and my three to use while to put on or take off their shoes. "If you need me tomorrow, just knock," he said, tying his laces.

"Probably will. It's supposed to snow again," I said. "Thank you."

"You're the one doing the hard work," Micah said. "I get to stay inside and be warm with the kids, and you're out there making me a path to walk." He straightened again. "Pretty sure I'm coming out ahead on that deal."

"It's not hard work," I said, because it really wasn't.

"Says you," Micah said. "Do you know how long it would take me to shovel all that snow, one handed?" He lifted his cane.

"It would take me longer to draw a book, though," I said, and he chuckled. "When we were kids, my brother Clark used to say he got the little body but the big brain, but that I got the big body and the little..." I paused letting it hang in the air the way Clark always did. "And then he'd just grin at me, because if he didn't *say* I had the little brain, he wouldn't get in trouble for it."

Micah laughed, but he also a flinched, like he was embarrassed for laughing. "Sorry," he said.

"He wasn't wrong." I shook my head.

Micah looked like he wanted to argue with me. Like I said, he's kind like that. "Good night, Hunt," he said, opening my apartment door, and then turning, he smiled.

I always noticed Micah's smiling, because when he does—he *changes*. When he wasn't smiling, Micah looked thoughtful. And not just smart, but clever. He had brown eyes, dark ones, and they moved around when he looked at you, as though maybe you were a puzzle he wanted to figure out.

But the smile changed his eyes, and the way he looked at a person. When he looked at me like that and smiled?

I don't know how to describe it, really. Maybe... like he'd figured out that puzzle after all, and he felt proud or glad about it.

Either way, making Micah smile was a great way to end a day.

"Good night," I said, and I watched him to make sure he got back to his apartment before I closed my door.

It DID SNOW, and stopped early enough that I knocked on Micah's door as soon as I got my three home from school and had a casserole ready for the oven. He took over, and I headed down to the street to start my work, waving to a couple of my neighbours and making sure I had Marion's path done first, in case she got home early today.

She used a walking stick too, like Micah. Only in her case it was because she was much older than me and a little arthritic, too, not because it something had been so badly broken. She never slowed down, though. It made me worry about her. I didn't want her to fall.

By the time I'd cleared the snow and made it back to the apartment, my three were holding out their plates while Micah served them each their portion, and I considered eating before cleaning up, but I felt gritty and dirty and my mother would never have let me sit at the table all filthy from a day of renovation and shoveling, so I told them to start without me and had a shower.

Scrubbed up and changed into sweatpants and an undershirt, I rejoined them.

Micah was looking at me strangely, so I checked my undershirt. "Did I miss something?"

"No," he said.

"Your hair is all flat," Nellie said. "You look funny."

"He looks fine," Micah said, shaking his head at her, and she giggled at him.

I sat and listened to Johnny talk and Nellie gush about their days at school, rarely letting Susy get a word in edgewise, but Susy was a bit like me, so I didn't try too hard to force it.

I don't mean Susy isn't bright. Susy's very bright. But she always liked to listen more than talk. We had that in common.

After Johnny talked about his school Christmas party, and Nellie asked Micah if he would stay and read her her bedtime story, Susy did speak up.

"Are we going to see Santa this year, Uncle Hunt?"

"If you want to," I said. Their first year with me, I'd taken them to see a local Santa, and hadn't been smart enough to realize they'd expected the *same* Santa they'd all seen their whole lives, the one Clark and his wife had always taken them to. Nellie, especially, had found it confusing—even though my brother had told them the Santa they'd always gone to wasn't *Santa*-Santa, but a Santa-*helper*.

I don't think I did a good job of explaining part of Santa's magic meant he had helpers everywhere.

"I think I do," Susy said.

"Then we will," I said, but wanted to make sure she understood what I could—and couldn't—offer. "It won't be the Santa-helper from Toronto."

She smiled. "I know."

"There's a great Santa-helper who comes to the library," Micah said.

"The sunflower library?" Nellie said. Her favourite branch of the library, and our closest, was on Sunnyside, and the librarians there planted sunflowers in all the boxes outside. In the summer, our walks to the library were a twice-a-week event, and while all my three enjoyed it, Nellie *loved* it.

"That's the one," Micah said. "My friend Nat works there. They're a librarian. Have you met them?"

"I know Nat! They have cool bowties," Nellie said, nodding emphatically. Nat was one of Nellie's heroes, and now she seemed completely on board. "Can we see that Santa-helper, Uncle Hunt?"

"I'll look at what days," I said, not wanting to promise until I knew. That lesson had come quick in our first year together. My construction schedule was nothing like what my brother and his wife had worked, and made things more difficult to plan than they were used to. There'd been tears more than once when they realized Saturdays and Sundays didn't mean Uncle Hunt would be available for whatever they might like to do.

"I'll find out for you," Micah said with a small shrug when I frowned, about to tell him it wasn't his job. "I brought it up."

"I want a story book," Nellie said.

"You *always* want a story book," Johnny said, shaking his head like it was a waste of her want gift. "We *always* get a book, anyway. 'Something to read,' remember?"

"But two books is better than one," Nellie said, sounding an awful lot like a teacher.

"One cannot argue with that," Micah said, with one of those nice smiles of his. "It would be folly."

Nellie blinked. "What's 'folly'?"

"Oh," Micah said. "It's another word for foolish. Sort of like *silly*."

"*Folly*," Nellie said the word carefully, and I knew it was going to be her new favourite word, at least for the next few weeks, until she found another. The last one had been *susurrus*, which meant any sound like soft whispers.

Once we were done eating, I wrangled my three through their after-dinner baths and got them changed into their pyjamas. When I brought them back out to the couch for their goodnight story from Micah, I found he'd loaded the dishwasher and run back to his apartment and brought a book back with him.

The man was so kind, and so good to my three.

"What's that book?" Nellie said.

"It's a collection of stories by Samuel Brunswick," Micah said.

"Brunswick?" Nellie's eyes went wide. "That's your name."

"That's because this is a book my ancestor wrote," Micah said. "A great-great-uncle or something like that." He waved a hand. "He wrote a lot of stories, and I think you'll all like some of the stories in this one."

"Are there horses?" Susy said.

"There are definitely horses," Micah said. "In fact, Samuel Brunswick wrote a whole series of stories that start with a really great story about a horse-drawn sleigh ride."

Johnny sighed, and I snuck him a little squeeze on his shoulder. Putting up with the stories your younger siblings wanted to hear wasn't always a fun part of being the big brother, but he was usually up for it. He was a good kid that way. He smiled at me. He was probably getting too big for bedtime stories at all, come to think of it. He already did a lot of things for himself.

"Have you decided what your want is?" I asked him quietly, while Micah listed off the choices of stories in the book for Susy and Nellie—though I had little doubt we were in for the horse story.

"New skates?" Johnny said, and I heard the question in his voice. *Is that okay?* All my three did that some, but Johnny's voice did it the most, and it broke my heart every time. They'd lost something important, and sometimes it seemed like Johnny thought he had to be a very good boy, or else he'd lose something else. He struggled with asking me for anything, no matter how much I told him he could always ask. Our family Christmas tradition had been one of the few ways I had to get my three to tell me when they wanted something.

"I'll let Santa know," I said, winking. He smiled again, and then Micah was settling down on the couch to read them their story. I put away the casserole while he read them a story about a man with a russet-coloured beard—another new word for Nellie, who stopped to ask Micah what "russet" meant and learned it meant a colour somewhere between red and brown—who had an adventure when riding a horse-drawn sleigh and getting lost in a snowstorm.

While I put my three to bed, Micah waited for me and he pointed to his phone when I came back into the living room.

"The library has Santa for Thursdays, Fridays, and weekends in December, and the week leading up to Christmas Eve," he said. "I'm so sorry. I should have run it by you alone, first. It's kind of a drag show, too."

"That sounds great. And it's fine," I said. Nellie loved going to the Drag Story Times. "I'm sure I can go to one of them. We'll make it work. Thank you again for looking after my three."

"I adore them, Hunt." Micah shook his head, smiling that nice smile he had. "And I've told you before, it's no trouble."

"You're a kind man," I said. He looked at me for a while, and for a second, I thought maybe I had something on my face from dinner. But if I did, he didn't tell me, which made me think probably I didn't. He wasn't the sort of person that let other people look foolish if he could help it. Just another way he was handsome, really. An *inside* way, rather than the outside.

Not that his outside wasn't handsome either. Which I continued to notice maybe more often than I should.

"Good night, Hunt," he said, picking up his book and his walking stick.

"Good night," I said. I walked him to the door, and made sure he got into his own apartment, like I did every night, then I went back to my apartment, and looked up ice skates on my computer, setting my mind to find some with dark blue, which was Johnny's favourite colour.

"THEY'RE *BEAUTIFUL*," SUSY said, her eyes wide, staring at the Santa who'd just arrived, two green-clad elves to either side of him. I recognized the elves as two of the drag queens I saw most years at Pride, though though their shiny, green-sequinned, fur-trimmed dresses were new to me. The Santa I didn't recognize—a drag king—but honestly the performer was one of the coolest looking Santas I'd ever seen, with a long red greatcoat over a red plaid double-breasted suit vest, matching red pants, shiny black boots, and although the neatly shaped white beard had to be fake, it looked *perfect*.

I didn't know Santa could look so *nice*.

"Santa looks *fancy*," Nellie said, which was probably a better description than mine.

The rest of the library was fully decked out in decorations that included Christmas, Kwanza, and Hanukkah and other festivals I didn't know, but all the attention had turned to the arrival of Santa and his elves.

"Look at their glitter eyes!" Susy said, as the two elves passed right by us, waving and escorting Santa to the large chair set up by the window. It took me a second to realize both the drag queens had glittery gold and green eyeshadow.

"It's very pretty," I said, knowing how much Susy liked everything glittery, and wanting to make sure I agreed out loud. When Clark had first told me Susy had told them she was a girl, he'd called me. She'd wanted Clark to let me know, right after she'd told them.

"It's our job now to make sure she knows we support her, Hunt. Susy is her name now. Okay?" He'd sounded so scared, so unsure of himself. I'd never heard him like that before. "I mean, I know you get it, you're gay. You've kind of done something like this already. In fact, she says that's why she knew we'd be okay with it, and God, Hunt, I'm so terrified I'll screw this up somehow."

"You won't," I'd said. *"You're the smartest person I know. Tell Susy I love her."*

When Susy appreciated something glittery or fancy, I always remembered Clark's words. Susy and I hadn't done much with makeup ourselves yet. She was still young for it, but I'd watched a few videos on the internet just in case, and hopefully I wouldn't be all thumbs if it wasn't much like Venetian plaster or caulking—but we did play around sometimes when she felt like dressing up as a princess or a fairy.

I wondered if this was her way of letting me know she'd like something similar. Like Johnny, sometimes Susy wasn't quick to tell me that sort of thing. More than once I'd had to tell my three they couldn't hint to me if they wanted me to know things. Better to come out and say it, if it was important.

"Have you all decided what you're going to ask for?" I said, after the Drag Elves and Santa took their places, and the first child in the line had climbed onto Santa's lap.

"New skates," Johnny said, nodding firmly, then giving me a small, embarrassed shrug. Maybe I'd get one more year before I had to have the talk about becoming a Santa for his sisters after all.

"I want a doll," Susy said.

"Dolls are folly," Nellie said.

"They are not," Susy said, and her cheeks turned red.

Oh no.

"Hey now," I said, and knelt down in front of the three of them. "Nellie?"

Nellie squirmed. Me kneeling down meant serious business, and she knew it. I did it whenever I wanted them to understand something was *important*. It put us eye-to-eye, on even footing, asking them to listen and understand me. I think Nellie already knew what I was going to say, too. But I still needed to say it out loud, for Susy especially.

"Yes?" Nellie said.

"Just because *you* don't like something, doesn't mean something is bad," I said. "Dolls included. I never wanted storybooks when I was a little boy. Does that mean you wanting a storybook is folly?"

Nellie gave me a guilty shake of the head. "No."

I looked at Susy, who didn't seem quite as upset as before. "Is there one doll you're hoping for?"

"One like me," Susy said, shrugging.

Huh. I nodded to her and stood up again. *One like me.* I wasn't sure I knew exactly what that meant, but I had some time still. The line moved quickly, and soon Johnny was taking his turn, and then Susy, and finally Nellie. When all three had had their turn, we started to leave. To my surprise, one of the Drag Elves took my arm and pulled me towards Santa.

"Not so fast, Mr. Big Man," she said with a big smile, tracing one of her brightly painted green nails across my forearm all the way up to my hand. "Your turn!"

"What?" I said. But a second later, I understood. I glanced over and saw Johnny, Susy, and Nellie all hopping up and down, laughing and clapping, Johnny with his phone out, ready to take photos, and realized I'd been set up. My three were no doubt behind this.

"Your nieces and nephew want you to tell Santa what you want for Christmas," the Drag Elf said, confirming it.

I didn't want to crush Drag Santa, so I sat on the armrest of the chair, and he aimed a big smile up at me. "Ho ho ho!" His voice was impressively deep. "So what's your name?"

I felt like a—Micah's word—folly, but I did my best to play along. "Huntington. Everyone calls me Hunt," I said.

"Ah, of course!" Drag Santa boomed. "Uncle Hunt!" He leaned in close. "Have you been a good boy this year?"

"I try to be," I said, because my three were watching, and I always said being good is something you had to keep *trying* to do forever, not something you ever *were*.

Drag Santa laughed. "And what do you want for Christmas?" He crooked one white-gloved hand, and pointed at his ear. "Whisper it in my ear!"

What did I want for Christmas? I had no idea. All I could think of was to say, "I want my three to have a good Christmas."

"*Ho, Ho, Ho*, that's very nice, but not what I meant." Drag Santa shook his head, and lifted up one white-gloved hand, wagging his finger at me like I'd done something wrong. "Something for *you*, Uncle Hunt."

"I—" I shook my head. My little brain had *nothing*. I took a breath and tried again. I'd never gotten the hang of thinking quickly. "I don't... I don't know. You choose for me?"

I think this time, Drag Santa realized I wasn't very bright and didn't do well at this sort of thing. I've always needed time to plan things, to make my thoughts line up better. He took pity on me, and patted my shoulder. "I'll get you something just right!" Drag Santa boomed, and then I was off to collect my three, who were delighted at having seen their big Uncle Hunt whisper into the ear of the fancy Santa-Helper.

"How DID IT go with Santa?" Micah asked. He'd come out of his apartment and stood at his door while my three filled up our own entrance shedding their coats and boots. I waited outside for my turn at the stool, leaving them to getting their coats and boots off and joining him a few steps back.

"Really good, thank you." I waited until my three weren't watching. "Though they made me sit on Santa's knee and tell him what I wanted."

"Did you at least tell him?" Micah laughed, and I might not be very clever, but the way he was laughing? It wasn't just my three who'd come up with the idea. His brown eyes twinkled, and he looked like he was trying to hide half his smile.

He'd been in on it.

"I said a good Christmas for my three, but Santa said it had to be something for me." I shook my head. Now I *really* felt foolish, knowing Micah had been a part of it and I'd been so blank. "I didn't know what to ask for so I told him to choose for me. I had to sit on his chair, and I wasn't ready." Why was I telling him this? "I couldn't think all quick like."

"I'm sorry. It was supposed to be…" Micah shook his head, the smile gone now. The twinkle in his eyes, too. "Sorry."

"Nah," I said, holding up one hand. I didn't like making Micah sad. It wasn't his fault. His idea was fun and funny. "They liked it, that's what matters."

"Fair enough, but…" He glanced at the door to my apartment and now it was now empty, the door only partly ajar. No doubt my three were already on their way to their various weekend favourites: video games for Johnny and books for Nellie—always harder to know what had Susy's attention at any time, though.

Susy. I still had to figure out a doll for her.

"Actually, do you have a moment, Hunt?"

I blinked. Micah didn't often ask me for a moment. "Sure," I said, and I stuck my head through the door of my own apartment long enough to say I was just going to talk to Micah for a few minutes. Johnny and Susy's replies of "okay!" told me they'd heard. Probably Nellie already had her whole brain lost in a book. A train could crash through our apartment and if Nellie was reading, she wouldn't notice a single car.

I closed the door and went back to Micah's, taking my boots off in his entrance way. His one-bedroom apartment was in the corner of the building, with two big windows. He kept the place very tidy, and even his small kitchen always struck me as clean and proper. Some of his paintings hung on the wall, and I couldn't help but look at my favourite: a self-portrait Micah had done from a photograph of himself swimming in a lake. It *looked* wet, with droplets spraying as he broke the surface and spread his arms out to the side. Micah wasn't built big like me. In the painting, you could see how narrow and graceful he was.

His skin in the painted sunlight looked so real, warm and soft like you could reach over and touch, and your fingers would come away cooled by lake water.

"I'm heading to that meeting with that new publisher in Toronto tomorrow, and then I'll be heading to my sister's place after that for the holidays, but I'd like your permission for something before I go," Micah said, and I turned around to see he'd moved behind his easel.

I frowned. "My permission?"

"I know you have a tradition," Micah said. "Four gifts for Christmas. Well, and the dinner present and stockings." He smiled again, probably remembering how last year my three had decided a perfect thank-you gift for Micah should be a stocking of his own.

He'd never had one before, apparently.

"That's right," I said, still not sure what he needed from me.

"Well, I'd like to give them this." Micah said, and he used his foot to unlock the wheels on the round platform beneath it. He moved his easel around and showed me the painting.

"Oh," I said. I wished I had a different word. I'm sure there were better ones.

It was a painting of my three, laughing and happy, pushing their way through a field of giant sunflowers. Only, after a second, I realized the sunflowers weren't giant, my three were little—and they'd each got wings. Johnny's wings were a bright, vibrant blue offset with black stripes; Nellie's wings silver and white in a very pretty, feather-like pattern; and Susy—*oh, Susy!*—had wings every shade of purple and pink.

My three painted as fairies. Or at least, fairies if fairies still wore sneakers and jeans like Johnny's. Only Susy looked particularly fairy-like, in a pretty dress. Nellie's dungarees, glasses, and sandals were perfectly *her*, though.

Oh, who was I kidding? All three of them looked perfectly like themselves, but Susy truly looked magical.

"Since I'm not going to be back until Boxing Day, if it's okay with you, I'll wrap it up here and you can come get it when the kids aren't likely to see it. I'll give you a copy of my key." Micah was still talking, but I barely heard it, I was just staring at my three, who looked so magical and wonderful and happy...

"Oh," I said again, and I reached out to the painting, though I knew better than to touch it.

"You like it?" Micah said, and I almost laughed, because he sounded worried, like it's possible I might not like it, which made no sense at all. The painting was *beautiful*, and I couldn't wrap my little brain around how he created something like this with paint and his own skill.

"It's wonderful," I said, still wishing I had better words. "They're going to love it." Then I realized this is something that must have taken Micah days, maybe weeks to do, and normally he was paid a lot of money to do it. "But I can't let you just give it to us. I can pay you for it."

Micah shook his head. "Hunt, I want to give this to them," he said, and then he looked at me, and his voice got quieter. Softer. "I want to give this to you." His eyes were flicking back and forth, like I was a puzzle again.

"I..." I didn't know what to say, so I did the thing I always do. Be polite. "Thank you."

"You're welcome," Micah said. He smiled.

That's better. It's always better when he smiles. Sometimes, Micah can get inside his own head, too, I think. This one time, he told me all about some paintings he was working on, and how the author and the publisher he was working with couldn't seem to agree on what they wanted, and I could tell he didn't like letting anyone down, even when it wasn't possible to make everyone happy.

It's not the same, and it's not like I'm an artist like Micah is, but I've had that problem with renovations sometimes, where even Mick knows we've got no way to make it perfect when multiple people can't agree on what's perfect.

He was so *good*.

"You remind me of my brother," I said, because Clark was like that too, always trying to find a way make things as good as possible for as many people as he could—but also he was smart, and talented, and good at pretty much anything he tried, too.

"Ah," Micah said, and his smile got wobbly, like he was upset or let down.

"It's beautiful," I said again, pointing at the painting, hoping his smile would go back to the way it was before.

"Thanks." But his smile didn't come back, not the way it had been, not even when I said goodnight and he walked me to his door and watched me go into my apartment.

I spent over an hour after my three were in bed trying to figure out how to find a doll that Suzy would like—one that's "like her"—and I started to realize I just wasn't smart enough to figure it out, so I went to bed and tried not to let it stop me from sleeping.

I ended up tossing and turning anyway.

I'd ordered the skates for Johnny, and I'd made sure they could be exchanged if he preferred another style or brand. Nellie's storybook would be even easier. She asked for a copy of the storybook Micah had been reading to her from, the one his grandfather or great-grandfather or whoever it was wrote. I'd stop by Ian's bookstore and ask him to order that for me. And the rest of Christmas I could keep on track, with some effort. We'd already visited Santa. I could find time to bake.

But if I couldn't figure this doll out for Susy...

The urge to ask Micah for help again didn't help the way it usually did. He was always so clever, he usually had an answer to anything I asked him. But this time I remembered the way he looked at me when I talked to him back at his apartment, and I wondered if maybe I relied on him a bit too much.

He seemed sad.

And maybe *tired?* Sometimes visiting his family did that to him, but he hadn't gone to see them yet. Or maybe it was my fault, for trying to pay him. Or for how often he watched over my three while I shoveled the back walkways. I knew he didn't like it when people treated him like he was fragile just because he used a cane, but did I go to Micah more often than I should? Had I asked too much of him?

I bit my lip and rolled onto my back, staring up into the dark.

Micah wasn't just clever. That was the real problem. I thought of the painting of him swimming in the lake, the one that made me think it would be wet if I touched it.

No, the problem here was me.

Because it wasn't just the painting I wanted to touch.

★

MORE SNOW WAS falling by the time I made it to the Second Page, and even though Ian was keeping the bookstore open later all month because of Christmas, I ended up getting there only a half hour before he was closing. At least I wasn't the only customer. I could see someone's toqued head just barely visible at the back of the store.

"I promise I know what I need," I said, going right to the counter, where he was opening some boxes and pulling out new books.

"Don't worry about it," Ian said. "I'm going to be here another couple of hours at least." He gestured to the boxes. Ian's eyes don't match. One of them is green and one of them is blue, and even though I know it, I always notice the first time I see him face-to-face on any given day.

"Nellie wants…" I paused and pulled the paper out of my pocket. Even though I'd written it down first thing in the morning before work, it had gotten dirty. "*The Collected Tales of Samuel Brunswick.*" I said it carefully, then looked up.

"Oh. I know that one. Just came out this month. In fact…" He went to the far side of the store from the counter, where the kids books were, and he reached up to the second shelf. "Ta-da." He pulled down the book. It was the exact same version as the one Micah had.

"Actually, Micah did all the illustrations in this one," Ian said. "The author was his great-great-uncle, and when the stories went into public domain, he put it together himself. I don't even think he used his usual publisher."

"Really?" I followed Ian back to the counter. "He didn't tell us he'd published it."

Ian glanced at me, raising one eyebrow. "Us?"

"Oh," I said. "He reads to my three a lot, and he brought that book over the other night."

"Ah," Ian said, with a funny little smile. I wasn't sure what was funny.

"Hey," I said. "Susy wants a doll that's like her. Do you know of anywhere I might be able to find something like that?"

Ian stopped to think about it, but it wasn't him who answered.

"Urbane Myth."

I turned. The peach-coloured toque I'd seen before belonged to Marion, and she was walking up with two paperback books in her free hand and her cane in the other. It had a little spike attached to the bottom of it for the potential ice rain. She put the books on the counter beside us.

"The clothing shop?" I said, not quite following. I'd only gone into the place a couple of times. The stuff they sold was a bit too fancy for me, but they'd had some really bright colours for scarves that Susy and Nellie had both liked.

"Phoebe does amazing hand-made doll clothes for Christmas every year," Marion said. "And she stocks some dolls as well. I'm pretty sure the dolls are made by students from the university art program, and given it's Phoebe, you can bet on there being queer dolls with queer doll outfits to match." She smiled. "Also, thank you for salting this morning, Hunt. Turned out we needed it." She nodded to the windows of the bookstore where the snow was definitely turning into something icier and wetter now.

"My phone warned me," I said. "Do you know if Urbane Myth is open late, too?" I asked Ian.

"I don't think so," Ian said, shaking his head. "But Phoebe's on the Village website like the rest of us."

That would work. A couple of years ago, the Village Business Association had put together a website for all the stores in the Village.

"I should have thought of that."

"Nah," Ian said, smiling. "This way we got to see your face." He paused. "Oh! And before I forget—are you done with the stockings yet?"

"Not quite," I said. I always bought the books from Ian, but he sometimes had other things that were good for my three's stockings, too.

"Check this out," Ian said, turning the little spin-rack he had on the counter for bookmarks around until one side faced out in particular. They were bookmarks, though smaller than usual, and I was about to point out my three lost their large-sized bookmarks on the regular when Ian pulled one out and opened it, revealing it was folded over in half and had magnets attached to it.

"You clip them around the page," Ian said. "They won't fall out or get lost."

"That is clever," Marion said. "And I'll be needing one of those, too."

There was a pretty purple one that was perfect for Susy, and one with piles of books on it that Nellie would like. It took a bit longer for me to pick one for Johnny—I ended up going with a night sky, mostly because it was blue more than the stars or moon—but in the end, I got the storybook and three more things for their stockings.

"Thank you, Ian," I said, taking the paper bag from him. I turned to Marion. "And thank you. I'll check the website."

"Merry Christmas, Hunt," Marion said.

"Merry Christmas," I said.

BACK AT HOME, I paid Rhonda, who told me my three had been no trouble at all, and I finally got to shower off the long day. When I went to the kitchen, I was surprised to see Nellie there, in her pyjamas, blinking up at me. She was holding a copy of *Scaredy Squirrel*, which was a book that was probably too young for her now, but also one of her favourites.

"You're supposed to be in bed," I said, though I wasn't really bothered. They were off school now, so it wasn't a school night.

"I couldn't sleep." She lifted the book. "Couch cuddles?"

"Couch cuddles," I agreed, and she grinned.

Couch cuddles usually required our softest blanket, two pillows, and snuggling up on the couch while I read to her, and tonight was no different. Scaredy Squirrel's antics made her giggle as always, and she leaned against me while we worked our way through the book.

When I closed it, she sighed. Probably she knew what came next, which was me tucking her back into her bed.

I kissed the top of her head, and noticed she looked off. Not *sad*, exactly, but something was going on in her head.

"Everything okay?"

She nodded, but she didn't say anything.

"Are you sure?"

She sighed again. "I wanted something to happen, but it didn't happen."

I frowned. Had I missed something she was hoping for? I wished I could convince my three to speak up more. "What did you want to happen?"

But Nellie shook her head. "It's okay, Uncle Hunt." She looked up at me, and I tried to decide if she meant it or not, but I couldn't really tell.

Which was always the problem.

"Nellie," I said. "You remember how I asked you three to tell me when you want or need something, right?"

"I know."

"Because you know I'm not good at guessing things," I said, repeating it anyway. "I don't always understand hints and things like that. It's better just to say things to me as plain as you can."

She blinked. Then she smiled, and then she grinned. "Right," she said, in almost a whisper. "That's *right*."

I squeezed her in our little nest of blanket. "So, *is* there something you want to tell me?"

"No," she said, but all that sadness was completely gone, and she looked really, really excited again. "No, I'm okay." She managed to get her arms out of the blanket and wrapped them around my neck, pressing her forehead against mine. "I'm ready for bed now. Thank you."

I tucked her in, and she grinned the whole time.

Whatever it was, she'd tell me eventually, I figured. And if not her, maybe she'd do her usual thing and talk to Susy and Johnny about whatever it was that was on her mind, and Johnny would let me know if it was important.

"Goodnight, little bean," I said, at her doorway.

"Goodnight, Uncle Hunt," Nellie said, in a voice just shy of laughter.

THE LAST WEEK before Christmas always got hectic, given my three weren't in school for half of it, and added to that Mick had me finishing off the plaster at two sites, but Rhonda was happy for the extra money and I juggled everything in the end, even if we ended up relying on takeout a few times for supper, something I tried not to do very often.

Urbane Myth had indeed had the perfect doll on their website. It had the same hair colour and eye colour as my Susy, and was tall and slender like her. The owner, Phoebe, had been there when I came to pick it up, and she helped me pick out two outfits for the doll, which it turned out she'd made herself, like Marion said. The doll clothes even had little tags inside the dresses that said "Phoebe Original," just like the ones she made in the store.

It was the final present I'd needed, and I'd wrapped it once my three were in bed on the twenty-third. By the twenty-fourth, I had only one more thing to pick up: the painting from Micah's, and while all the jobs for Mick had meant we were going to have a delivery Christmas Eve dinner, my three definitely weren't going to complain about that.

When I got home on Christmas Eve and asked what everyone wanted on their pizza, I had them set the table while I took Rhonda aside to pay her for her time.

"Thank you again," I said.

"They were great," Rhonda assured me, then she glanced at the kitchen and took another step into the hallway with me. "One thing," she said quietly.

"Okay," I said, following her.

"This morning they had a call with a friend, on the computer," Rhonda said, biting her bottom lip. "Johnny said it would be fine, and they've done it before, so I didn't think anything about it, but I'll feel more comfortable telling you. It wasn't a kid they phoned, it was an adult."

"An adult? Who?"

"Apparently your neighbour?" She lifted one hand. "Micah, I think his name was. Nellie wanted to talk to him about something, and—like I said—Johnny seemed to think it would be fine."

"Oh," I said with a smile. "It is. Micah is in and out of here all the time, and he's away in Toronto right now for his work and for the holidays." I relaxed, though I hoped Nellie hadn't interrupted Micah while he was at anything important, like those meetings with the new publisher or time with his family. I knew he didn't always enjoy either as it was. "Nellie adores him. They all do. We all do. Thank you for telling me, though."

Rhonda shrugged into her jacket. "Oh, good. I'm glad."

"Oh, wait, I have something for you..." I said, remembering just in time after she'd put her boots on. I went to the hall closet and came back with a little bag from Sweet Temptations, the candy shop in the Village. When I held it out to her, she laughed.

"Did you buy me *gelt?*"

"Happy Hanukkah," I said. "I know I'm early, but I won't see you again before."

"Thank you, Hunt," she said, looking at the small bag of chocolates. "Are these hand-made?" She sounded surprised. "They smell really nice."

"They're from Sweet Temptations," I said. "Avery makes all his chocolates in the store." I paused, suddenly worried I'd made a mistake. "Is that okay?"

"It's probably going to be the best tasting gelt I've ever had, Hunt," Rhonda said, laughing.

After she'd left and the pizza arrived, I gathered my three around the table and watched them open their dinner presents. They'd been surprised when all their

170

presents were exactly the same shape—bright red envelopes—and Johnny had been the first to reveal what was inside.

"Hockey tickets?" He bounced in his chair. "For real?"

"For real," I said. "I already booked the games off with Mick."

He was hugging me when Nellie saw her gift certificates for the bookstore and cheered, adding herself into the hug before he'd even let go. Susy had a quieter reaction, as always, but she smiled at me.

"Art camp," she said, and her eyes were wide. "Like... sleep-away?"

"Micah found it," I said. "It's an LGBTQ camp for two weeks over summer." I watched her face, hoping it wasn't going to overwhelm her. "If you don't want to do the sleepovers, though, you don't have to."

She shook her head, considering and thinking it through like she did most things. "I'd like to."

I exhaled, relieved. They watched me open my gift from them, which was a new hat and scarf, both of which were very soft and a dark blue I was pretty sure meant Johnny had picked them out.

"Thank you," I said. "These will be great when I'm shoveling the back paths."

After that, we ate. Johnny was on his third piece before Susy had even finished her first, and Nellie had barely stopped talking about all the books she wanted to use her certificate to buy long enough to eat her first piece, but they all seemed to be in a really good mood.

"You had fun with Rhonda?" I said.

"She's great," Nellie said, speaking for all of them as usual. "Did you know she and Lyndsay are getting a dog for forever this time?"

I fought off a smile. Rhonda and her girlfriend were, in Nellie's opinion, two of the coolest women she'd ever met, and she tended to see anything they did in the best light. Lyndsay volunteered at a dog rescue, and Rhonda often showed them photos of whichever dog they were taking care of in their home when she babysat.

"That's great for them," I said. "They like dogs, and since they live with Lyndsay's grandmother, there's always someone home to take care of it."

Johnny pointed his half-eaten third piece of pizza at Nellie. "Not like us. We can't have a dog, Nellie."

Nellie sighed. "I know." Then she pushed her pizza around on her plate. "But if someone was home?"

"That'll have to be a someday wish," I said.

They all got very quiet, and for a moment I thought about reminding them that pets weren't something we could fit into our lives, but they didn't seem upset or anything, so I let it go. In fact, they were smiling at each other, which felt good.

This year, it didn't seem like Christmas was bringing them too many memories of their parents.

Once dinner was done and everyone had been tucked into bed—two stories for Nellie tonight, who seemed very excited still, which wasn't unusual for Christmas Eve—and then once the girls were asleep I leaned into Johnny's room, where he was sitting up in his bed playing on his phone, like he did most nights before finally going to sleep.

"You okay to hold down the fort for a few minutes?" I said. "I'll be right back."

"Sure," he said.

I got the key Micah had given me and went into his apartment. He'd left the painting in the middle of the room, wrapped in crisp white paper and a red ribbon, with a tag hanging from the bow. I flipped the tag, just to make sure, and it said: *To Johnny, Susy, Nellie and Huntington, from Micah with love.*

I was just about to pick it up when I heard the sound of a key in the door behind me, and turned, surprised. When the door opened a second later, Micah looked even more surprised than me.

"Oh," he said. He bit his lip, then pulled his small rolling suitcase through the door. "Hey." He stopped in the doorway after that, just looking at me.

"You're back early," I said, because I'd thought he was supposed to be back on Boxing Day. Then I realized I was standing in his apartment, and I pointed at the wrapped painting. "I came to get the painting."

He smiled. "I figured." He took another step inside and leaned his cane against the wall while he took off his jacket and hat and hung them up, and then he stopped again. "Hunt, I…" he said, then he sighed. He looked good in his brown sweater, even with his hair rumpled from his hat. He always looked good, But he also seemed worried or nervous or something.

"I'm sorry," I said. He might want to go to bed, I realized. "You're probably really tired. I should go."

"No," he said, holding up one hand when I took a step. "Don't."

I stopped. "What?"

"I spoke to Nellie today," he said, and he looked at me, and then he looked away, staring at the ground.

Oh no. Had I missed something after all? Rhonda hadn't said anything had seemed wrong, and I hadn't noticed anything at dinner, but maybe there was. "Is everything okay?" I said. "If something is wrong, please tell me, Micah." What had I missed?

He frowned, and then shook his head. "Oh, God, no. No, Hunt, it's nothing like that, I'm sorry…" He took a breath. "I'm so sorry, no, everything is fine. Really."

"Okay," I said. "I don't really understand. If everything is okay, why did Nellie call you?" I frowned. "Wait. Is that why you came home early?"

"It is," Micah said. "She told me I needed to speak plain. That you weren't good with hints."

"That's true," I said, but now I was even more confused. "But I'm not sure why she said that to you."

"Oh, because I was being a coward," Micah said, crossing his arms and smiling at me, and making me feel like a puzzle he'd just solved, even if I was still completely puzzled myself. "I was definitely hinting, rather than saying."

"Hinting at what?"

"I really like you." Instead of his usual voice, the one that made him sound smart and confident and most of all *clever*, he seemed almost embarrassed. "And sometimes I think you like me, too, but then you told me I reminded you of your brother, which wasn't the most romantic analogy, and so I thought I'd maybe imagined it, and then—"

"Micah?"

He looked up at me again. My heartbeat felt loud inside me.

I've never been good with words. I didn't really have any now, either, beyond the obvious ones.

"I really like you, too," I said. Then I stepped forward and leaned in, careful to go slow in case I'd misunderstood, though I didn't think I had. He didn't pull away, so I kissed him. He held on to me, and I pulled him against me and it turned out his lips felt about as perfect as I'd thought they'd feel.

I don't know how long we kissed. I was too busy enjoying the little noises he made and how nice it felt to hold Micah Brunswick in my arms, but eventually we stopped, though both of us were breathing heavy and I really, really wished I didn't need to go back to my three before Johnny fell asleep.

"Okay," Micah said, in this husky voice I'd never heard him use before. "So we cleared that up."

I laughed and loosened my grip. "I... need to get back to my three."

"Right. Right. Responsibilities and things." He looked up at me, his brown eyes dancing back and forth. "Remind me to thank Nellie for the advice."

"Did she know?" I said. "That you were coming back?"

"Yes," he said. "They all did. They all wanted me to tell you."

They all wanted him to tell me. They all knew? That explained how excited they all were. I looked at Micah. Micah who *liked* me. I shook my head. "I should probably be worried how much they arranged things behind my back."

"Maybe," Micah said. "They also invited me over for Christmas Day tomorrow. If that's okay."

"It is," I said. I wanted to invite him to spend the night, but I couldn't. Not with my three asleep in the apartment with us. We'd have to talk before Micah could spend the night. I'd never brought someone home like that, not that I'd been with anyone these last few years.

But I wanted to bring Micah home.

"Good night," I said, forcing myself to step back.

"I'll bring the painting over in the morning," Micah said. He stepped back to lean against his wall, like he needed to have some space between us. I understood that. I wanted to kiss him again, but if I did, I was pretty sure I wouldn't leave.

I *really* liked kissing Micah, and the way he fit against me. I wanted to put my hands under his sweater, to see what that skin in the painting felt like beneath my palms, to see if I could make him make those little noises in his throat again.

We stared at each other. He swallowed.

"Good night," Micah said, and I managed to make it out the door and across the hall.

NELLIE LEAPT ONTO my bed before dawn, and I remembered at the last second to pretend to be asleep.

I'd been tossing and turning most of the night, because even if my three had wanted Micah to tell me he liked me—and he did, and I liked him—around three in the morning, I'd heard the hiss of ice rain against my bedroom window and then my brain had realized something.

I *counted* on Micah Brunswick. So did my three. He watched over them. It wasn't just me, either. Micah was important to Johnny and Susy and especially Nellie. He had a friendship with each of them they treasured. Nellie might have wanted a storybook ending for Micah and me, but there was no way to know if that would happen.

By four in the morning, I remembered that kind of thing had *never* happened to me before. I'd had four boyfriends before my three had come into my life, and the truth was they'd all gotten tired of me for the same reason when it came right down to it.

Micah was talented and skilled and not just smart but *clever*. More clever than any of the men I'd been with. Those men had all been more like me, guys I'd met at the gym or the club, who'd liked the way I looked enough to not care so much about anything else. If those men had gotten tired of me not getting their jokes and not understanding their hints, how long would it take Micah?

Nellie landed on the bed before I could come up with any answers.

"What time is it?" I said, pretending to be sleepy and confused.

"I waited until *seven*," Nellie said, with so much frustration in her voice I had to laugh. I grabbed her in a hug and she laughed into the blankets.

In the kitchen, Johnny and Suzy were already up, and the smell of cooking bread was already coming from the toaster. I worked with Johnny and we managed a quick assembly-line of toast and jam and peanut butter, which Nellie devoured without barely saying a word between bites, something that really only happened when there were presents waiting for after.

"Does anyone want a hot chocolate?" I said, teasing and stretching after they were done eating. "I might have a cup of coffee first..."

"*Uncle Hunt!*" Nellie pleaded, putting her forehead down on the table.

"Go get the stockings," I said, and they were off like a shot, even Johnny. I cleared the table, though I'd get to the dishes later, and joined them in the living room where they'd each staked out a spot—Johnny and Susy on either end of the couch, Nellie on the floor—and my own stocking was sitting on the chair.

"Merry Christmas," I said to them, and they smiled and said it back and started tearing into their stockings. I watched, forgetting to even pull the first thing from my own stocking. Johnny took his time, ripping open each gift and really looking at it—even if it was just some candy or a hockey puck—and Susy was even more careful, trying not to rip the paper on her presents as she went through them.

Nellie shredded her wrapping like she was trying to make confetti.

I loved them so much. They were very much the centre of my life. My brother's kids, who I was lucky enough to call my own. I couldn't risk—I *wouldn't* risk—

"Uncle Hunt?" Susy said. She looked at me, and I realized she'd undone the package of hair ties, ribbons, and clips and had put her hair back with one of the clips.

"Sorry, what?" I said, tapping my temple. "I was in my head."

"You're not opening your presents," she said.

"Oh, right." I laughed. "I like watching you all."

She smiled at that, but she didn't open another present until I started with mine, the first of which was a bar of soap. I filled my own stocking, of course, but I'd forgotten I'd gotten that for myself, so it was easy to pretend surprise.

"Why does Santa always get you things like soap and stuff?" Nellie said. She'd paused tearing her way into a chocolate orange to ask the question.

"I like soap," I said. "You've seen how I look when I come home sometimes."

Nellie took a second with that, then nodded, going back to her work.

The doorbell rang.

For a second, they all froze, and then they grinned at each other. Nellie leapt up and said, "I'll get it!" and was halfway down the hallway before I could have said a word.

I'm not sure what word I would have said, anyway. I wasn't ready. I didn't know what to do. Because if this was Micah—and who else could it be?—I still hadn't figured anything out.

Susy looked at me, and a little line formed between her eyebrows, so I tried to smile for her.

"Come in, come in!" Nellie was practically dragging Micah—because of course it was Micah—into the room, and he was barely holding on to the wrapped picture and his cane, and I got up to take the package from him and then he smiled and...

Oh. Micah had come dressed the way we dressed for Christmas morning: his pyjamas. For Micah, that was a pair of red flannel pants and a plain white t-shirt and he looked wonderful.

"Surprise," Micah said, with a crooked twist to his lips.

Right. I wasn't supposed to know he was home.

"You're here," I said. I couldn't tell if I'd fooled any of them with that.

"We invited him," Nellie said, grinning and looking back and forth between Micah and me. "Is that a present for us?"

"*Nellie*," Johnny groaned. "At least let him sit down."

"I'll get your stocking, Micah," Susy said.

"But it is a present for us, right?" Nellie said.

Micah had been looking at me, and I couldn't tell what he was thinking, but he finally glanced down at Nellie. "It is. It's for all of you."

"Take my chair," I said, and Micah sat down as Susy gave him his stocking, and I put the painting down beside the tree, and then realized I wasn't sure where to go myself, but given my stocking was by my chair, I ended up sitting on the floor beside Micah, who put a hand on my shoulder.

I looked up at him.

"Merry Christmas," he said. That crooked smile was back.

"Merry Christmas," I said. *How long will he look at me like that?* I swallowed and glanced away. Susy was looking at me again, that little line back between her eyebrows.

Micah and I made it through our stockings—Nellie noticed most of the things were the same, right down to the bar of soap—and then Micah asked if my three could open the gift he'd brought first.

"Okay." My throat had gotten raw, and the word came out a little choked.

Micah waited until my three had their attention on the wrapped painting before he leaned in.

"Are you okay?" he said in a soft voice.

"I don't know," I whispered back, and he frowned, but then Nellie was basically screaming and we turned to see they'd torn the paper off and all three of them were looking at the painting.

Johnny glanced back at us, first. "That's really cool, Micah."

"Thank you," he said.

"We're so small!" Nellie said. "We're *fairies*!"

"It's awesome," Susy said. She turned to look at Micah, tears in her eyes. "Thank you. It's really beautiful." Her bottom lip trembled, and Nellie frowned at her.

"Why are you crying?" Nellie said.

"Oh, honey," Micah got off the chair, sliding to the floor, and he opened his arms. Susy gave him a big hug, burying her face in his shoulder.

"Thank you," Susy said again.

"I don't understand why she's crying," Nellie said.

"Sometimes good things make you cry," I said, rubbing Susy's back with one hand. I wasn't entirely sure I understood myself, really, but I think it was because Susy the fairy in the painting was so very *perfect*. It looked like her so much it *was* her.

Micah had tears in his eyes, too, and when Susy finally pulled back, sniffling, he said. "Lucky for us I got handkerchiefs in my stocking." He opened the box of white cotton handkerchiefs and pulled one out for her and another for himself.

Susy laughed as she blew her nose and Micah wiped his eyes.

Nellie sighed. I could tell her patience with crying and feelings was about to completely run out.

"I'm going to go get coffee started for me and Micah," I said, raising one hand when Nellie opened her mouth to complain. "But he can hand out the first presents for me while I do that, if he doesn't mind?"

"I don't mind," Micah said, and Nellie cheered.

I gave Susy one more squeeze and then I ran away. I needed to think, and I couldn't seem to think while I was watching Micah with Susy. Before I got too lost in my head, I got the coffee started, and then I just stood there.

I liked him. My three liked him. If it didn't work out, then it wasn't just me who'd lose him. Susy needed people like Micah in her life. People who *saw* her. I leaned against the counter, my arms to either side of the coffee machine, watching the dark liquid start to fill the jug. I couldn't find the answer.

I wasn't even sure what the question was.

"Okay, that's really unfair," Micah said, his voice snapping me out of my thoughts. I turned to look at him. He was in the doorway, one hand on the wall. He'd left his cane in the living room, I noticed.

"Sorry?"

"When you lean like that? Your arms." He grinned. "Very distracting."

"Oh," I said, pushing off the counter.

He shook his head. "That wasn't a complaint, Hunt." He made his way carefully toward me. Using the counter and looking at me with that eye-flicking thing he did, only this time he didn't seem to be figuring me out. "They're going to riot if we don't get back in there soon—well, Nellie is—but you seem upset." He paused, and took a breath. "Is it because of last night?"

"Yes," I said, and he flinched so I shook my head. "It's not the kissing. I liked that. A lot."

He smiled. "Me too."

178

"I'm just…" I looked out through the open doorway into the living room, and then back at him. "I don't want to ruin anything. For them."

"Oh," Micah said, frowning. "I'm not sure I get what you mean by ruin."

"When you get tired of me—"

"Sorry, what?" Micah held up one hand.

"Uncle Hunt!" Nellie's voice interrupted. "Is the coffee done yet?"

I groaned, and Micah put a hand on my shoulder. "You and I will finish that conversation, Hunt, but just to be clear?" He leaned in. "I am *not* going to get tired of you." Then he looked back out through the door. "Of *any* of you."

I swallowed. "You're sure?" I said. "You know I'm not very…" I tapped my temple with a finger.

"You are kind, you are wonderful." Micah leaned in closer. "You are very much the man for me, Hunt." He kissed me, and I kissed him back, and I probably would have forgotten all about everything else, only—

"Uncle Hunt!" Nellie cried.

"We're coming," Micah said, pulling back. He sighed, then he winked at me, nodding to the machine behind me. "Coffee's ready."

Micah made his way back out, and I followed with two mugs of coffee. Micah liked his with cream, something I already knew. When we got back to the living room, I saw my three had rearranged themselves. Johnny had the chair, Susy had one side of the couch, and Nellie remained on the floor. They already each had a present in front of them.

"You two sit there," Nellie said, pointing at the remaining space on the couch.

Micah's lips twitched, but he sat in the middle. I took the end.

We each opened our "something to wear" present—my three had chosen this one for me, and I found myself the proud owner of a new Sens jersey, which would be great for taking Johnny to the games—and Johnny seemed happy with his new black hoodie, Nellie pretended to be enthusiastic about her dungarees even though we all knew full well she cared more about the books to come, and Susy shook out the lavender dress and beamed at me. "It's purple!"

"I'm glad you like it," I said.

"She *always* likes purple," Nellie said.

"And you *always* like books," Johnny said, though he wasn't being mean, and Nellie stuck her tongue out at him playfully enough.

They'd all also gotten packets of socks and new underwear in their packages, but unsurprisingly, no one brought them up.

"You're up," I said to Johnny, and he handed out the next round of presents—"something to read"—and this time it was Johnny forcing some excitement rather than Nellie, though he at least opened the *Ottawa Walking Tours* book and flipped through it, glancing up at me with a questioning look on his face.

"I thought you could pick out the ones you want to do, and we could all go exploring," I said.

He smiled. "Okay." That sounded more genuine. I'd hoped a book that led to going somewhere and doing something would hit the right spot.

Susy had an art book—a how-to-draw kind of book—and she bit her bottom lip, looking at it. I wondered if I'd gotten it wrong, but then she turned to Micah and said, "Will you help me with this?"

"Of course. I'd love to."

My throat got rough again, and I had to drink some coffee and look at my own book, a cookbook I'd picked up that promised all the recipes were healthy and quick to make. I'd see if that was true in time, I supposed. Once I was sure my voice wouldn't choke again, I said, "Should we do it out of order this year, and do the 'something you need' next?"

All three groaned, and Micah laughed, and Johnny said, "That wasn't funny when Dad did it, Uncle Hunt. It's not funny when you do it, either." He shook his head, but he laughed, and I realized he was *really* laughing. The memory of my brother doing the same thing every year—and Clark had always done it, Johnny was right—didn't seem to be sad this time.

"Whose turn is it?" I said, honestly not remembering if Nellie or Susy had been the one to hand out the "something you want" gifts last year, but Susy raised her hand.

"My turn," she said, getting the most coveted gifts to pass them out.

Nellie barely let Susy hand it over before she was tearing into the paper and cheering at the reveal of another storybook—and this one the very book Micah had published. Johnny seemed just as happy with his skates, but I was watching Susy the closest, and her slow smile at the reveal of the doll I'd gotten from Urbane Myth was *everything*.

She looked up at me. "She's perfect."

"Just like you," I said.

She bit her lip and pulled out the two changes of clothes that came with the doll and laid them out beside her.

"Are you going to name her?" Micah asked Susy.

Susy thought about it. "What's a good Christmas name?"

"How about Noelle?" Micah said. So clever.

"Hi, Noelle," she said to the doll.

My gift was a new coffee thermos for work, one that stayed hot because you charged it, and Johnny watched me open it and while I made sure to thank all my three for it, I knew he'd been the one in charge of getting it so I made sure he knew I knew with a wink aimed just for him.

The "something you need" gifts never gave the same excitement as the third gifts, but Nellie liked her new school backpack well enough given her old one had been starting to rip, and Johnny's attempt to pretend to be excited about new bedsheets was funny in its own way. He really tried to ham it up, reading the label and talking about thread-counts the way he'd normally talk about game scores. I was pretty sure he knew how much the season tickets had cost, and was being a very good sport about it. Susy had also needed new sheets, but her new ones were purple, so that was just fine by her.

I'd needed a new frying pan. Now I had one.

"What about Micah?" Nellie said after Johnny's performance ended. She frowned, and I tried not to smile, because it had only seemed to strike her that Micah had no presents after the excitement of her having presents had worn off.

"I loved my stocking," Micah said, which was nice of him, but I could have told him that would never work with Nellie.

"But you didn't get a *want* gift," she said.

Micah looked at me, and then said, in that wonderful soft voice of his. "Hunt?"

You are very much the man for me, Hunt. He'd meant that. Micah wasn't the sort to say things he didn't mean. I still wanted to ask him more questions. There were so many things we needed to talk about, but I knew he meant what he'd said. So I nodded, because my throat was going all choked again, and I wasn't sure I could speak.

Micah leaned in, I put my arm around him, and Micah took my hand, lacing our fingers together after. Micah turned back to Nellie, and said, "I got the best want gift. Your Uncle Hunt and I are going to be boyfriends, if that's okay with all of you."

All my three were watching us, but Susy broke the silence first. "Really?" She clutched Noelle to her chest and grinned.

"Really," I said. "I know you'll all have questions——" I started to say, but the three of them jumped up and dogpiled us, and Micah and I found ourselves buried in hugs and laughter and the demand to be allowed to call Micah "Uncle Micah" from now on.

I rode it out, smiling across their heads at Micah who looked back at me even while he answered all their questions almost as fast as they could ask them, something I'd never been able to manage, and I let him, and I realized just how much he'd already been a part of all of us over the last two years.

We tidied up a bit, and when my three—*our* three—were busy bagging the shredded wrapping paper, Micah leaned in close to my ear.

"For the record?" he said. "I do have a 'something you need' gift in mind you can help me with."

I frowned and glanced at him. He had that crooked smile again. "What do you need?" I said.

"Tell you later," he said, squeezing my hand. "*After* their bedtime."

I may not be very bright, but this time I knew *exactly* what he meant.

I wrapped my arms around him and squeezed him tight, putting my mouth to his ear. "Santa did say he'd get me something for Christmas."

Micah laughed, but before he could reply Susy was back with her art book asking him if he'd like to draw now, and Nellie wanted to know if we could watch a Christmas movie, and Johnny suggested *Rise of the Guardians*.

Thoughts of later tonight would have to wait for both of us.

It was funny. The past three years had changed my life in every way, and somehow, they'd gone by faster than I could have imagined.

I had a feeling the next few hours were going to seem very slow in comparison.

Still, as the movie started and we all settled in and I listened to Micah quietly explaining how to hold a pencil for Susy, I had to admit Santa had delivered.

It all felt just right.

ACKNOWLEDGEMENTS

As I MENTIONED in the dedication, this book wouldn't be here without some of the most wonderful editors and authors I've worked with over the years, so I'll say it again. Thank you to Matthew Bright, Anthony Cardno, Nicci Robinson, Victoria Villasenor, and Jerry L. Wheeler. You are the glitter of the holidays I still find stuck to things mid-March.

I mean that in the best way, really.

I need to further underline Jerry L. Wheeler and Matthew Bright, Jerry for his always-brilliant editing and Matt for making this book so darn *pretty*. That's right, he's not just an editor, he's a massively talented artist. Trust me, I understand you might want to try to hate him for it, but he's just too nice and cuddly.

More massive thank-yous go to Marie Bilodeau and Lydia Hawke, who are so very often my wing-women when it comes to self-publishing (by wing-women I mean they take my panicky texts because I have to fill in a form somewhere and remind me I'm a human adult and capable of filling in forms and calm me down again).

Last, of course, but by no means least, my husband, Dan and our rescued husky, Max. If it weren't for my husband, I couldn't do this. Every time I finish a book I realize how freaking lucky I am to have fallen in love with such a brilliant man. (That's not rose-tinted glasses, by the way, he graduated university with a literally perfect GPA, which a friend pointed out just before our first date, so let's all cheer how incredible it is I made it past the sheer intimidation factor alone.)

Max gets thanked mostly because if I don't people get mad at me, and he's a husky and if he feels left out there'll be hell to pay. Also, I love him.

ABOUT THE AUTHOR

'NATHAN BURGOINE is a tall queer writer of (mostly) shorter queer fictions, but novels keep happening. His stories tend to live somewhere in the Venn Diagram of romance, young adult, and spec-fic—often where at least two of those circles cross—but always queer. He grew up a reader and studied literature in university while making a living as a bookstore manager for a couple of decades.

'Nathan's debut novel about a telepathic and telekinetic not-quite-superhero trying to save Pride Week, *Light*, was a finalist for a Lambda Literary Award and his debut young adult novel about a hyper-organized gay teen who develops a teleportation problem two weeks before high school graduation, *Exit Plans for Teenage Freaks*, was a Prix Aurora Award finalist. His other novels include the contemporary paranormal Ottawa-set Triad Blood trilogy, *Triad Blood*, *Triad Soul*, and *Triad Magic*.

For young adults, 'Nathan also wrote the "don't forget, queers have always been here" novella "Hope Echoes," included in *Three Left Turns to Nowhere*, and his first hi-lo queer YA rom-com about two frenemies stuck together on a long train ride who realize they've completely misjudged each other and actually would maybe like to kiss, *Stuck With You*. If you don't know what a hi-lo is, don't worry, he didn't either until someone asked him to write one. They're accessible "high-interest, low-complexity" books written to be accessible for reluctant readers, readers with reading disabilities, or those who read English as a second language, but still telling interesting and relevant stories for young adult readers.

On the novella side of things, romance lovers can find the Little Village Holiday Novellas: *Handmade Holidays*, *Faux Ho Ho*, *Village Fool*, and *Felix Navidad* where awesome queer dudes with chosen families find other awesome queer dudes to fall in love with alongside some holiday cheer; the more magical romance novella *A Little Village Blend* where a tea-shop owner can brew magic into his teas; the far more spicy (and comedic) disaster-cute romance, *Rear Admiral* where a nurse meets his porn-star crush and it gets awkward, fast, and the wibbly-wobbly timey-wimey romance *In Memoriam*, which has, well, time-travel.

His first collection of linked short fiction was *Of Echoes Born*, which shares the dubious dual honour of being both his favourite and the book that sells the least. Writing is fun.

A cat lover, 'Nathan managed to fall in love and marry Daniel, who is a confirmed dog person. Their ongoing "cat or dog?" détente officially ended with the rescue of huskies. They live in Ottawa, Canada, where socialized health care and gay marriage have yet to cause the sky to cave in.

nathanburgoine.com.

ALSO BY THE AUTHOR

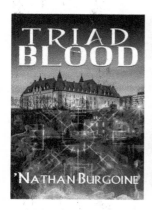

Printed in the USA
CPSIA information can be obtained
at www.ICGtesting.com
CBHW021322081124
17141CB00006B/61